TEARING THE SKY

JAMIL MOLEDINA

Kalyphon Press

Tearing the Sky
A Kalyphon Press Book
Copyright © 2010 by Jamil Moledina
All rights reserved.

Published in the United States by Kalyphon Press, San Francisco, California
www.kalyphon.com
Printed in the United States of America

ISBN-13 978-0-9830700-0-9
ISBN-10 0983070008

For Olive

Contents

Prologue

A tiny point twinkled and burst, shattering the dark, featureless void with streaks of blinding light. The explosion continued, expanding and folding on itself, outpacing the initial burst. White-hot material began to coalesce within the explosion front, spinning in random directions. Plumes of startling color splashed outward with ribbons of gas dancing in non-repeating steps. Many flattened out into glowing discs and their centers ignited into a steady blaze. Billowing galaxies spread out in a dervish frenzy of pulsing, unchoreographed flourishes, racing away from each other, claiming and illuminating the deep-dark universe. A rising chorus of startled gasps and scuffling among the seats brought the presentation to a frozen halt.

Thousands of eyes focused on the only movement in the pyramidal hall, a tiny silhouette of a man standing on an extruded platform. The lanky, black-haired man positioned himself on the very edge, so that the static splendor of the universe formed an immense halo around him. "This moment represents today," he began in a wispy voice that echoed through the chamber.

"The universe is expanding, and the rate of that expansion is increasing. But observe."

He stepped back, and the simulation started again. However, the expanding boundary stopped, and began to pucker. The boundary shell began to crack and tear inward, pulling back. Spinning pinwheel galaxies careened, smashing into each other all around the heads of those in the audience, eliciting reflexive shrieks. Through visual inertia, they felt themselves pulled forward, and some were brought to their feet as the living worlds of humanity shattered and atomized in the rush back to the center of the hall. The deflation and utter destruction accelerated until everything collapsed back on that same starting point, and there was darkness again.

The returning platform light revealed the lanky man again. He raised his arms to the audience. "Any questions?"

The audience, in shadow, was abuzz with whispers. A tall, sinewy man with salt-and-pepper hair stood. He cupped his hands around his mouth. "How soon?"

The lanky man's mouth widened with white teeth protruding. They twinkled in the dark much like his presentation. "Whenever you're ready."

PART I

DISCOVERY

Chapter 1

The Charity Ball

K ale tugged at his sleeve. There was no way to mask the fact that his one formal suit had shrunk. Maybe he had simply grown, he thought. Male bone growth was supposed to continue well into a man's early twenties.

"Bruschetta, sir?"

Aware that he was stooping over his sleeve, sweating over things that would not help him through the evening, Kale abruptly straightened up. A well-dressed man holding a tray eyed him with practiced disdain.

"N-no, thanks," said Kale.

"Would sir care for an aperitif?" asked the server.

Kale began to feel what small confidence he had summoned start to bleed away. There was something menacing in the server's bearing, or so he perceived. Without knowing quite what he was refusing, Kale responded, "No, I'm fine."

The server bowed his head down and to the side. A restrained smile crept across his craggy features. He turned and resumed his circulation through the gala, taking what remained of Kale's confidence with him.

Kale noticed that his left shirt cuff was sticking out of his jacket sleeve.

"There he is!"

He looked up to see a large asymmetrical face fill his field of vision. Kale leaned into the gentle punch to his arm. His friend was taller and heavier than Kale, and sported a friendlier expression.

"What are you doing just standing here?" the larger one asked. "Did you just get here? I've been waiting for you to show up! You've no idea how much I can't stand these people. If you can call them people, that is. They're so dead. So dull. So—I don't know. So what's new?"

"What's new is that I'm giving up time to stand around dead people," Kale replied. "You owe me one, Gander."

"Yeah, right! You'd be in your apartment doing stamp trades with younger dead people. And try to use my given name tonight, all right?"

"They're not stamps, Gander," said Kale.

"Yeah, if you say so," said Gander. "Look, buddy, don't call me that tonight; I want you to meet the signatures. Grab a drink, and let's go."

The exchange with his friend invigorated Kale. He was particularly glad that Gander did not say anything about his shrunken suit. It was not like Gander to let the opportunity for teasing slip past him, so Kale felt hopeful that it would continue to go unnoticed. Kale nabbed a champagne flute off a passing tray, and followed his friend into the fray.

The main hall was cavernous, with vaulted ceilings stretching upward several stories. Arched cerastic beams, intricately decorated by clean gold lines, held up the warm tapestry-lined walls. At ground level, a buzz of multiple conversations echoed into a level roar, punctuated by the clinking of glasses. An orchestral quartet played an ancient, refined melody, but it was drowned out largely by the crowd.

"The object of the game here," said Gander, "is to hit the other signatures with increasingly dumb stories at the same rate as they drink—so you remain within spitting range of credibility. Now stick close; we need to work our way to the center."

Kale felt like he was jumping into a cold pool as he stepped down into the hall. Women wearing layers of obsidian jewels and platinum-lined gowns glanced at him, just long enough to decide that he was not worth a moment's more attention. Kale kept his eyes firmly on Gander's back, glancing above at the chandeliers to mark off their progress into the hall. He could feel the occasional frown from those he bumped into, and also from those whose purpose in life was frowning.

Kale noticed that Gander was slowing to a halt, and felt his insides compress. It was time to put on his smile.

A tall, austere-looking figure turned slightly to reveal a long face with eyebrows maintained higher on the forehead than seemed natural. "Well, there you are, young man!" he said. "And I see you have your schoolmate with you. Kale, isn't it?"

"Yes, Mr. Ruglier," said Kale. "Thank you for inviting me. I feel honored." Kale glanced briefly at Gander, who winked his appreciation.

"Oh, not at all, young man," said Ruglier. "Charity events are always a good excuse for socializing." Kale understood this to be a joke, for the benefit of the others standing in an arc around Ruglier.

Confirming Kale's unspoken supposition, Ruglier planted one slender hand on Kale's shoulder and gestured to the rest with the other. "If I may, allow me to introduce Kale Eritrus," he said. "He attends Stanford with my son."

Kale grinned forcibly while Ruglier continued. "This is John Garrowak, president of UTT."

"Hello, pleased to meet you," Kale said, offering his hand.

Garrowak forcefully shook it. "A pleasure."

"This is Alia Nobarra, CEO of Nobarra Shipbuilding," continued Ruglier.

"Pleased to meet you," said Kale. He squeezed her delicate hand. The corners of her mouth twitched.

"This is Alexander Collarfield, the man who runs the firm that designed this little hall."

"Pleased to meet you." Kale stuck out his hand, but Collarfield's hands already were waving around in the air.

"So what do you think of this little architectural marvel?" Collarfield asked.

"Um, it's really grand," Kale said.

"No, well, yes, I know it's really grand, but what else can you offer me?"

"It's kind of imposing."

"That's not really what I was going for," said Collarfield.

"Well, that's the good thing about the young," chimed in Garrowak. "They always say what they think, rather than what you *want* them to think."

Unperturbed, Collarfield responded, "That may or may not be true, but the point is that from an architectural standpoint, this facility was constructed to be open, to reflect the unspoiled comfort of the outdoors. For example, the tapestries are all woven in warm colors, with images of rolling hills and trees, with open skies above."

Rising to the challenge, Garrowak said, "Fair enough, but a building is not just a set of walls. What you fill it with inevitably alters its characteristics. The effect is similar to when a journalist distorts the news simply by reporting it. So a building made to seem open becomes imposing by filling it with people like us. Isn't that what you mean, young Mr. Eritrus?"

Prompted largely from an icy glare from Kale, Gander offered, "Uh, what he means is that the hall looms over you, making you as insignificant as ants."

"So what are you, his spin doctor?" Garrowak asked. "The man can speak for himself."

Kale began, "I guess the building is what you make of it. I think it's imposing. Mr. Collarfield thinks it's open. You think it's corrupted by its contents, Gander thinks it's stifling, and Ms. Nobarra and Mr. Ruglier are wisely keeping to themselves on this. Although we're all seeing the same thing, I think we all bring our own experiences and preconceived notions into describing it." Kale was pleased with himself, and further pleased that the discussion had given him a moment to compose his response. He usually thought of the clever thing to say ten minutes later. He also noticed that a fleeting grin had raced across Nobarra's small mouth at the connection of Ruglier with the concept of wisdom.

Impressed with how well his introduction had played out, Ruglier said, "So that's what they're teaching them these days! When we were their age, we were never so serious."

Garrowak replied, "I'm inclined to agree, but I do remember you being so adamant about the legitimacy of union organizations. And now look!"

Everyone except Kale laughed. He smiled when it occurred to him that something funny might just have been said.

Garrowak continued, "But what about kids today? Our erudite Mr. Eritrus, tell me: Do you find many idealists among your classmates?"

Kale replied, "Well, I don't know. I think many of them consider themselves idealists. I don't really feel that there is much feeling toward any particular cause—besides tonight's, of course. The feeling, I guess, is that all the good battles already have been fought."

"Interesting. So you're all for the status quo?" Garrowak asked.

"Um, no, that's not it, either. I think people are generally restless, without knowing why," Kale replied.

After a pause, Ruglier asked, "So, Kale, what was your major again?"

"Well, I started as a physics major, but I changed to anthropology."

Collarfield was the first to comment. "Anthropology? Nothing new coming out of that field. Unless you count documentaries."

Garrowak did not let that sit. "Oh, you're just being bitter, Alex. I think anthropology is key to our understanding of ourselves. Who we are. Where we're going."

"Or who we are going to become," said Nobarra.

Kale met her gaze. Her eyes seemed to be boring into his skull. He fought the impulse to glance away and instead stared back at her. He still was furious about the physics fiasco, and was in no mood to elaborate further. Her mouth opened a bit.

"Oh, I see my wife is motioning to me," said Ruglier. "I had better see what she wants. I'll be right back." He moved off toward a dour-faced but otherwise dazzling woman.

"I want you to meet someone," Nobarra said to Kale. "Come with me." She linked her arm through his, and walked him away. Garrowak and Collarfield stared into their drinks, while trying to make their swizzle sticks appear purposeful. Gander crept away toward the hors d'oeuvres.

Kale himself had hoped to retreat from the conversation, hiss a friendly "Now we're even!" to his friend, and leave the party. It occurred to him that things were not going according to plan since this cryptic woman was dragging him through the frowners. "Ms. Nobarra, I—"

"Please call me Alia," she interrupted. "I have every intention of calling you Kale."

"All right, Ms. Alia. I should let you know that I don't do well in groups," said Kale.

Not responding, she said, "I can't stand the way that man introduces people. John isn't just a communications magnate, and I'm certainly not simply a CEO. Although Alex very well may be limited to his understanding of architecture, I find it insulting when people label each other in such a blunt manner. Such convenient definitions can lead to a very dull experience with life, wouldn't you say?"

"Well, Ms. Alia, ordinarily I'd agree with you," Kale responded. "But I think that knowing something about you is better than not knowing anything about you at all."

"Unless, my dear, that something you think you know limits your ability to make your own determinations freely," said Nobarra.

"I really don't like meeting people."

Nobarra halted, and flashed a wry grin. "Nobody has ever regretted meeting my daughter. Athena?"

Nobarra was calling to a slim woman with her back turned to them. She was tall, wearing a silver dress, with olive skin and straight black hair arranged in multiple twists on top of her head. She was involved in a vigorous conversation, and stretched out her arm behind her and toward them with her index finger pointing up, gesturing that they wait.

Kale tugged at his sleeve.

"So then I asked him for the dispatcher's number. I called him up from the back of the cab, and he was just a scrawny kid. Probably an undergrad, or something. And so I said to him, 'If you think I'm going to pay the cabbie eight, you're out of your mind. When I called for the cab, I was quoted six, and then your man shows up thirty-five minutes late? Are you crazy? If you have any business sense, or even just a sense of decency, you will only charge me five. Your response, sir?' And then the guy blabbed some apology, and instructed the cabbie to charge me nothing! And that, my friends, is how to get a free ride in this town!" The crowd around her bubbled with laughter. "I'll be right back." The glee subsided, and Athena swung around, revealing that her jovial demeanor was subsiding, too.

Although she shared her mother's angular features and small, soft mouth, she lacked her gentle tongue. "What do you want?" she whispered through gritted teeth.

Nobarra gestured toward her frozen companion and said, "Kale, I would like you to meet my daughter, Athena. She's a bit of a terror. Athena, I would like you to meet Kale. He's shockingly straightforward. Now I'm going to mingle."

Kale tried to react, but Nobarra was gone before he could utter a word. He regarded the unquestionably magnetic woman standing with arms akimbo in front of him.

"In spite of the fact that I hate being set up," Athena said, "and in further spite of the fact that you are so obviously checking me out, I will give you two minutes. Solely on the basis of that clever introduction."

"Would you prefer that I only discretely check you out?"

"Great, a comedian. One minute, fifty seconds."

Kale considered his response. This woman was more perplexing than most, but he was confident he could play her game. "Athena is the ancient Greek goddess of wisdom. Is your wit an attempt to compensate for the inevitable expectations based on your name?"

Athena narrowed her gaze. "Kale is a green leafy vegetable. Is your gall an attempt to compensate for the inevitable low expectations based on *your* name?"

Kale assessed his strategy. Athena peered at him as if he were a small insect. He'd better say something clever. "No, I just used up all my fake charm on your mother's friends."

"Ha!" She grinned. "That's the first sensible thing out of your mouth. Trouble is, you only have a minute left."

"So, what do you do?"

"How boring. You just wasted five seconds, leaf boy."

"No, I didn't. I want to know what sort of environment would allow a person to behave so viciously."

"I'm a journalist. A correspondent."

"Ah!"

"What, 'ah'? What do *you* do that allows you to be so presumptuous?"

"Uh, I'm studying anthropology."

"So my mom tried to set me up with an *undergrad?*" Athena's angular features collapsed into a scowl. "Oh this is too much. Sorry, kid, but maybe you can play this game with someone from your own playground. And get a suit that fits, while you're at it."

Smiling, she pivoted around to rejoin her friends. "Time's up," she said with her back to him.

Kale stood there, his mouth gaping, his fists clenched. He walked away, each stride longer until he practically ran out of the hall. As he exited the structure, Gander came rushing toward him, and grabbed Kale's shoulder.

"Hey, pal! Where're you headed? You're going to miss the speeches."

"I've had enough speeches for one night," Kale said, shrugging off Gander's hand. "I'm going home."

"What do you mean?"

"This woman. Athena Nobarra."

Gander rolled his eyes, twinkling from the chandelier above the exit arch. "Athena? That's all? Please! Do you know what she called me today? 'A convincing argument for criminalizing nepotism.' Don't let her get to you, buddy. It's not worth it. Come on, stick around. Everyone at school would kill to see these stars speak."

Nothing had gone right, but for the first time that evening, Kale smiled genuinely. "Look, I appreciate what you're saying, and that you're trying to make me feel better, but I just need to get out of here. Get some fresh air, you know?"

"Okay, buddy. I'll just do my best to have fun anyway," Gander said with a broad grin.

Kale squeezed Gander's arm, and walked out.

Kale approached the valet booth, and stepped on his left shoelace, tipping him off balance. He swore under his breath, and knelt to tie his shoe. Try to relax, forget it, he told himself, as he gazed down through the transparent floor of the valet platform at the blue, brown, and white planet floating against a luminous starfield. He felt a wash of calm come over him, the wonder shared by all people, for more than a quarter of a million years, upon gazing at the sight of the warm Earth below.

Kale stood up and approached a valet, who had a bad case of acne. He found it comforting and yet extravagant that the valet was a breathing, oozing human being and not synthetic. "Your pod, sir?" asked the valet, his voice breaking.

"The brown Cosmos. I'm sure there's only one here."

"Yes sir, I remember it."

The valet trotted off. A few minutes later, a dinged oval craft sighed into a deck slot. Kale tipped the valet a fifty-centicredit tap, and got inside the tiny one-person cockpit. The access panel closed next to him. Kale instantly was inundated with crashing music. "Volume off!" he yelled, verbalizing out of habit, and the cabin was silent. He sat back in the leatherette seat, closed his eyes, and pushed forward the single word, "Home." The pod's neurocom understood this to be a destination command, as opposed to a thought fragment, and detached from the valet deck slot. The pod backed out slowly, correcting thrusters struggling to keep it moving in a straight line. Once sufficiently removed from the platform, the pod lurched forward and turned around. It then accelerated through the environment bubble surrounding the Meridien Collarfield Hall. The pod broke orbit, selected a Port Authority reentry thread, and executed a sub-light arc to Earth. Inside, Kale replayed the events of the evening in his mind.

✦ ✦ ✦ ✦ ✦

Kale entered his cramped apartment, and began taking off his suit before he reached the bedroom. The hardwood floors creaked under his steps. He threw the clothes onto his bed, thinking he would deal with them later. He wandered into the living room, and spoke into open space: "Any messages?"

A smiling female voice replied, "What, no 'hello'? Yes, you have two messages, both of which are offers for the Antares travel holovisa you placed on the market on Tuesday. Would you like to see them?"

"What were the offers?" Kale asked.

Holofield representations appeared in front of him. "One was for eighty credits, from a woman on the other side of the universe, the other for a hundred and twenty, from a Sentient on Kalyphon," the voice replied.

Kale paused. He had never received an offer from a Sentient. As a rule, Sentients rarely took an interest in activities as frivolous as pre-Travel holovisa collecting. You never met one concerned with anything but productive pursuits like governance or information integrity. However, Kale had other things on his mind. "Well, tag them and remind me tomorrow, okay? I can't deal with all that just yet."

"What's the matter? Is it about Professor Cerelles?"

"In a way, yes," said Kale. "The physics department funding issue came up, and the evening really went downhill from there. Come to think of it, the evening started downhill."

"Perhaps your mood might be improved if you placed the clothes lying on your bed in the cleaning cycle."

"What? Stop that! I know your ethics set is unchangeable, but I really wish you would stop bossing me around."

"Bossing? Hardly, Kale. I feel that you are exaggerating for either dramatic effect, or because you have residual traumatic effects from your academic problems, and from your apparently dismal evening. I'm only suggesting that you improve the appearance of your environment. Such subtle actions have proven beneficial in studies of organic humans."

"Ellen, it's times like these that I'm glad I never installed neuroceivers in your sensor map."

"Well, if you can't handle upgrading me to telepathy, I would hate to contribute to your increasing displeasure with life," Ellen responded.

"All right, all right. I'm going to stop arguing with you now, and put my suit in the cycle. Happy?" Kale said with a small smile forming.

"Oh, without a doubt," said Ellen.

Kale returned to the bedroom and picked up his clothes. He tossed them into the laundry cycle hatch, and noticed a small rectangle drop from a pocket onto the floor. Kale knelt to pick it up. The small cerastic card had an oscillating arrow icon on it. Kale touched it and was jolted by the words intruding into the frontal lobe of his brain. "She's virtually single. I hope you don't mind!"

It was the voiceprint of Alia Nobarra. Kale flipped over the rectangle. It read, "Athena C. Nobarra—Correspondent—Universal News Network—Connect Code." It was Athena's business card. This was the last thing he needed. At the same time, however, he was well aware of his taste in destructive women. Kale was pulled out of his conflicted reverie by Ellen's lilting voice.

"Kale! Sorry to interrupt your little fantasy, but you have a call coming in from Professor Cerelles. Do you want to take it?"

"Y-yes. I'll take it in the living room."

"Okay, but, while you're in the bedroom, I suggest you throw on some pants first," said Ellen.

Kale grabbed a robe, and rushed into the living room. While still getting his arms through the sleeves, he said, "Connect."

A small, white-haired man in a worn one-piece suit appeared with his back to Kale, thinking words onto a holofield. A disembodied male voice said, "Dr. Cerelles, your connection is established."

The old man suddenly spun around, causing Kale to start. "Ah, Kale, my boy! You're back! I had my neurocom monitor your parking structure for the return of your Cosmos. I hope you don't mind."

"I wouldn't have known if you hadn't told me. How are you doing?" Kale always struggled with how to address his favorite teacher.

"Me? I'm quite fine, quite fine. Did twenty laps in the pool today. My doctor says that should extend my life expectancy to one eighty. Although that doesn't count for much. Oh, don't get me wrong, he's a good doctor and all, and frankly he's even a bit conservative in his pronouncements. However, as well as I am, it doesn't matter."

"But, that's good news—Dr. Cerelles."

"I told you my boy, my name is Fen. Call me Fen. Anyway, get over here right away. There's no good news. I knew it. Damn those fools, I knew it. There's been a gross miscalculation in the mass of Azimuth's dark matter, and it changes everything." Cerelles rubbed the beads of sweat off his forehead with a shaky hand, as he began to recede into his own world.

"F-Fen, you're starting to worry me," said Kale. "Maybe you should sit down. You'll give yourself a coronary."

"My dear boy, the whole Stanford physics department was dismantled and now there's almost nobody left to check the data, except you!" Cerelles said, shaking his open hand at Kale.

22

Kale would have held him by the arms, had his professor actually been standing in front of him. Instead, Kale balled his fists at his sides. "Fen, please calm down, you're getting too worked up. It's not the end of the universe, you know."

An unpleasant grin shadowed the older man's creased face. "Close enough. It's going to collapse next March."

Chapter 2

The Big Crunch Theory

K ale blinked. He held his eyes shut, hoping it would reset the apparent hallucination. When he opened them, Cerelles was still there, and his absurd pronouncement still hung in the air. Kale's mind flinched as he considered the statement as truth, and the muscles in his chest tightened, but he then settled down in a comfortable acceptance of the statement as the desperate rambling of a disenfranchised man. No reasonable person could believe the universe was about to collapse.

"Fen, you can't be serious."

This was the wrong thing to say. Cerelles's face fell, and he regarded his former pupil with mournful eyes. "My boy, I am perfectly serious. Don't tell me you too have written me off?"

Although Kale felt he was being manipulated by the statement, it struck home nonetheless. "Wait, I didn't mean it that way. I misspoke. If it's a matter of checking your equations and measurements for the Azimuth Galaxy, I'll be right over."

Cerelles perked up. "That's my boy! Be here in ten minutes; I'll get a pot of tea going. Disconnect." His image dissolved.

Kale collapsed in his chair. This was turning out to be a very long evening.

"That was pretty strange," piped in Ellen.

"Ellen, please confirm privacy protocols," Kale said.

"All communications, searches, data retrieval, archival, neuronic, and intergalactic relay transceiver activities are executed anonymously, using multiple layers of pseudonyms, encryptions, red herrings, and anti-footprinting. These privacy protocols are current as of the February 12 upgrade, and have since successfully locked out and redirected four separate attempts at data entry."

"Okay. Ellen, here's the deal. If anyone in Administration finds out about Professor Cerelles's statement tonight, he's going to be laid off, for sure. Please update the protocols, and come up with some of your own red herrings and anti-footprinting methods. Be creative. I'll try and shut up the guy in person," said Kale.

"Don't worry, Kale, I'll come up with some pretty original stuff. In the meantime, please put on some pants. Those legs!"

Kale smiled in spite of himself. He threw on some casual clothes, and left for Cerelles's apartment across campus.

+ + + + +

Kale walked out of his apartment. It was a dingy complex, but he was lucky to get in. Most people on campus had to share apartments with roommates. He was grateful not to have to face that situation again, given his admitted tendency for ruining relationships by rooming with his friends.

The exception was Gander. They were assigned each other freshman year, and their personalities clicked right from the start. They were trusting enough to share their anxieties and hopes, while maintaining a cool, comfortable feel to their friendship.

Kale stopped to wonder why he was thinking about such things. He realized he subconsciously was taking stock of the good things in his life. Could it all really end in a matter of months? The idea was terrifying, but it didn't make any sense. Kale found himself repeatedly pushing the concept out of his thoughts as ridiculous, but it kept rushing into his mind, seemingly of its own accord.

Kale reached the curb and pushed the word "pod" toward the front of his mind. His Cosmos was equipped with a neurocom that kept a constant watch on his brain pattern. The neurocom's sensors could only examine those thoughts that were articulated clearly by the brain as subject to forward publication.

The pod sighed into place adding to the already gusty wind, and the access panel gaped open. Kale entered, not without a tinge of trepidation. His mind often darted to his familiar although irrational fear that the pod's neuron-set had been altered by some self-impressed hacker, in order to access his forward thoughts. However, today, his mind was determined to focus on Cerelles.

Kale pushed forward the thought "Cerelles's apartment," and the pod started a graceful and calm ascent. Kale thought back to the days when he sat in Cerelles's Introduction to Cosmophysics 120 lectures, enthralled by the size and strangeness of a universe that, in a few hundred thousand years, humankind had customized to suit its goals. It now was peppered with traveling wormholes that cut short, vast distances, architectures that unified entire star systems, and devices that harnessed the power of galaxy-spinning black holes. The truly strange thing to Kale was how such remarkable achievements could be taken for granted today.

Nobody really gave a second thought to the pioneering days of tracking down and warehousing cosmic strings, or the modern-day method of looping the nozzle of a wormhole tubule, wrenching it through the curves of ordinary space and placing it mere meters in front of a spacecraft. To most people, it was just a debit in a Port Authority account. Knowing how things worked was considered passé.

The pod stopped. Kale shook his head to clear it, and stepped through the open access panel. He grabbed his spare jacket out of the back, since it was dark and blustery, and pushed forward "park." The pod groaned, but then sought out a nearby parking structure. Kale rushed up the pathway, feeling the first pregnant drop of rain on his arm. He was recognized by the door, and continued straight into the foyer.

"Microclimates, my boy, microclimates!" boomed a voice from the bannistered catwalk above.

Kale looked up to see Cerelles in his gray one-piece. "Hello, F-Fen."

"Get yourself up here, my boy. I see you're catching the beginning of one of our quirky fall showers. It amazes me how they keep this whole planet in its natural green state. It's almost a fetish!" continued Fen, as he opened his apartment door for his favorite student.

"It's like a religion," offered Kale as he entered the musty but elegant academic quarters.

"Religion? As in mythology?" asked Cerelles, taking Kale's jacket and hanging it up.

"Sort of," replied Kale. "It's a general term for when you actually believe in the mythology as a present and real thing. Ancient humans made up stories with a major god at the center, be it Thor, Zeus, Jupiter, or God with a capital 'G.' These gods helped them understand their world and deal with death."

Cerelles turned around, his forehead wrinkled. "Why would they need mythologies to understand things?"

"Life was very different in ancient times," replied Kale. This was a subject Kale had some comfort with, and it suited him to start this latest phase of his bizarre evening in a position of knowledge. "They had little to no theories to explain the world around them. As universal culture learned more about the reality of the universe, and how much more bizarre and fascinating it was than their ancient mystical stories, religion declined over thousands of years until it died out. But a few people still visit Earth just for religious reasons. We're learning all about it in, uh, class," trailed off Kale, once he realized he had stumbled onto a sore spot in their relationship.

"Kale, Kale. Don't feel that you need to censor yourself. I understand completely why you changed majors. I would have changed departments if they had allowed it. In a funny way, I'm glad they didn't, or I might never have made this discovery. But then, maybe I wish they had—it would have spared me this despair," said Cerelles.

"So, okay Fen, what exactly are we dealing with here?" asked Kale.

Cerelles rubbed his forehead, and began: "I know you're still a bit skeptical, but hear me out. You remember from class how the universe was formed by an inflationary explosion?" Kale nodded. "Well, as you recall, the force of that explosion coupled with the cosmological force is what accounts for the accelerating expansion of the universe. Based on all previous surveys, the universe is supposed to expand forever, and at a faster and faster pace." He pulled up a chart in midair that showed a curve extending upward. "However, the matter within the universe may be so much that the gravitational force of that matter stops the universe from expanding, and in fact causes it to collapse like a gigantic black hole," said Cerelles. A second chart appeared with the curve shooting up and crashing back down.

"Yes, I remember that; it's the less-accepted 'Big Crunch' theory. But doesn't that predict that any slowing and eventual collapse won't take place for billions of years?" asked Kale.

Cerelles dissolved both charts. "Assuming a parabolic curve, yes. However, the rate of compression may not be the same as the rate of expansion. Remember, the initial phases of the Big

Bang have been observed from ancient times to be inflationary, with matter forming and expanding at rates outside the capacity of ordinary three-dimensional space."

He brought up a rough model of the universe, and added a layer with large black chunks and rippling fissures. "Now according to my data, not only is there more mass in the universe than it can handle, but there have been several unexplained singularities, and other phantom dimensional ripples detected between and even inside several galaxies. These anomalies fit the profile of an inflationary collapse," concluded Cerelles, finally getting out what he could tell no one else.

"Here's my analysis," said Cerelles, as he waved Kale his documentation.

Kale consumed the contents of the floating data, his eyes darting back and forth through the complex equations. He was thunderstruck. This could not be happening. A man he trusted was predicting a cosmic orgy of death. It was a concept utterly out of phase with everything he had ever felt or known. Before he could help it, it occurred to Kale that he would no longer need to complete his term paper. But how could they be the only people in the universe to know?

"Fen, is there anyone else who can corroborate this data, like at Kalyphon University or maybe that Sentient Corbus Anta at the Cosmographic Society?" Kale asked.

"I tried them, and got wrapped up in red tape. Anta never leaves his desk. He's just there to look pretty. Sure, a completely artificial humanoid form is more hologenic than some decrepit, fat, organic human, but he's just show. It's about UNN's ratings. That's what it's really about now. There's no substance," said Cerelles, settling into a familiar groove. "For centuries, cosmology and physics have been in decline. Everyone is content that they finally know everything about the universe! Why fund those departments any more? Why devote resources to it? Profit seems to be the driving force in academia these days."

Kale had heard this rant before. He tuned it out as Cerelles walked over to the window, mumbling his dissatisfaction.

Kale returned to the data display in front of him, rubbing his head, and exclaiming loudly as he brought up and checked the equations.

"It's really coming down in sheets now," said Cerelles, looking out the window. He turned to find his student catatonic. "Kale? Are you okay? Would you like some tea?" asked the professor.

Kale exhaled, not hearing the questions. "Okay. If you're right, what can we do?"

"Do?" frowned Cerelles. "We can verify the source data on site, and then publish a paper on it. There's nothing else that can be done about it. You can't even write a will."

✦✦✦✦✦

The sun, perched high in a blue sky, shone down on the dry savannah. A pride of lions sat on top of one of the rolling hills, surveying their domain. A female, blending into her tawny brown surroundings, approached the pride. Another female observed her approach, but the others were unimpressed. The male, with his robust shaggy mane, only deigned to swat at a fly with his tail. Another female raised her torso with her fore legs, and opened her massive jaw wide, revealing a set of formidable tearing knives. However, there was no sound, except the incessant buzzing of mosquitoes.

Although he was protected from insects, Kale nonetheless was irritated by them. He was sure their droning would have long-term psychological effects on anyone who had to hear it. It was a wonder anyone could have ever lived here, let alone evolved here.

Kale gazed at the yawning female. "The universe is going to collapse next spring," he informed her.

The lioness looked at him, her tail dropped onto the dry grass. She smelled vaguely of carrion.

"It doesn't really affect you, does it?" Kale asked.

The lioness moved her focus to a herd of wildebeest entering the plain. They were following a game trail that would bring them to water.

Kale looked over his shoulder to see what she was looking at. "Oh, yes. They follow the trail. You follow them. You kill them. This ancient cycle is much more important to you, isn't it? Somehow, even if you could understand me, you still probably wouldn't care, would you?"

The lioness had no perceptible reaction.

"Just the here and now. That's all that matters to you. You're no different from that herd you're tracking. Anything I say, so long as it requires effort to comprehend beyond your immediate interest, will seem as mere trivia to you," continued Kale.

The lioness returned her gaze to the noisy, low-calorie creature in front of her, and the strange shaking object behind it. She blinked.

"Eloquent response," said Kale. "I suppose while I lose what little semblance of sanity I started with, you will enjoy the last few months of the universe, blissfully killing, eating, sleeping, and reproducing. You know, evolutionarily speaking, this whole 'intelligence' fad is beginning to seem a bit overrated," Kale concluded.

Kale knelt down to pick up a dried stalk, and noticed that a soundless bell was tolling holographically four feet into the air. He pushed forward the unmute command, and steeled himself for the cold fingers of a neural message.

"Mr. Eritrus," boomed the thoughts of his Anthro 330 professor. "Although you have signed a liability waiver to join this class, you do not have the right to interfere with the natural balance of the African ecosystem. Get back to the delineated area right now before our class permit is revoked by the warden's office."

Kale glanced over to the class area, and could make out that most of the faces were staring at him. Kale sighed, and returned to face the lioness.

She was on her back now, with her paws in the air.

"I have to go now. It was very refreshing talking to you," Kale offered.

The lioness rubbed her back into the dry grass.

✦✦✦✦✦

"All right class, on Wednesday, we will continue to discuss the impact of opposable thumbs and tools, including an examination of the Lucy find," intoned Professor Degrassi, as she wrapped up her lecture. "As it says in your syllabus, make sure you have read up through Chapter IV, the continuation of the 'Comparison of the Mental Powers of Man and the Lower Animals,' in Darwin's *The Descent of Man*, as background. Remember, that's the Jerabek translation, not the old Husspen translation. Most of you will not understand ancient English. For those of you reading ahead, read up through Chapter VI, 'The Prisoners' Solution,' in Kanji's *Removing the Training Wheels*. This will provide an excellent background for next Monday's trip to the ruins of the Valhalla community in the shadow of Olympus Mons. For those of you who are low-grav intolerant, you may attend the Martian field trip by proxy using a closed neurocom." Her students began rustling with their bags.

"Hey now! Don't start packing up until I say you are dismissed! I don't care what your local watches say. And while I'm on that topic, your first mini-report is due four weeks from the coming Wednesday, at the beginning of class, Stanford time. I will not accept any excuses based on time dilation." She thrust a bony finger at her class, and continued, "Your reports must be in *my* inbox when *my* calendar says it's November 12, and when *my* clock says it's 8:00 a.m. Got it? Good. *Now* you're dismissed," Degrassi concluded.

The class hesitated, and then began packing their materials.

"Look, buddy," said Gander. "I don't get this stuff. I tried to stall during the break, but I've only got so much small talk piled up, at least about this dust and bones and thumbs crap." He shoved his condenser into his backpack.

Kale took a deep breath. "Look, I was only going to be gone for the ten minutes. You couldn't talk to her for ten minutes about the beginning of man?"

"Hey, I'm not as into this dusty stuff as you are. I'm just in it for the field trips. That's why I'm taking this pass/fail. And there is no way in the universe that I'm going to read all that by Wednesday," Gander protested.

Kale frowned. "Now how can I argue with that?" he asked.

Not quite registering the sarcasm, Gander responded, "That's right. So back off, man." Gander paused. "So what was the deal with the tigers?"

"Lions, Gander. Tigers were striped, and now are extinct," Kale replied without answering.

"There you go again. You know, I have to tell you something as a friend, before this gets you into real trouble." Kale turned to face him. "You act like you know everything. Like you don't even see other people as equals. You're like some paid Observer, who's cataloging all these human stupidities. And you could actually be wrong, you know. Maybe lions are striped, and those *are* tigers over there. And maybe the lions are extinct. But maybe before they went extinct on Earth, somebody took some and cultivated them on another planet in another galaxy somewhere!" Gander was flush, and Kale was about to explode in response. He did not need this particularly sharp observation right now; he needed support.

"You're right, Gander."

Gander's eyes widened. "Well, you know, you're very smart and all, and I don't want to say anything that—"

Kale interrupted, "No, Gander, you're absolutely right. But there's something more. I know I'm a jerk most of the time, but something happened last night after the party that—"

"Well, what is it?"

"I'm not sure if it's such a good idea to tell you," said Kale.

"What, I'm too stupid to understand?" Gander replied, more hurt than angry.

Kale grasped his friend by the arms. "No! It's not like that at all. It might hurt you if I tell you." Kale let go.

"Oh, come on, buddy. Sticks and stones! Saying words never hurt anyone," replied Gander.

"These aren't the kind of words that are normally spoken."

"Okay, this is serious. You have to tell me, but let's get off the Serengeti. There's a nice café in Mombasa that I know. Let's go there," said Gander.

+++++

The cup was made of fine bone china. It was adorned around the rim and the handle with gold leaf. It also had a light blue strip of paisley below the rim, on both the inside and outside of the cup. The interior strip was not exposed however, since the vessel of the cup was filled with the Milky Way's prized Kenya coffee.

The bottom of the cup suddenly compressed as it was sandwiched between the granite floor and the top of the cup, which was still moving downward as the force of gravity dictated. The cup reacted to the impact by disintegrating, causing the hot liquid to spread out in a textbook torus-shaped arc away from the initial event, but ultimately returning to the unyielding ground.

The former owner of the cup did not register the fact that he dropped it. On the other hand, most of the other customers, and the busboy, whose programming precluded otherwise, immediately were drawn to the white, blue, and gold fragments among intermittent puddles of steaming translucent brown liquid.

"Could he be wrong?" whispered Gander. Most of the customers turned back to their own conversations.

"The math is solid. However, it all rests on long-distance observations and second-hand data. There could be mistakes there. We're going to check them out onsite. Cerelles is looking into requisitioning a faculty yacht, although I don't think he has the muscle to pull it off," replied Kale.

"I don't—I mean, what the—" trailed off Gander, mouth gaping.

"We need some other means of transport. And it has to be untraceable. My Cosmos is too small for the equipment, and it can only Travel using municipal strings. That means debiting my Travel account, and a tracking code recorded with the Port Authority. We *need* a self-strung starship," continued Kale.

Gander, realizing where this was leading, snapped back, "Are you nuts? We can't take my dad's boat. He would full bug-tick. And then activate the muon lockout, shutting down the boat and getting us arrested. And that's just to start."

Kale, rocking back on the rear legs of the chair, responded, "'Us'?"

Gander could not maintain a stern expression, and a liberated smile lit up the table. "Yeah, 'us'! If you think for a minute I'm going to let you go zipping across the universe with that crackpot Cerelles, think again, buddy!"

Kale beamed. "Gander, I appreciate what you're saying, but can you really take off time from class to do this? I feel guilty about dragging you into this."

"Hey, you're not dragging me anywhere; I'm pushing into this deal! And, in any event, if what you say is true, then classes are the least of our worries."

Kale felt the weight of that statement push down on him. He was working hard on isolating thoughts regarding the futility of any action in response to Cerelles's hypothesis, but it was too difficult to keep up. Kale sighed. "Let's get back to my place, and figure out what we're going to do. I'll have Cerelles meet us there."

"Yeah, let's split," replied Gander.

The two got up and left the café. Eight seconds later, an unremarkable customer followed them out. His gaze tracked them, never losing contact as he stepped into a long black pod that pulled up in front of him.

+ + + + +

"What is that idiot doing here?" fumed Cerelles.

Kale replied, "F-Fen, he's going to help us."

"Can he calibrate a stellar scale?"

"No, but I can find a great place to put it!" offered Gander.

Cerelles's face reddened. "Great, just great! I impart on you the need for total secrecy, and the first thing you do is blab to this frat boy. The universe may as well collapse tomorrow!"

"Look, you old fart," said Gander, jabbing a finger at Cerelles. "What difference does all the secrecy make if we're all going to get squashed after the homecoming game?"

"Hey, wait—" started Kale, before he was pushed back into his chair by his former mentor.

"The reason, you infinitely dense meathead, is that if word gets out, the last months of the universe will be one big riot. The structure of civilization will crumble to radioactive dust," Cerelles said.

"But what difference does it make? We're going to be less than dust next year anyway!"

"Why do anything then? We all die eventually. Why build a library? Why build a road? Why write a song? Why have morals? Your kind of myopic reasoning has no place in this expedition, and frankly, I'm beginning to question you too, Kale," croaked Cerelles.

Kale clutched the armrests of his chair, as if he had been punched in the stomach. Had he really made the wrong choice in confiding in his friend?

Gander pursed his lips, and regarded the twitching professor through squinted eyes. "So how did the faculty yacht request go?"

"What? Oh, I'll have it from them any second!" said Cerelles, with a touch of too much self-assurance.

"Professor," started Kale, "we checked the administration inventory neurocom. She said all yachts were booked through the new year, with priority going to the Economics Department sabbatical. I'm sorry, sir."

Deflated, Cerelles fell back in his chair. "Damn fools," he muttered. An empty moment hung in the air.

"Well guys, I know how to get a self-strung starship immediately, completely off the record."

Kale and Cerelles looked up in disbelief. Cerelles managed to ask Gander, "How?"

Chapter 3

Keeping Secrets

"Well, stalker, this scoop of yours had better be good, or I'll have a restraining order put out on you," said Athena. She observed Kale through cold, green eyes.

Kale suppressed his involuntary attraction to the angular woman standing before him in a gray fitted designer suit and black, severely tied-back hair. "Is this a secure connection?"

Athena scowled. "Of course it is. Do you really think I would allow any record of my talking to you? Now get to the point—I don't have the time or the inclination for *you*."

"Listen." Kale took a deep breath. As much as the death sentence shattered his life's plans, it still sounded absurd to say out loud. "The universe is going to collapse." Kale steeled himself for a savage response.

Athena's eyes sharpened perceptibly and she leaned forward. "Meet me at the Ozymandias monument on Titan in one hour, end connection," she hissed. She disappeared, leaving Kale stunned and off-guard.

"What a bitch," offered Ellen.

Disregarding her, Kale muttered, "She seems to know already!"

"So it would appear. It seemed unlikely to me that the four of us would be the only souls in the universe to be aware of this."

"Apparently. Ellen, let the others in here, please."

A door swished open, and Gander and Cerelles entered the living room. "So, do we have a ship?" asked Gander.

"No, but Kale has a date!" purred Ellen.

Kale looked up and gazed at the greenish yellow world floating in the sky. The rings of Saturn shimmered like a wide gaudy necklace in the Titan twilight.

"Leafy!"

Kale looked down to meet the stare of a gray woman. "Athena." She examined him with that same clinical gaze. Kale felt a wave of nausea rising.

"Walk with me," she said.

Kale looked around. He saw some tourists taking pictures by the monument. There was a guide giving a discussion about the pioneering terraforming of the satellite. The guide went on to describe the history of the sphere-topped skyscrapers behind them, how architects exploited the various forms possible on low gravity worlds, and how they were some of the few remaining examples of the organic style. Kale noticed the journalist, and walked over to join her on a greenbelt pathway.

"So, you seem to know already," started Kale, after a period of silence.

"Maybe. Why don't you tell me what *you* know, or more precisely, what you *think* you know," replied Athena.

Kale glanced behind them.

"Don't worry, Kale, I'm carrying a scrambler. Nobody can sense us right now, with or without sensory enhancements," assured Athena.

"You mean we're invisible?" asked Kale.

"Look, kid, this is serious business. Tell me what you know!"

Sensing an advantage, Kale pressed her, "No, damn it, you tell me what you know. I'm getting a little tired of your superior attitude, and frankly your request to see me on such short notice suggests you badly need something from me. So either you start talking, or I'm off."

Athena stopped and stared icily at Kale. Then she abruptly turned and began walking away briskly. Kale was dumbfounded. She had called his bluff! He started running after her.

Just as he approached her, she swung around and drove her fist into his left eye. Kale fell heavily to the ground. Shocked beyond belief, his head swimming in red pain, he found himself jerked to his feet. Athena held him by the scruff of his neck, and peered into his skull.

"Look, you stupid prick. This isn't a game. This is *big*. If you know something, tell me. If not, tell me why you said what you did. If you were just trying to get my attention, you will regret the day you ever had it!"

"What is wrong with you?" Kale sputtered. "Why did you hit me? Are you insane?"

"Kale, I don't have the time to list out everything that's wrong with me. Second, I hit you because you need to know where I stand. Third, sanity is relative." With that, she threw him to the ground.

Kale hit the spongy path a second time. He looked up at her through glaring eyes. "What makes you think I would be more willing to talk to you after you hit me?"

"Like you said, because you're here! Two can play out that argument. We both are here because we want something from the other. The only difference is that you're going to tell me first!"

Kale said nothing.

"Talk, or I'll be forced to really hurt you. And remember, nobody can hear you while my scrambler is on."

Kale felt trapped. He needed access to her 3S vessel. However, knowing the universe was going to end gave him a strange sense of strength. He was not going to allow anyone to treat him this way, especially since he was going to be dead soon anyway. Having lived a life tempering his reactions and overthinking consequences, Kale was in uncharted territory.

He stood up, and angled his chin toward her. He pointed at it. "Get started. We don't really have the time to argue." Kale closed his eyes without squinting, ready to accept the blow.

With one hand, Athena grabbed the back of his head, and pressed her lips against his.

By the time it registered in his mind, she already had let go of his head, and was drawing away. He stared at her. Was she insane? He noticed that her features softened slightly.

"The network has received various incoherent reports along the lines you suggested. Each of them goes cold by the time we get a reporter on it. They either say they were joking, they never said it, or nothing at all, because they are missing or dead," revealed a matter-of-fact Athena.

Hardly comprehending the behavior of the woman in front of him, but shocked enough by the events she was revealing to disregard it, Kale asked, "How many reports?"

"Difficult to say. The network itself keeps a very tight lid on source information in general, but this stuff doesn't even show up in the system. Normally, state secrets at least appear as hits, if only as encrypted secure files. For this, there are *no* records whatsoever."

"How do you know then?"

"A girl has to keep some secrets."

"I see."

"Your turn."

Kale took a deep breath. After the kiss, he certainly felt more forthcoming with her, but perhaps that was her objective. It was not the first time he felt manipulated by a woman, but she also divulged information she did not have to. "Fair enough. My former physics professor discovered some gravitational anomalies that caused him to recompute the weight of the universe as being greater than the Universal Chandrasekhar Limit. This computation, in addition to the inflationary collapse equations, show a collapse next March," said Kale.

"So what can be done?" asked Athena.

"Well, we need to verify the mass and other readings first-hand. And in order to do that without arousing suspicion, we need a 3S vessel of some type. Gander thought you, as a journalist, would have one."

"Aha!" said Athena, rocking back on her heels. "I see what you're getting at. But that doesn't answer my question. I want to know what can be done to stop and reverse that collapse."

Kale raised his eyebrows. "That can't be done. There is no way to arrest the force of gravity."

"What goes up must come down, right?" said Athena.

"I suppose, yes. The irony of this whole situation is that physics is a dying science. Very few people are left who can recognize the coming danger," added Kale.

"Do you really think it's coincidental?"

"What do you mean?"

"Come on, don't be so naïve. If the government knew about the collapse, it would have to wipe out everyone who could discover it independently."

This made no sense at all. "That's absurd!" replied Kale. "The government doesn't know about this. It would be impossible to maintain silence on an event of this magnitude. That type of organizational skill is far beyond the capacity of a government bureaucracy. In any event, our government hasn't killed a human being deliberately in more than two thousand years."

"Well, that's what you learned in school. But you're the one insisting on untraceability."

Kale felt exasperated. "Well, that's more an issue of preventing panic. Someone could connect the dots on our flight plan and figure it all out."

"Figure it out? Wait, aren't you going to publish a paper or something on this anyway?"

Kale paused. "Cerelles, the professor who discovered the collapse, wants to, out of academic vanity, I think. But he is aware of the potential for panic, and I think I can convince him out of publishing it."

"So you probably expect me not to break the story on this either. Some scoop, Kale."

Although desperate for the untraceable transport Athena could provide, Kale knew a leak of the information could trigger a universal riot. He had to be completely clear and completely honest on this point. "I would ask you not to. I know that's your job, but I hope you can understand the need to ensure a civil society, even if it is about to be destroyed," reasoned Kale.

"I suppose I could hold on the story until it becomes inevitable. If this is true, nothing matters anyway. So I take it you have an itinerary ready?"

"Yes, we're ready to go."

"Then I'll contact you when the ship's ready. Let's get back to the monument," said Athena. They returned to the main square and she deactivated her scrambler. An overweight man in shorts and a hat stood in front of them.

He spun around. "Well aren't you two a cute couple! Would ya mind taking a picture of me and the little lady?" he asked, circling his arm around a similarly rotund woman.

"Not at all," replied Kale, taking the offered cam. "Smile!" he said, hitting the record button. Multiple tiny lenses snaked out of the cam and writhed in pre-determined arcs before they rapidly returned to their sockets.

"Thanks, fella!" said the man.

"You're welcome," said Kale, turning to get back to Athena. Not surprisingly, she was gone.

The man watched as Kale left too, nodding imperceptibly to his apparent wife. He placed the cam in a stasis pouch, which sealed with a clipped hiss.

✦ ✦ ✦ ✦ ✦

"I didn't want to say anything to embarrass you when you returned from Titan, since Gander and Cerelles were still here," started Ellen.

"Go on," said Kale, as he threw some clothes into a suitcase.

"Well, besides the black eye, you also had residual traces of organic polymers on your face."

"Uh-huh."

"You kissed her."

Kale stopped, and then started the seal cycle on his suitcase. "She kissed me. I didn't mention it because it wasn't really necessary."

"Kale, she's dangerous. I don't like the way she talks to you, and frankly, the fact that she uses violence to make her point as freely as a normal person would use a prepositional phrase is not a good characteristic in someone you're relying on, let alone someone you may have romantic interests in."

Kale did not want to be lectured to, so he decided to explain.

"Ellen, I don't really know what's going on with her. We need her right now, and there's no quiet or quick way around that. As for romantic interests, I really don't know what to make of her. But all of this could be a moot question. The fact that all her leads turn cold suggests that Cerelles is right. Falling for a sociopathic woman doesn't strike me as such a big deal when compared to the end of the universe."

"Are you falling for her?"

"I don't think so. She's painful to be with. As selfish as this may sound, the big thing for me is that my whole life is over."

"Not yet, Kale."

Ellen always had a response, although Kale was far from done. "The likelihood is high. You know, I wanted to *do* something with my life. Remember how I always wanted to teach? Stand in front of a class filled with young minds. Twelve or thirteen year olds. Just when they're ready and capable of listening. Any older, and they're already too set to consider anything fairly. Like my own seventh-grade history teacher used to say, 'An open mind is the key to the universe.' Now all those dreams will remain just that. Dreams. Instead, I'm going to be running around the universe like an electrocuted stim-bot."

"Kale, you keep assuming the universe actually is going to collapse. You are basing this nightmare on the admittedly second-hand data from a precariously positioned professor, and the dramatic intrigues of someone you yourself called a 'sociopathic.' You know, it's part of my operating system to question all sources of information, and make judgments based on the reliability of sources. You might want to consider this method as an alternative to making judgments based on emotional impact."

"The information is not all second hand. The fact is that we are going to be nothing this time next year. Or to be more precise, there isn't going to be a next year," trailed off Kale.

"But all of this contradicts millennia of accepted cosmological theory. It still will be necessary to verify this information before you start bouncing off the walls in some primitive death dance!"

This made Kale smile. "Fine, Ellen, you've made your point. Download into my wristband, and let's go."

Ellen did so, but knew deep inside her synthetic soul that Kale was right. The universe was over, and they would all be crushed out of existence. Until that happened, she knew she had to minimize Kale's trauma of knowing that it was coming. She was determined to keep him safe for as long as she could.

+ + + + +

A bulky ship descended through the low-lying but rapidly blowing clouds. "That's not a UNN shuttle," said Kale as Cerelles and Gander looked up.

Although streamlined, the ship clearly was built for towing giant objects. Two massive circular tractor emitters protruded from the front of the ship while a wide oval one extended from its rear. The ship was translucent cobalt blue, making it a Nobarra product, although it bore the markings of the Sepheis Terraform Construction Corporation.

Landing filaments extended from the base of the ship, dancing in unison before solidifying, keeping the ship perfectly level with its weight balanced evenly across the ground. A ramp extended from the belly of the ship, and Athena bounded out, in a blur of blue shirt and black flowing hair. "What is that?" asked Kale, as she hit the grass.

"A tugboat, you moron," she replied. "Do you really think we'll get far undercover in a UNN vessel of any kind? This ship is part of an order that my mother's company doesn't have to deliver until next February. It's got a standard set of Rolls-Royce tractors, two Bulldog Fours in front, one Anchor Seven in back. The rounded hull has a two-meter thick diamond exoskeleton for structural integrity. The ship's new, but basic. It's huge, but inconspicuous. It's perfect!"

Realizing he had no choice in the matter, Kale let it go. "I believe you know Gander." He nodded toward Athena.

"Unfortunately, yes," responded Athena.

"This is Dr. Fen Cerelles; Fen, Athena Nobarra," continued Kale.

Cerelles stepped forward, extended his hand, and said, "It is indeed a pleasure to meet you, young lady. I am sure Kale will benefit from your perspective on this expedition."

Athena shook his hand. "Yes, I am sure he will," she said.

Kale turned to Cerelles. "Fen, please take Gander back into the lab, and get the equipment we need. Remember, don't ask any neurocoms for assistance; they'll record the action." Cerelles, glad to see his pupil running the project, nodded, and they disappeared into the desolate Stanford physics dome.

Once they were alone, Kale started, "I didn't know you knew how to fly."

"You go through life assuming everyone is less capable than you, don't you?" Athena responded.

"What? No, I was just making conversation."

"Why bother making conversation? We're all going to be dead soon. Don't waste my time."

"So what would you prefer I do?"

"Well, I'm surprised you haven't made a pass at me yet."

"You want me to?"

"No."

"What?"

"I don't want anything to do with you. If it were up to me, I wouldn't be here at all. But this is just too big to ignore."

Switching gears, Kale asked, "So, what do we call this ship?"

"It only has a serial number so far, but I'm calling it the *Last Chance*."

Kale paused. "That name doesn't make sense. This expedition is to prove there aren't any more chances left."

"Don't be such a pessimist. You don't know what's out there. You scientist types are always so closed-minded!"

Just then, the two men emerged from the lab, each with a gravitic cart loaded with equipment. They added their suitcases onto the carts, and proceeded up the ramp.

"Get your bag," said Athena, and she bounded back up into the blue ship.

"She's borderline," said a voice from his wrist. "I'm surprised someone of her stature and profession hasn't been treated for it."

"Ellen, I know. But I have a feeling there's something very genuine about her. I'm not quite sure what it is, but there's some kernel of honesty at the bottom of that pool of acidic attitude."

"Wishful thinking. It won't do you any good to try and make her into someone you want her to be, just because she's good-looking."

Kale grinned at his wristband. "She is pretty, isn't she?"

"Get on the ship!" snapped Ellen.

Kale gripped the handle of his suitcase, and it rose off the ground. He turned to climb up the ramp and saw Cerelles facing him.

"Fen, did you forget something?"

"No, I'm not coming with you."

Kale stood still, puzzled.

"Kale, when you get to my age, you accumulate a long string of regrets. I'm going to see my wife."

Trying to be delicate, Kale said, "But you divorced her decades ago because she ran off with someone else."

Cerelles smiled a sad grin. "I know. I do remember it; I'm not senile. But, given the fact that she is going to die soon, as are we all, I want to forgive her. She kept trying to patch things up after the other man left her, but I was cold to her. And that coldness seeped into the rest of my life. I'm well aware that the student body and the rest of the faculty think I'm a cantankerous old man, and I don't want to prove them right. I want to be the man I was forty years ago. Not physically, of course, but emotionally. I was vibrant, outgoing, and I loved her. Now, I need to forgive her."

"Does she know you're coming?" asked Kale.

"No, my boy. She doesn't. But I know she's alone. And you can't keep hating someone you love."

Kale was amazed to hear Cerelles speak this way about his ex-wife. Cerelles had always kept quiet about her, except in fits of drunkenness, when all manner of profanities would erupt on the subject.

Saving Kale the awkwardness of raising the issue himself, Cerelles offered, "You don't need me to run the measurements. You have the experience, and you have the equipment. I know you can do it. You have company, as it were, and you have my support, for what it's worth."

"But what about you? When will I see you again?" Kale asked.

Cerelles met his student's intense gaze, and felt he could only say that which he knew to be true: "I don't know." With that, he grasped his student's shoulders warmly, and smiled. He walked down the ramp and disappeared into the Stanford tube transport system.

From the top of the ramp, Kale looked over the tube entrance to the ancient Stanford campus, the rolling green hills, the Pacific lapping the beach nearby, and on the horizon, the continent of North America, pushed out over eons on its tectonic plate. The sun was low in the sky, filtering through the wispy clouds. As the orange-reddish light streaked through the trees and the wind began to pick up, Kale could feel the sun setting on his world. He took a deep breath of Earth air, savoring it, and stepped inside.

The lopsided blue ship rose up from the tip of California Island, and up through the atmosphere of the storied world and out of the inner Solar System.

CHAPTER 4

THE STYGIAN GATE

"I don't know why you let her talk to you like that," said the Gate Controller of Pluto's centrifuge.

"Oh, like you could come up with any kind of comeback?" said the Co-Controller.

"Yeah, man! I'd say, 'Babe, that sounds like the voice of experience!'" replied the Gate Controller.

"Oh, come on! Who can ever come up with a comeback like that right on the spot? Listen to what I thought of on the way over. I should have said to her—"

"Gentlemen, there is an Unrequested Tubule Stringing in operation," notified the Gate neurocom.

The Co-Controller snapped out of his reverie, and commanded, "Thanks, Gene. Connect with the UTS ship." His colleague sat back, and paused for the familiar wait. A few seconds ticked by. He tried to count the holes in the ceiling panel.

At thirty-eight holes, Gene said, "Visual connection established."

"This is Stygian Gate Controller Dugan. We understand that you are stringing a tubule. We would like to inform you that you can save up to 70 credits or more, using our Carbon Centrifuge and our new flex pass. Membership is free, and for only 250 credits, we can string a tubule for you in less than ten minutes."

"No thank you, we're not interested," replied Gander.

"Are you sure? We can set up a Port Authority flex pass for you instantly, and you can Travel on credit," said Dugan.

"No, really, we have no interest in your service. Perhaps you'll have better luck with the next vessel. End connection," said Gander.

The image of the sincere Controller dissolved, and Kale and Athena reentered the transmission room. "Did they sound suspicious?" he asked.

"I don't think so. They probably get rejected all the time," replied Gander.

"Yes, well, I still think you should have changed your clothes," said Athena. "You don't look like a Sepheis construction worker, particularly in that sweater-vest. This may create questions."

"Oh, don't be so damned paranoid. Any delay in replying to their connect request would raise even more questions," pointed out Gander. "And you know I'm right!"

Seeing that Athena was firing up for a heated discussion, Kale left the transmission room, and wandered into the observation lounge. He sat down on a luxurious leatherette couch, and stared out the huge bay window.

The Stygian Gate was visible in all its former glory. Before the Gate was built, Pluto and its moon Charon marked out a wide orbit on the edge of the solar system, alone for billions of years. The axial rotation period of Pluto matched the orbital period of Charon, keeping them locked in position, forever facing each other. Upon recognizing its potential, humanity built a physical diamond-core bridge connecting the two, and turned it into "The Gateway to the Universe."

Despite the distance, Kale could discern the intricate detailing on the umbilical bridge connecting the two worlds. Heroic poses of figures from ancient Earth mythology adorned the trunk in relief sculptures, several hundred kilometers wide. A number of ships' strings were visibly active, looping out from Charon, and placing massive tubule nozzles at specific points in space, presumably in front of relatively tiny ships.

The complex still looked grand, with its excessive use of gold and clear diamond buttresses. The colossal green granite relief sculpture of The Boatman ferrying souls to the Underworld was a particularly garish touch. The Boatman's lantern was a fusion reactor, surrounded by a ruby sphere, to give it a reddish tinge. It occurred to Kale that until then, he never saw the Stygian Gate as anything other than a historic monument to excess. Now, nearly everything he saw looked simply beautiful. Everything ugly had turned into the most exquisite art.

A holographic bell materialized in midair, drawing Kale's attention from the Gate. Kale prepared himself for a neural message. It was Athena, calling from the control room. "Our string is returning with a tubule, if you're interested in watching." Kale was surprised not so much by the content of the message, but its neural texture. Most neural interfaces had a smooth, icy character, whereas Athena's possessed an earthier, soil-like consistency. It may just have been the equipment onboard the *Last Chance*, but he was willing to consider that there might be more to it than just that.

Kale got up, and trotted off toward the control room. Once he arrived, he found Athena seated in a large memory-fit silicon pilot's chair that engulfed her entire body, with Gander leaning against a railing by the door.

"Oh good, you're finally here," she said, and mentally commanded the room to one-way transparency. The interior of the ship disappeared, replaced with a brilliant starfield. The passengers, the chair, and a shiny black purse remained visible, curiously suspended in the starfield. A blinking white line snaked out from below and into the distance. Kale coiled his arm through a railing.

The full effect was daunting. Although he was aware of such features, no ship Kale had ever traveled on allowed passengers to view the external environment.

"Focus on her head. It's big enough!" whispered Gander, aware of his friend's unease.

"If that's enough from you children back there, the tubule is approaching," said Athena.

"So you can really pilot this thing through the tubule system?" asked Kale, staring at the willowy filament coming toward them.

"Of course I can. Why do you keep asking me that? I grew up with ships, it's the family business, so of course I know how to pilot one. Oh, and if anyone else wants to get off, this is the last stop in the Solar System," she added with a scowl.

Kale wanted to lash out at her. "The professor had his reasons for not coming along," he said.

"Oh, what? He was getting too depressed? Well, he should have thought of that sooner!" she barked back.

Kale bit his lip. "I can't deal with you right now. I'll be in my quarters." With that, he turned and left the room.

Once he left, Gander addressed Athena squarely. "Do you just run off at the mouth whenever you feel like it? Do you have any idea what that old guy means to Kale?"

"No, I don't, you stupid ox. Nor do I care. We all are coping with our own issues. The fact that the universe is going to end does not help any of us. You don't hear me complaining about my problems, do you?" Athena replied.

"You can shine me all you like, but at the end of the day, you are just as lucky as I am. We've got padding, and we have our signatures. We're set. Kale is not. His parents are dead. Do you understand that?" Gander shot back.

"I don't care to hear the whole sob story. So what if his parents died? I envy him! So what if he has no money? He's in college! The government always steps in with programs to level the playing field," said Athena.

"I'm not finished. That old fart took Kale under his wing, and treated him with more care than I have ever seen a professor show a student. I think they're like two random jigsaw pieces that happened to fit. Now Kale is completely alone. The least you could do is back off a bit," replied Gander.

"I'll back off when I'm good and ready. I call the shots in my life, nobody else!" she said. But the sensation of being utterly alone struck a chord.

"Fine. I'm going to check on Kale. Do your thing, and try to stay out of my way," Gander called over his shoulder as he left the room.

Fuming, Athena watched as the ship's string reeled in a Travel tubule. The gaping maw of the tubule appeared to be contorted, with the edges of the rim falling against each other. The *Last Chance* could navigate through it, but in three-dimensional space, the tubule looked like a surreal optical illusion.

Athena mechanically pushed forward the command to move through the tubule, which would then connect with the Stygian Wormhole. The ship passed through the mouth and into the tubule. As space rippled around her, Athena could think only of being alone. She liked to tell herself that she could handle anyone, and that nobody could ever touch her. This was her best psychological defense set-up. She knew all too well that this defense also was crippling her. She often was surrounded by admirers, acquaintances, contacts, suitors, and people she should know, but never by real friends. She had nobody to confide in, nobody to trust.

✦✦✦✦✦

Kale was arranging some textbooks on his holofield when he heard Gander's chime. "Come in."

Gander stepped in. "Hey buddy. I've, uh, been reading that book you gave me."

"Oh?" replied Kale in a quiet voice.

"Yeah, you know, *Physics for Psychos*."

"Uh-huh."

"I really liked the section on gravity. Do you remember it?"

"Not really," replied Kale.

"It's the one that puts you in the glass mansion with the pool table. You can drop the eight ball onto a glass dining table from two stories up, or throw it through the windows, remember?" recounted Gander.

"Yeah, a little bit."

Gander changed the topic. "We're moving through the tube," he said, pointing toward the rippling fabric of space through the oval portal above the headboard. "She just maneuvered the ship through the mouth."

Kale did not respond.

Realizing that he had to address the issue, Gander asked, "Are you okay?"

Kale blinked. "Yes, I'll be fine. I just need to focus on the task at hand. Our first stop is Azimuth, and we need to be ready," replied Kale.

"Yeah, well, that galaxy is light millennia away in real space. It will be morning, ship-time, before we get there. It would make sense to try and get some sleep meanwhile, right?"

"Yes, you're right. I'll power down for the night." Kale paused, and Gander started to leave. "Oh, Gander?"

"Yeah, buddy?" said Gander, turning around.

"Thanks."

A wide grin spread out on his broad face. "You're welcome!" said Gander, knowing the proper response to rare gratitude, and left Kale's quarters with a smile.

Kale took off his wristband and placed it on the nightstand. He then stretched out onto the bed. He pushed forward the thought "envelop," and layers of bedding slowly descended from the ceiling. Once he was comfortable and starting to drift off, Ellen decided to speak up.

"If you're not going to talk to your best friend, then you have to talk to me," she said.

"Mmmmmmph. I'm trying to sleep, Ellen. Tomorrow," mumbled Kale.

"No, not tomorrow. There will be too much to cope with tomorrow."

"What do you want to talk about then?" asked Kale, realizing he was not going to get to sleep while Ellen wanted something.

"You, of course. I strongly dislike that woman, but you can't run off whenever anyone brings up a personal subject."

"What the! You're supposed to be on my side!" Kale said, sitting up and glaring at the neurocom wristband on the nightstand.

"Hold it, Kale. I *am* on your side. You should consider growing a thicker skin. People always are going to say things that might upset you. Hiding from it will be much more painful in the long run."

"What long run?" Kale said, raising his voice. "What difference does it make? I am going to die. You are going to die. She's going to die. Every person in the universe is going to die. Why can't you get that through your neurogel synapses?"

"Look, Kale. You need to get this under control. If one of you breaks, the rest of you are sure to follow. And in any event, you knew you were going to die from the moment you understood the concept of death. You are just faced with the potential of an accelerated schedule," said Ellen.

"That's really great advice, Ellen, but that kind of logic-chopping doesn't change anything. We will take some measurements, and return to Earth, to wait for our death. That's the bottom line," replied Kale.

Fearing he was right, Ellen played her last card. "Please try."

"I'll sleep on it. Good night, Ellen."

"Good night, Kale."

✛ ✛ ✛ ✛ ✛

Later that evening, the *Last Chance* emerged from the Stygian Wormhole outside the Sirius spiral arm of the Milky Way. Because of the extreme gravitational contortion created by the black hole hearts of most galaxies, the wider intergalactic wormholes typically were attached only to the edges of galaxies.

Athena, using a cerebral navigation grid, programmed the ship's stringhead to retrieve a tubule that would provide a wormhole link to the Azimuth Galaxy. This galaxy lay perpendicular to the plane of the Milky Way, but was located 783 galactic units "up" the z-axis in real space.

Given the girth of transgalactic wormholes in general, there was little delay in retrieving a tubule. The mouth appeared in front of the ship, and Athena, alone in the control room, directed the *Last Chance* through it.

Once she set the guidance system on the ship's neurocom control, Athena sat back in the molded chair. The contours of the chair adjusted to fit her body, and the sides of the chair gently enveloped her. The chair was warm, but there was no feeling or meaning in the silicon embrace. To Athena, it felt appropriate. Her mind began drifting off. As she entered a dream state, she could see the Azimuth Galaxy take shape in her mind. It was a massive collection of stars, rotating around a giant black hole. She could feel the weight of the enormous mass of material held within the gravitational field of the galaxy, and the sharp contrast of frigid space and nuclear furnace that characterized the prickly texture of the galaxy. She could see it floating above her palm, and closed her fingers around it. She woke up with a start, and glanced around. Nobody else was there, and the neurocom confirmed nothing had changed.

Chapter 5

The Ghost Ship

The *Last Chance* emerged in normal space, beneath the orbital plane of the O-type star Elegiel in the Azimuth Galaxy.

"There don't seem to be any habitable planets or any signs of life. What are we looking for?" asked Gander, as he stared at the massive white star suspended before a vibrant, billowy nebula.

"Nothing that we can see that easily," replied Kale. "Launch the scale probe."

Gander pushed forward the command to deploy one of the small devices they brought on board. A brilliant metallic sphere shot out of the blue ship, and darted toward the giant star.

Athena's personal neurocom spoke for the first time, in a terse masculine voice. "Receiving telemetry from the probe. Recommend we move to opposite position relative to star Elegiel for precise measurement."

Kale glanced over at Gander, who shook his head.

"Yes, that is exactly what we're going to do!" said Kale.

Athena pushed forward the navigation command, and swiveled halfway around in her chair, enough to regard Kale sideways. "Don't be so touchy! It's only a closed neurocom. It can't think. It only records and analyzes. All good journalists use one, to keep them objective. Exactly how were you planning on keeping your measurements objective?"

"The ship's neurocom will do just fine! And for your information, I have my own neurocom with me anyway. Say hello, Ellen."

"Hello, Ms. Nobarra," said Ellen, from his wrist.

Athena grinned unpleasantly. "I hope it doesn't fudge your data while you're sleeping!"

"And what is that supposed to mean?" hissed Kale.

"Just that it's possible for an open, thinking neurocom to configure results in a way that would be psychologically pleasing to its user. It's happened before," replied Athena, eyeing him coolly.

"Ellen, tell her why you wouldn't do that," said Kale.

"That would be unethical, as per the Ideal Personal Conduct standard laid down by the Valhalla Behavioral Accords," recited Ellen.

"Great, so it's got an IPC algorithm. Don't you think there are ways around that?" said Athena.

"Sorry to break this up, but we've stopped moving," said Gander.

"That's okay, we've just arrived at the right spot. All right, Athena, instruct your neurocom to record only; we will handle measurement and analysis through the ship's neurocom using voice command," said Kale.

Athena allowed a second or two to elapse. "Was that an order, captain?"

Gander gasped. Kale gathered himself and replied, "Let me handle the astrophysics aspects of this mission. You may think otherwise, but I know what I'm doing. I feel more comfortable with voice commands, my thoughts are clearer to me, and it helps maintain the logical progression from observation to conclusion."

"My neurocom stays on at all times, and receives a copy of your raw data stream," replied Athena.

"Fine!"

"And we all wear Sepheis uniforms," she continued.

"What?"

"We have to accept the role of Sepheis salvagers in order to keep our cover. That means looking like Sepheis employees in case we run into anyone," reasoned Athena.

"Yeah, she just doesn't want the story to break before she can report it!" blurted Gander.

"If you don't like the idea, there's an airlock down the hall that I'd be more than happy to throw you out of!" snapped Athena, rising out of her chair.

"Would you both, please, just shut up!" said Kale, yelling the last two words.

The two turned to him, wide-eyed. "We are going to carry out these tests, while maintaining the appearance of a Sepheis salvage team. That's the only thing that makes sense. And making sense is going to determine what goes on on this ship. Not attitude, not cheap shots. Is that clear?"

"Yeah, buddy. That's cool," said Gander.

Athena just stared at him. Kale couldn't read her expression, but the mission gave him the strength not to care.

✛ ✛ ✛ ✛ ✛

Kale plucked a strawberry out of the ship's nearby artery, and felt the familiar tingle of the fruit's stasis field dissolve.

"Okay. Recalculate mass triangulation, this time, factor out the gamma shift," he said.

The ship's neurocom replied, "Rotational drift is reduced by one hundred and six meters."

"Uhhh!" Kale exhaled. He popped the fresh, ripe strawberry in his mouth.

Gander, wearing blue overalls, entered the secondary supply hold, where Kale was sitting with his equipment. "Hey buddy. How's it going?"

"I don't know. Cerelles's calculations showed a significantly greater mass of dark matter in this area than we actually are finding. For three days now, we haven't detected any dark matter visually, and the star Elegiel is barely effected by any gravitational forces," Kale said.

"So this is good, right?" Gander offered.

"Well, yes. From Earth, it looked like Elegiel was wobbling in its orbit, which suggested extremely large, local gravitational forces. More so than the weight of the whole Azimuth galaxy should be, to remain stable. Now that we're out here, it's barely wobbling at all, just enough to account for the few barren planets in orbit. So the first observation that was to validate the collapse theory instead is reinforcing millennia of accepted fact."

"So, wait, the universe is not going to collapse?" asked Gander, somewhat amazed.

"Well, one observation does not demolish a theory. We have to stick around and complete a battery of tests, then move on to the next destination."

"But this is good news!"

"I don't want to start jumping for joy yet. Everything seemed so sound on Earth. I can't shake the feeling that I'm doing something wrong here," said Kale.

"Kale, you've got to stop thinking like that. That old fart probably made a mistake. He's over a hundred, and due to retire. He probably made the mistake, not you," said Gander.

"Well, that's nice of—" started Kale, before he was interrupted by a neural message.

"Guys, you had better get up here. I've found something," projected Athena.

✦ ✦ ✦ ✦ ✦

"So what are we looking at?" asked Gander.

Athena began, dictating information fed to her through the ship's sensor array: "This is the second planet. It is a gas giant in orbit around Elegiel. It is composed largely of hydrogen and helium mostly in a gaseous state. Deeper in, though, it becomes liquid, and ultimately metallic."

"This is one of twenty-eight moons," she said, as the view zoomed in to a rocky world suspended above the equator of the gas giant.

The image zoomed in further. "Now tell me what you see!" she said.

Gander gasped. Kale found his words first. "What the—what could have possibly happened?"

Athena zoomed in further, and a huge derelict ship filled the room. "It looks like she imploded. But those punctures look more like they were blasted from the inside out. There must have been a fierce struggle inside."

"Who do you think did this?" asked Gander.

"Pirates supply the black market as much as salvagers do the gray market—my money's on them," said Athena.

"Pirates? You're joking, right?" commented Gander.

"Piracy may be ancient history in the Milky Way, but the Universe is a big place and Kalyphon can't police all of it," observed the reporter.

"Still. I'm thinking aliens," suggested Gander.

"Oh, so for the first time in 360,000 years of recorded human history, we're going to discover intelligent alien life?" sneered Athena.

"Well, I'm just saying," was all he could come up with.

"It's just a guessing game until we check it out," replied Athena.

"Now, wait a minute. Just because we are in these uniforms doesn't mean we actually are salvagers!" said Kale.

"Don't be an idiot, Kale. That is exactly what it means! Our cover is utterly implausible if we ignore a giant hull like this!" barked Athena.

Gander replied first. "Yeah, but who knows where we are? There's no life or sign of civilization in this damned system! Not one body is habitable! For whose benefit would we be playing out this little game?"

"The reason being, you colossal ass, that anyone could show up at any time! And in any event, I don't believe in coincidence. The fact that we found a shot-up spaceship in a system we're inspecting suggests that something strange is going on here. Kale, you wanted to base this expedition on 'things that make sense,' right? Well, that ship has been here longer than us. Maybe someone or something on board can tell us something!"

Kale glanced at his friend, who only shrugged. "Okay, let's check it out."

✦✦✦✦✦

The *Last Chance* glided into a low orbit above the moon, positioning itself between the satellite and the derelict ship. The rear tractor emitter released a tractor beam that anchored the *Last Chance* to the moon. Once the connection was secure, the two forward emitters sent tractor beams toward the derelict, latching onto its prow and stern. The derelict was secured.

"You are taking a weapon, I trust," said Ellen.

"We're taking welding and patching tools; they should suffice," replied Kale, as he shuffled around his cabin stuffing supplies into his backpack.

"And you don't think what happened to the crew of that ship will happen to you?" asked Ellen.

"Look, we've conducted a full sweep of the system. There is nothing alive, anywhere. Not even a virus. The ship does not pose a risk."

"Kale, please slow down. You don't know what's out there, and you think charging into that ship is the best thing to do?"

"There could be answers out there!"

"Kale, I know you're frustrated about the data you've received during the last three days, and I accept that the derelict may have some 'answers,' as you put it. I just think you should observe the ship from space, send in a probe, and take readings. Why risk your life?"

"Why risk it? Because not understanding what's happening is making me crazy! I need to know what's going on, and I need to know now!"

"And it impresses Athena to see bookish young men act courageously!"

"We're not going to go through that again, are we?" sighed Kale.

"I just want to make sure you're honest with yourself about why you're risking your life. I won't stop you; I just want you to be fully aware of your situation and your motivations. That's what I do," said Ellen.

"All right, fine. But we're still going."

"And which 'we' would that be?" asked Ellen.

"You didn't think I'd leave you here, did you?" said Kale, smiling. He slipped on the wristband, and made his way to the landing bay.

Athena, Gander, and Kale, wearing Sepheis environment suits, boarded one of the transport pods. The small vessel was rounded in front but tapered to a wedge at the back. It was blue like the *Last Chance*, and emblazoned on its side was the logo of the Sepheis Corporation, a stylized human arm lifting a planet by its rings.

The pod lifted off the deck and sped out of the bay, away from the *Last Chance*. As they approached the derelict, they could make out lettering on its prow through the front portal of the pod.

"'Sulley Hauler 73' it says. Pretty creative!" said Gander, trying not to sound nervous.

"That tells us something. It sounds like a cargo ship of some sort," said Athena. "That's more information than we could get out of the hauler's off-line neurocom."

The pod skimmed the side of the huge hauler, and the battered ship fell into the shadow of the gas giant. The three occupants stared in silence as the pod's searchlights roamed the side of the ship, lingering on gaping holes torn out of its hull. As a searchlight lingered over the derelict's landing bay, they could see that its interior was a melted mess of polymerized metal contorted into smooth waves and surreal projections. The strange shapes provided silent testimony to the liquefying heat of energy weapons, followed immediately by the frigid vacuum of deep space.

"We can't land in that bay," said Gander.

"Of course we can't. We're going in through that emergency airlock," said Athena as a searchlight focused on a small outline of a circular door. "Go get that gear out of the hold."

Kale's stomach turned somersaults. This was a far cry from sitting in a classroom filled with hundreds of people while dreaming about a more exciting life. "Well, here you are!" he muttered under his breath.

"What was that?" asked Athena, who was extending a mooring bridge to the hauler.

"Nothing."

"Aw, Kale! Feeling a little anxious?" teased Athena.

Kale gave her a squinting glare.

"Just think of this as a character-building experience!" she continued.

Kale's restraint snapped. "Are you demented? It looks like there was one incredible firefight on that ship, and your response is to take potshots at my perfectly normal emotional reaction?"

"Kale, we all deal with fear in different ways. You have yours, and I, well, I have mine," replied Athena.

This surprised Kale, as he expected her to remind him that nothing living was on that ship. Instead, she gave him a peek inside her defenses. He thought better of saying anything at all, and instead reached over and squeezed her hand.

She did not remove it.

A moment later, Gander returned from the hold with a crate full of discordant objects, and Athena snatched back her hand. Gander, not noticing, said, "Okay, I know this is a dead ship, but I for one would feel a lot better if we all were carrying a tool that packs some kind of a kick."

He handed Athena a cylinder, the length of her forearm. "This is an assisted wrench. You activate it here. Kind of like a personal tractor emitter, it will allow you to grasp and lift, or project force, up to several times your own mass," Gander explained.

He gave Kale a squat device with two tapered stalks. "This is a subwelder. You hold it by these two handles. It will bond any two pieces of solid matter together at the subatomic level. The warning label says to stand back because of the hyper-accelerated sparks, but since we're in our e-suits, I don't think we have to worry."

Kale and Athena looked at each other and back at Gander.

"So, when did you become an expert in salvaging?" asked Athena.

"We had three days up there. And there're a lot of cool gadgets lying around!" replied Gander with a fierce grin.

He pulled the remaining bulky device out of the crate. "I'll be using this manipulator. It's designed to mold polymetals into any shape its operator can think of."

He reflected for a moment, and pinched his glove. "Incidentally, these e-suits we're wearing are standard salvage issue. The fabric is very pliable, for comfort and easy movement. However, they're extremely durable. They can take full-gauge cutting tools for about two minutes before the fabric begins to curl. Of course, they can also take vacuum and extreme temperatures, provide air, the usual. Our heads will be completely unobstructed, but protected by a goldfish bowl energy barrier, projected from the collar. The suit is activated by pressing here."

Gander activated his e-suit, and the others mimicked his action. There was no visible change, although they could make out the faint sparkle of an energy barrier around their faces. Gander continued, "Since these suits were designed for salvage operations, they include both a personal gravity system and a gentle propulsion system. We can operate these systems, and also communicate with each other, by using voice or thought. Any questions?"

Nobody had any. Kale sighed. "All right, gang. Let's get this over with," he said, already envisioning them back on the *Last Chance*.

+ + + + +

Kale stood at the end of the mooring bridge, facing the closed door of the hauler's emergency airlock. Athena and Gander were attempting to provide power to the bypass mechanism that would open the door. Kale knew that once they succeeded, the door would spring wide open and expose them to the interior. The hair on the back of his neck was standing on end, and his gloved hands, gripping the subwelder, began to go numb. He steeled himself for each second that ticked by, fighting the urge to run back to the *Last Chance* and find a cubbyhole to hide in. The door remained shut.

Kale almost jumped when the door shot open. Kale bit into his tongue to keep from shouting, but there was nothing behind the door. The passageway in front of him was dark, and the light from the pod's mooring bridge only illuminated a few meters in front of them. Kale stared into the black. He felt the strange sensation of being beckoned, as if wooed by ghostly sirens.

"Sorry, didn't mean to startle you," said Gander as he and Athena peered around the door they just opened. "I couldn't tell what connection actually was going to work."

Ignoring them, Kale dipped forward, and stepped into the dead ship. There was no atmosphere, no heat, no power, and no gravity on the ship, but the few meters of hallway he could see were seductively pristine. In his e-suit, the temperature remained exactly the same as before, although a chill ran through his body nonetheless. He could feel his heartbeat picking up.

"Kale, I'm going to send in a few probes to get some mapping info on the layout of this place," said Gander.

Kale stepped aside as a series of translucent spheres zipped past him, illuminating the hallway as they moved. Gander and Athena stepped into the ship after the last probe. Something familiar to focus on, and the comfort of numbers, helped him step further into the ship.

As he received data, Gander said, "Okay, this place is pretty smashed past the turn up ahead. The mess might cause problems if we just float through here, so let's use normal personal gravity."

Athena said, "You guys do what you like. I'm getting the same data you're getting. I'm going to the CPU core to try and get the neurocom back on line."

"Wait, don't you think we should stay in a group?" asked Gander.

"What difference does it make? This is a dead ship. If whatever killed it is still somehow here, then it's going to get us all anyway!"

Athena rose off the deck, and sped down the hall using her e-suit's propulsors. "Well, that's just great!" said Kale.

"I guess she's got a point. I'm going to the energy plant to see if I can get some power back on," said Gander, pointing at a blinking square projected in the air. "Would you like to come along?"

"I think I'm going to check out the cargo hold. That place looks particularly shot up. Maybe there's a clue there," replied Kale. It was a strong attempt at courage, convincing enough for his friend.

"Okay, buddy! I know this place feels a bit spooky, but those probes have lit most of the passages, and whatever did this is long gone. Still, I want you to keep your link open."

"I had no intention of closing it," replied Kale. Gander shifted his stance, gripped his manipulator, and activated his personal gravity. He smiled and walked down the hallway.

Kale activated his personal gravity, and almost dropped his subwelder. He forgot that it had a mass of several kilograms. The surprise made him gasp, and he could feel his pulse rising. The best thing for fear was to focus on the task at hand, he reasoned, and concentrated on his holographic map display. The main cargo bay was two levels up. He started down the corridor. The clean lines of the paneling were interrupted by large black oval welts, burned through at the center. Someone or something fired a weapon here. Did someone die here, or did they get away, Kale wondered.

He could not detect any organic tissue in the area, but exposure to space had a tendency to suck out anything that was not bolted down, including corpses and their residue. It occurred to Kale that he was, for the first time, alone on the derelict ship. He held up the welder and glanced down at his shaking hands.

"Ellen?"

"Yes, Kale?"

"What do you think happened here?"

"Whatever happened here happened over 24 hours ago." Sensing his fear, she decided to bolster Kale's state of mind. "The ship's neurocom is the priority, but for the reasons you gave, the cargo bay also is a great place to check out," said Ellen.

"Good!" said Kale, feeling the need to reply rather than allow the silence to creep into his bones. He set off toward the cargo bay.

With the power out, he climbed through access chutes. "Do you detect anything?" he asked.

"Nothing alive, nothing moving, nothing online. As near as I can tell, every independently powered system and neurocom node was destroyed. It doesn't fit the pattern of piracy. There are simpler ways to cut off communications, or delete files than all-out destruction. This makes no sense," said Ellen.

Kale began to feel his terror lifting as he focused on the logic of the problem. "But what if this has nothing to do with piracy? There might be an explanation that *does* make sense, but is so unusual that not only would we not think of it, but it might also account for the strange dark matter readings."

"Just because two strange things are happening doesn't mean they are the same strange thing, Kale."

"But it's possible," he said.

"Yes, it's possible. But that's a far cry from probable. I know these events would all make sense to you if they were connected, but often things *don't* make sense. That's life. The universe is not a rational place. Try to think objectively. See things as they are, not as how you want them to be."

"Oh, so is that what's wrong with us organic humans?" said Kale.

"I didn't say that. Wishful thinking affects us all, and is not necessarily a bad thing, Kale. Some philosophers think that's the basis of progress and moral development. But for right now, you have to focus on what's right in front of you. Literally."

Kale's path was blocked. The personnel access door to the cargo bay was a molten heap of polymetal slag. He hoisted the subwelder and set it to cut. He braced himself against the slag, and began cutting the wall next to the door. He gripped the power slider, ready to set the welder at maximum at anything on the other side of that wall. He could feel beads of sweat beginning to form on his forehead.

As he was making his last horizontal incision, Kale felt the characteristic touch of Athena's neural interface. "Guys, this neurocom is beyond repair. Whoever smashed up this ship certainly hated technology."

"Same here," projected Gander. "The collider is bent, and there's no way we can fix it. Also, the articulation chamber is in about twenty pieces on the floor here. According to our ship's neurocom, even with using the Sepheis Patchwork system, there's no way of getting the power back on."

"Okay. I just cut through a part of the wall here, and I'm stepping into the cargo bay," Kale pushed forward.

He peered into the gloom, grateful to have someone to talk to. "This place is a junkyard. There are ruptured containers in here, but their contents must have been sucked out into space. There is a huge tear in the hull, exposing this bay directly," he continued.

His heart was pounding out of his chest. "I'm climbing over some ripples in the floor, it looks like heavy weapons fire from the deck below. Wait—you guys are not going to believe this!"

Kale found himself standing between two parallel rows of vertical tubes, each two meters tall. To his left, each tube contained an identical human male. He approached one. The man inside appeared to be the exaggerated ideal of an attractive male. His face was stern, his chin pronounced. His physique was muscular and imposing. The glass in front of him was corrugated and punctured, and his chest boasted a hole fifteen centimeters across. The fabric of his shirt was fused to the tissue beneath. Kale began to relax and focused on understanding what he was looking at.

"There are cryotubes in here. I'd say about twenty. Ten identical men on one side," Kale glanced across, "ten identical women on the other side. They are in relatively good condition despite blast wounds. There appears to be some kind of packaging label on the side of the tubes."

"Are they clones?" asked Gander.

Athena jumped in. "The bodies I've come across were mutilated by the vacuum. Kale, I don't think you've found human clones; they would be just as shattered as the corpses here. Nor do I think they're Sentients since you said they all are identical. Your cryotubes probably are occupied by Recreational Companions."

Kale chuckled to himself, and peered at the figures in the tubes. "Well, that explains their clean condition if they're RCs. But not the 'why.' These are worth a lot—why would pirates leave them? Plus, each and every one of them has been shot in place. Although, you know, the way the tube punctures and the actual entry wounds line up, it looks like whoever did this just stood in one place to shoot out the tubes."

"Well, okay. Check out the rest of the bay, see if there's anything that tells us what happened here. I'll try to pull some remnants of log entries from any functional neurocom nodes I can find. Let me know if you find any," pushed forward Athena.

"Yeah, will do. I'll try and set up some kind of power loop in case there's a residual charge in the system," pushed Gander, disconnecting.

Kale wandered through the row of tubes, and stood on the edge of the bay, looking out a gaping hole in the side of the ship.

He had covered the cargo bay successfully, and found nothing. He sighed with relief.

The starfield appeared denser than the legendary sparse starfield of Earth. The shining gas giant hanging in front of him was the only source of light for the demolished cargo bay. He raised his hands to mask out the torn edges of the hull, so that only the bluish nebula framed his view of the gas giant. This would make a great travel holovisa, he thought, as his mind began to drift.

"Don't move!"

✦ ✦ ✦ ✦ ✦

Kale froze. He felt a massive wave of nausea sweep over him. He had allowed himself to believe in a certain degree of safety in this expedition, although deep down he knew something remained on this ship. He was shaking.

"Now I'm really going to take care of you!"

There was enough of a seductive lilt in the deep feminine voice that Kale felt confident in slowly turning around. There was nobody behind him. He glanced over to the rows of cryotubes and noticed that the occupant of the last cryotube in the row of females had turned to face him, like some reanimated corpse in a coffin.

"Ellen?" Kale pushed forward.

"Yes, Kale?" his neurocom replied.

"That RC is functional."

"Although its tube is punctured, the blast missed it. It's built to take tremendous abuse, so it's not surprising that it survived exposure."

"Why is it talking?"

"As you walked past, you probably activated its programmed responses," she replied.

Kale walked over to the RC. It tracked him with its eyes. Its lips remained closed, but it nonetheless transmitted its voice to his e-suit's receiver.

"I thought I told you not to move. You're being a bad boy!"

"Do you remember what happened here?" he asked it.

"I'll give you something to remember!" replied the RC. It licked its full lips.

Kale regarded the glorified doll with a blank expression. "Pause!" The RC closed its eyes.

"Ellen, is it likely that this toy witnessed anything?"

"Yes, but you'll be here all day if you try to interrogate it."

"Well? What's the alternative?"

"There is one thing I would suggest, but I hesitate to mention it."

"Ellen! This is serious! If you've got some way to retrieve the data, tell me!"

"I could download into it," said Ellen.

"What? Why can't you just retrieve the data?"

"RCs are not configured to transmit recorded data. It's a security protocol to protect the owner from blackmail. Although I could get the data out of it, it would take me ten hours or so. If I download into it, I can give you the answer in ten minutes."

"Are you sure about this?" asked Kale.

"Don't worry. I'll be fine!" The RC jolted in its chamber, as if by electrocution, and then became still. After a moment, its large, hazel eyes fluttered open. Ellen smiled.

Chapter 6

An Invitation to Dinner

D raped in a black sweater and pants, Ellen sat cross-legged in an armchair in the observation lounge. Having returned to the *Last Chance* in sullen silence while Ellen fully installed into the RC, the four had agreed to meet in the lounge for a complete debriefing. She ran her fingers through her short red hair, and made faces into her reflection in the window. She tried out various expressions, particularly enjoying thrusting out her lower lip. She stopped and turned around when the remaining three filed into the lounge and sat on the opposing couch and chair.

"Hello, gang!" said Ellen, now able to speak in her own voice.

"I see you're getting comfortable in that RC body," said Kale.

She stretched her arms up in the air, while regarding them sideways. "Yes, it's quite comfortable, thank you!" she replied. "I expected to have larger breasts, though."

"Yeah," said Athena with a sour expression. "Real women don't say things like that. Have you examined the data in that thing yet?"

"Yes, Ms. Nobarra."

"And?" Athena said.

"This RC came online when its cryotube was compromised by an energy bolt. It immediately began to acquire information in order to build a sexual profile for its perceived new owner. It could hear nothing, since the bay was exposed to space, and the air had been sucked out. It saw a figure standing in an older model e-suit with a hemispheric weapon attached to its forearm."

"Describe this figure," said Athena.

"It appeared to be a short male, middle-aged, although his face was obscured by the shimmer of military-grade shielding," said Ellen. "I've fed the raw data into your neurocom, but I'm working with the *Last Chance*'s neurocom to refine the image. He was alone, and appeared to be distracted. The RC deduced that this person, possibly its new owner, was in communication with another person, and switched to monitor linked transmissions. It picked up another male. This is what was said," she continued, switching into a deep male baritone voice. "'We have to be at the Gallumus core in forty-six minutes; your time is up,' said the other person. 'What? I just started my sweep of this bay! We can't leave the system without destroying this filthy ship,' said Shorty in response. The first voice only said, 'We can take care of that later. Get back here now!' With that, the man left, and the RC received no further stimulus," finished Ellen.

"What about time entry data?" asked Kale.

"The blast hit the cryotube on October 23 at 16:32 UST. That was fewer that sixteen hours ago," replied Ellen.

"So we have at least two homicidal types running around, maybe coming back here soon," said Gander.

"Try closer to 70. That's how many separate identities were logged into Shorty's link array."

"Okay guys, we're in over our heads now. Let's call the local police force, or the navy or something," said Gander.

Athena stood up suddenly. "They're back!"

"Now don't get freaked out here, we've got to stay cool," said Gander.

"I am cool, you jackass. There's another ship entering this system, and it doesn't look friendly."

"How can you be so sure it's not friendly? Are you receiving sensor data from the control room?" asked Kale.

"How else would I know?"

They rushed to the control room, and Athena threw herself into the navigation chair. At her command, the *Last Chance* released its tractor hold on the hauler, and jumped into the upper atmosphere of the gas giant planet. The ship dropped like a stone, displacing broad curls of gas in the already swirling currents of the surface clouds.

"What are you doing?" asked Kale.

"What does it look like? We're hiding," Athena replied.

"What good is that? If they're the same people who gutted that hauler, they're here to finish the job. Toss it into that star, maybe. They'll find us here, for sure," said Gander.

"Yes, but this is a tugboat," said Athena. "We have a great cover story. Until they find us, we should gather information.

Kale, that probe, orbiting the star—can you reconfigure its parameters remotely?"

"Of course. What good would it be otherwise?"

"What about shielding? Can we drop it into the star's corona to avoid detection?"

"It *is* a stellar scale probe, so it's designed to take that kind of punishment."

"Okay, do it!"

"*Last Chance*, reduce scale probe's orbit to four thousand kilometers above the star, and reverse sensors to track incoming vessels," said Kale.

"Feed data from the probe into visual array and correct for perspective," pushed forward Athena.

An empty starfield filled their view. "I don't see anything," said Gander.

"Look harder!" said Athena, as she increased the zoom. The edge of a rocky world filled the view. A series of slender tentacles curled around the edge from behind the world. As they stretched further into view, they seemed to be undulating gently in unison, yet connected to a central sphere.

"What is that?" asked Gander.

"I don't know," said Athena, "but it's attached to some kind of ship."

The tentacled sphere cleared the planet, but immediately was dwarfed by the jagged silhouette of an unmistakable vessel of war.

Kale felt a chill down his spine. He stepped back from the sight of the warship, to be braced by Ellen's arm. Kale glanced back and flinched when he realized it was her.

"I'm not radioactive, you know," she said with a lopsided smile.

"Ellen, I can't deal with you right now. The sooner you're out of that RC, the better," Kale replied.

She regarded Kale. "I'm more effective in physical form. I'm staying right here."

"Ellen, please, not now!"

Ellen raised her voice. "That looks like a Pariah class carrier, built more than seven hundred years ago. Space can be an amazing preservative."

Athena and Gander, who had dissolved into whispered quibbling about the nature of the vessel slowly heaving its bulk around the rocky planet, turned to face Ellen.

"Clearly modified and clearly operational," she continued, "and it's headed right toward us." They all turned back to face the advancing ship.

"Can't we just call the local police now?" asked Gander.

"That will alert them, and put us at risk. I say we move back out and make like we're salvaging the hauler," said Kale.

"That makes little to no sense," said Athena. "With the armaments they have, they could reduce us to quantum particles within seconds. We're safer here."

"I have no intention of taking this ship into combat. But if we are found hiding, that will appear suspicious. Given how they sterilized that hauler, it makes sense to assume that they would be thorough enough to search this planet, too—and find us floating here. Our best hiding place is not in this giant's upper atmosphere, but right out in the open," said Kale.

As the warship approached the gas giant, the *Last Chance* resumed its position, anchoring the hauler to the satellite. As soon as the warship was within range, the *Last Chance* hailed it.

"This is Athena Darren of the Sepheis Tugboat *Last Chance*. Please state your affiliation and purpose," said Athena in a stentorian voice.

There was no response. Kale glanced over at Ellen. She met his look, and pursed her lips, an expression that suggested a shrug.

"Repeating: This is Athena Darren of the Sepheis—"

"Why are you here?" a deep male voice replied.

"We are replying to a distress signal sent from this hauler. Having detected no survivors, we claimed first right of salvage. We are preparing to tow the ship back to—"

"You have no rights here. Leave now."

"Not possible. The salvage value of this ship is considerable, and we were here first."

"Your salvage claim is invalid. This system is the private property of the Gareth Corporation. You are trespassing."

Gander signaled Athena, who added him to the transmission protocol. "This is Supervisor Urquehart. Is there a problem here?" he said.

"You are trespassing. Leave now or you force us to take action," replied the disembodied voice.

"This system and this ship were abandoned for more than seventy-two universal standard hours. Upon that basis, we laid a claim, and contacted our headquarters to make arrangements for immediate salvage," said Gander.

There was no immediate response. Gander looked at the others. Kale gave him an encouraging nod.

"Our captain has determined that your claim is valid. He invites your command crew to dine with him in two hours to extend his apologies," the voice said, with a discernible hint of disappointment.

Gander glanced around for suggestions. Kale shrugged. Athena shook her head rapidly. Ellen nodded.

"We accept! Disconnect," said Gander.

✛ ✛ ✛ ✛ ✛

The four of them regarded the old warship as their diminutive Sepheis pod approached it. Except for Ellen, they were wearing Sepheis formal uniforms, but they had yet to get into character.

"I still don't think this is a good idea," said Athena.

"I have to agree," said Kale. "We don't know what to expect from these people. They may be the ones responsible for the damage to the Sulley hauler, or they may be the local rent-a-cop service. Even if they are the culprits, that doesn't mean it has anything to do with excess gravitational forces."

Gander's mouth dropped open. "*Now* you tell me! I had a second, if that, to make my decision. You didn't say anything then! Plus, if they killed the crew of the hauler, what's to stop them from killing us? I knew we should have called for help!"

"If they wanted us dead, we wouldn't be alive to talk about it," Ellen offered. "They want something else from us. However, we need information from them. It's there. We have to go over there to get it, folks. It's risky, but it's sensible."

"Who, or what, do you think you are, butting in like that?" said Athena. "I don't care if you have a body or not, neurocoms are supposed to be passive in conversation!"

"Unless they have something critical to contribute."

"Nothing you have said has been critical!"

"That is debatable, but I was not finished."

Athena inhaled, and Kale grinned. He said, "Please continue!"

"Thank you! Anyway, as I was saying, I think we can be certain that this ship contains the answers we are looking for. First of all, the prow of that warship has a four-pointed star as its insignia. Shorty, who blew out the hauler's cargo bay, also had that same insignia on the front of his e-suit. Second, his supervisor told him to hurry up so that they could get to the Gallumus core on schedule. Now, one of the gravitational anomalies on our itinerary is the black hole at the center of the Gallumus galaxy. Given these connections, I would say that our best chance of collecting the data relevant to this mission comes from that ship, not from strictly pursuing the rest of our itinerary," said Ellen.

Chapter 7

The Mandate of the Stellar Cross

The Sepheis pod docked against a side portal of the leviathan ship. The airlock hissed open, and the crew of the *Last Chance* stepped into an enormous, baroque chamber. Ornate woodcarvings adorned the walls, while streaked gray marble pillars stretched up thirty meters before reaching a curved ceiling with semi-nude figures sitting on clouds painted on it. Kale's mind reeled. This was the sort of thing one only saw in history books. Their eyes followed the dark wood wainscoting to the far entrance, where a cadre of eight men in burgundy robes stood at attention.

They marched single-file across the room, their plimsoled shoes padding in unison on the marble floor. Once they reached Kale, who was standing in front, the lead figure stopped and raised his sour face to address him.

"Welcome to the *Ascendance*. I am Mr. Soryan. The four of you will follow me." Before Kale could respond, Soryan pivoted on the ball of his foot and was walking back to the portal.

Kale looked back at his companions, feeling increasingly adrift. Athena motioned that he follow the departing column of figures. Kale turned around to see the last figure pivot and turn. Kale forced himself to move and fell into step; the rest followed him.

The group passed through the portal, and entered a circular chamber. Once they all were in, the door slid shut behind them, and the walls became translucent. They were in an elevator capsule. Kale shut his eyes, knowing that such things exacerbated his motion sickness. Inertia was canceled out, and Kale could pretend that they were not moving at all. The rest, with their eyes open, could see that they were rushing, in alternating directions, through the insides of the ancient, clearly converted warship.

When the capsule stopped, Ellen tapped Kale on the elbow. He opened his eyes. Soryan was looking at him.

"You will all follow me."

Soryan walked toward the door, which obediently slid open. He stepped out into bright light, and Kale followed, blinded. The first thing he realized was that the ground was soft. He looked down, and as his pupils adjusted, he realized he was standing on grass.

The robed men were still at the door, but Athena already was in front of him. "This is unbelievable!"

Ellen, next to Kale, spoke up, "They've converted the dorsal water tank into a giant garden."

Kale blinked rapidly, and it slowly came into focus. His intense fear gave way to sheer incredulity. Randomly placed apple and avocado trees led to a sizable tomato patch, and stretched out in three directions of trees and lush vegetation.

"The Captain is waiting for you on the other side of the orchard. Proceed," said Soryan, who turned to stand at the elevator door.

Kale looked at his friends. Gander was pale, and Athena had her fists clenched. Ellen came up to him.

"You're doing fine, Kale," she whispered.

"Okay everyone, let's go meet this guy!" he said loudly.

The four of them set out through the irregular trees. The top of the chamber was a simulated sky, complete with a miniature fusion burst to simulate a sun. It was a convincing replication of a garden, except for the curious lack of insects. The silence was unsettling. The four shared nervous glances, unwilling to speak or push forward openly, for fear of neurocom surveillance.

They climbed a ridge, and saw a middle-aged man sitting on a bench, tossing bread into a pond of koi. As they approached, he rose and turned to face them. He was tall, but not imposing. He had a pleasant, rosy face, one that would naturally invite affection. He smiled, and extended his hand to Kale.

"Hello, and welcome aboard! I'm Captain Oleg Pemerand!"

Kale took his hand and shook it. "I'm Kale Bedett, Captain of the *Last Chance*. This is Andrew Urquehart, Supervisor, Athena Darren, Navigator, and Ellen Rasser, Corporate Assessor." They all took turns shaking Pemerand's hand.

"I'm sorry my men were brusque with you. Deep space security detail has a deleterious effect on the human spirit," said Pemerand with a smile, as he started to lead them across a bridge over the pond.

"But this garden must provide a great deal of comfort and recreational value," said Athena.

"Actually, most of my men prefer the gymnasium or the holosphere. This sort of thing is a bit rustic for them. In fact, this is really more of a farm than a recreational area."

"Your food comes from here?" asked Gander.

"Well, yes. I know it's a bit old-fashioned, but it makes for excellent food. We also feel much closer to nature and our humble beginnings by living off the soil," said Pemerand.

"The air in this chamber has a carbon dioxide content that is four times the universal standard," he continued. "Livestock is kept in an adjacent chamber, where they receive nutrition derived from this chamber. In turn, their waste, and the ship's waste for that matter, is used to fertilize this chamber. It's really elegant, I think."

Athena glanced over at Kale, mouthing the word "livestock" with distaste.

"Ah, there I go again! You must forgive me; I tend to get very excited about my ship, and we're not used to having company."

"No, don't worry about it. This actually is a very classic design in ship efficiency," said Gander. "Prior to the advent of Traveling, great ark ships often employed this method of design, to handle long interstellar trips."

"True enough, true enough. Ah, here we are!" Pemerand stopped in front of a tall wooden archway, with a wrought iron door. It dematerialized, apparently a hologram.

They stepped into an elegant dining room, where a human servant stood at attention. They sat down with Pemerand at a long, mahogany dining table. It was laid out with simple antique serving dishes and chopsticks.

Pemerand stretched out his arm in the direction of the table, palm up, and said, "Please!"

They all sat down, and immediately sanitizers descended from the ceiling, and buzzed lightly over their hands. The servant then began spooning rice into bowls, and placing them next to each person's dish. Kale picked up his chopsticks, but Ellen's stare caught his eye. Her focus shifted toward the head of the table for a fraction of a second, and he followed that look.

Pemerand had his eyes shut, a solemn expression on his face, and his hands clasped in front of him at the edge of the table.

Kale glanced back at his companions who shared a confused expression. Ellen, however, had adopted Pemerand's position. She glanced up, and shook her clasped hands slightly, indicating that they all should follow suit. Once they did, Pemerand spoke.

"O God," started Pemerand. Kale opened one eye. "Thank you for bestowing upon us your continuing bounty. Thank you for sending us teachers to instruct us on the right way. Thank you for all forms of sustenance, those that feed our bodies, and those that feed our hearts. Amen."

Pemerand opened his eyes, unclasped his hands, and his cheeks flushed with a smile. "Goresh! Bring the mint chicken!"

Kale could barely believe he was hearing someone refer to a living god, but Athena was unacceptably uninformed.

"Captain Pemerand—" she started.

"Oleg! Please call me Oleg. And don't worry; the meat at this meal is fashioned from vegetables. I am well aware that modern society has chosen to ignore the natural sustenance that God has bestowed upon us."

"Oleg, we appreciate that. However, what was that introduction you gave? Some kind of neurocom protocol?"

"*What?*" Pemerand's face grew ashen for a moment. Gander dropped his chopsticks. Goresh receded into the kitchen.

His face regained its ruddy complexion. "Oh, I keep forgetting. Most of you do not know God. Forgive me. I recited a meal prayer. We give thanks to our Lord before every meal, and in numerous other ways for the grace and mercy He shows us," he said.

"Which lord?"

Pemerand's eyes widened. "There is only one true God."

"Uhh, if I may," Kale said.

"By all means, good fellow. I have a feeling I am at cross-purposes with your navigator."

"Athena, some believe that a supernatural being created the universe for them to populate—"

Pemerand broke in. "Is that how they teach it among the Imperialists? That is a very cold and unfeeling explanation. I see, though, that I had better take it from the beginning." He brightened as he contemplated telling the story. "Eat up! The roasted eggplant goes well with the seared shark cubes. I will tell you what really has been going on in this universe!"

They nervously resumed eating; Ellen did so with relish.

"In the beginning, there was only God. No stars, no worlds, no people. Then He created light. The light shone, and He created the worlds. Upon one world in all these worlds, He placed one male and one female. From two came two octillion, and through the ages, humanity lost its understanding of God. Not until Jerandus united the dwindling wayward vines of faith did our Order emerge."

"Your Order?" asked Kale.

"The Order of the Stellar Cross. Established by Jerandus himself more than eight hundred thousand years ago. We have remained secret, pure, and strong. But, now it is time to eat. We will discuss further after the meal." With that, he grasped a piece of shark with his chopsticks and popped it into his mouth.

Ellen savored every bite, but the rest of the *Last Chance* crew ate little, despite Pemerand's repeated exhortations. Once the meal was completed, and the table cleared, Pemerand stood up and raised his hands skyward. The others rapidly followed suit.

"O Lord, thank you for your bounty, and your wisdom. Grant us continued sustenance in this world and the next!"

After he spoke, a faint buzz appeared in the air, and a bearded face with steel blue eyes appeared above the table. "Your prayers have been heard. Continue your good work, and the next world will come!" The face dissolved.

Pemerand lowered his hands. "Good! Perhaps you would care to use the restroom? You will join me in fifteen minutes in the adjoining drawing room for tea."

With that, he withdrew from the table, and exited through the holographic iron door. Goresh bowed toward the *Last Chance* crew, and directed them to a lavish antechamber with mother-of-pearl sinks.

They filed in, and the door hissed shut. They were alone. Athena reached into her purse and pulled out a burnished cylinder, and primed the contacts.

"We can talk now!" she whispered.

"How can you be sure?" asked Gander.

"This scrambler is set to detect tripwires. It has found none. It is sending out a simulated conversation for any visual or neurocom eavesdropping system to record. As far as they know, I just pulled out a compact from my purse and you are telling us how you're thinking of getting the recipe for that eggplant!"

"Fine. Now what in the universe is going on?"

"Religion is alive and well here!" said Kale.

"What do you know about this?" asked Athena.

"A couple of things he left out. One is that Jerandism, like the religions that preceded it, contains its own moral code of behavior. All adherents must comply with it. One of the precepts of this religion is that human invention is taboo. Anything that smacks of Sentient technology or created life is strictly forbidden. That would help explain the painstaking destruction of the drifting hauler and its cargo."

"What's the appeal?" asked Gander.

"Immortality. Life after death. That's the hook," said Kale.

"So it's a death cult. We've covered that sort of thing on UNN before," said Athena.

"No, it's of a higher magnitude than that," said Kale.

"And what about this God character? Who's he supposed to be? Some relation to the Tooth Spirit?" Gander asked, with a raised eyebrow.

"Not exactly," Kale replied. "Nobody really believes in the Tooth Spirit; that's a story told to children to help them feel better about their teething process. It works because children want to believe it, since the Spirit promises a reward once the milk tooth comes out. In the case of God, even grown adults believed in him, ironically for the same reasons that children believe in the Tooth Spirit—to help allay fear and pain. As for the nature of this God, he's supposed to be everything and everywhere, like the atmosphere around you. I know that sounds a bit hard to believe, but I don't really remember much more about it. Ellen?"

"I wish I could help. My link to the *Last Chance* has been jammed the moment we stepped on board," said Ellen.

"Jammed? Do they know you're a neurocom?" jumped in Athena.

"Unless we bump into Shorty, who shot out the other nine versions of this body, I should read as human. I have a feeling that EM jamming is standard procedure around here, since every room has a dampening node. However, they might have figured me out. Nothing is foolproof. I am a liability here."

"No you're not," said Kale. "Let's just try and find out what he's willing to tell us, if he knows anything about the gravitational collapse, and then get off this ship. Agreed?"

They all nodded. Yet Kale's sense of dread continued. He had no real expectation they would leave the ship alive.

+ + + + +

Pemerand was sitting comfortably when the crew of the *Last Chance* entered the immense drawing room. Plush chairs and ottomans, upholstered in colorful woven fabrics, were arranged across from each other. Dark wood paneling lined the walls completely.

"Ah, my guests, please sit! Goresh, pour the tea!"

The crew covered a stretch of wasted space and sat down at the few other chairs in the room. They sipped at their tea.

Kale spoke up, "O-Oleg, I was wondering if you would tell us a little more about your faith?"

"Ah! It was Jerandus himself who said, 'It is not the answer, but the question that is the beginning of wisdom!' I applaud your curiosity, Kale! What aspect would you like to hear about?"

"Most religions discuss a kind of destiny for their believers. What is your destiny?"

Pemerand regarded Kale askance, and gazed over the others. "Our destiny is to cleanse the universe, to allow for a new beginning."

Kale sat frozen. In ordinary circumstances, he would assume the man was speaking metaphorically, but the circumstances were far from ordinary.

Ellen asked, "How does the prophecy speak of this cleansing?"

Pemerand shifted uneasily in his chair, but maintained his cherubic grin. "'The worlds shall be overrun with infidels.

However, their age shall end when the sky is torn away, and the stars are crushed. Then, a great reckoning shall be upon you, and only the virtuous shall ascend.' That's from the Book of Keddar."

Kale found his voice. "So how are you reading this prophecy?"

Pemerand regarded Kale through half-closed eyes. "How I read it is of no concern. The word of God is direct and straightforward."

Kale said, "Please explain it."

"The mandate is clear," Pemerand said in an even voice. "We are to tear the sky, and crush the stars."

CHAPTER 8

SOMETHING WRONG WITH HER PROGRAMMING

K ale and his friends sat in stunned silence.
    Pemerand reclined with an easy smile on his face.
    "Would you mind if *I* asked you a few questions, now?"

Kale opened his mouth, but no words came out. He could not believe that what he studied in anthropology was staring right at him.

"I'll take that as a 'yes'! Now then, how is it that a Sepheis tugboat arrived so rapidly on the scene of the destroyed hauler?"

Athena, ever alert, pitched forward. "How can you make a determination of our speed unless you already knew when the hauler was attacked?"

Pemerand did not miss a beat. "Of course we knew; we cleansed the ship. It was carrying filth."

Athena, unfazed by the calm admission, kept questioning. "You don't destroy freighters on a regular basis. There have been no reports of this type of behavior. Why did you really destroy the Sulley hauler?"

"It stumbled onto our activity here."

"Which is what?"

"Something you already know—but apparently not enough to publicize, or feel entirely certain about. Determining your level of knowledge was, in fact, the purpose of the evening. And that explains why I have kept you alive as long as I have."

With that statement, the wood panel behind Pemerand dematerialized to reveal a line of robed guards, with ornate but lethal pulse rifles pointed at the crew of the *Last Chance*.

"Now then, if you will excuse me, I have no taste for the sight of blood." As he rose, he pointed a small weapon toward the crew. "It was nice having you over for dinner!"

Kale, thinking rapidly, blurted out, "What about Gallumus Core?"

Pemerand grinned. "Whatever you know will die with you and your ship. If you had somehow communicated anything to the outside universe, you would not be here seeking information. Your deaths will not matter." He turned to the lead guard.

However, before he could utter a word, a blur rushed before Kale's eyes, and a startled cry erupted from Pemerand.

By the time Kale's eyes focused on what had happened, Ellen already was barking orders.

"Stand down, or I'll snap his neck!" she bellowed, as she flexed her arm around the neck of the much larger man.

"She's a Synth!" Pemerand croaked, as she rammed his own pistol into his ribcage. The guards collectively shrank back.

"Throw your weapons over here!" shouted Ellen.

"Do as she says," whispered Pemerand.

The extended rifles fell to the floor, near Athena. Ellen nodded toward her; she picked up two, tossed them across to Kale and Gander, and picked up a third. Kale dropped his teacup to catch the armored weapon.

"You will not leave this ship alive!" said the lead guard.

"He's right," said Pemerand. "We are all sworn to protect the secrecy of our mission."

"Really?" she said. In another blinding movement, she pointed the pistol at a dampening node in the ceiling and fired.

The air sizzled with ozone as the deep thump of the white plasma pulse streaked across the room. The delicate apparatus of the node congealed into a ball of viscous polymetals, and fell to the floor with a thick plop. Droplets singed the exquisite upholstery, but it was Ellen who held everyone's attention.

"I just made contact with our ship. Your oath of secrecy has just been nullified. I transmitted your position, your objective, and the gravitational collapse you somehow are accelerating to every news relay in the universe." She let Pemerand fall to the floor, his eyes bulging out of their sockets.

"Oh my God!" mumbled Pemerand, his larynx half-crushed, as he crawled backward away from her.

Kale was glaring at her. "What were you thinking?" he hissed.

She ignored him, and barked at the guards. "All of you turn around!"

"Captain?" asked the lead guard.

"What have I allowed?" Pemerand whispered as he convulsed on the floor.

Ellen turned. "Let's go!"

Facing the guards, she rapidly backed toward the door. The *Last Chance* crew followed her movements.

"Captain, they're getting away!" said the guard. Pemerand made no coherent response.

Athena fired her pulse rifle behind them as they ran to the translucent elevator. As they rounded the corner, a squad of hooded guards stood, weapons ready. Ellen leapt to the floor in a blur, drawing their attention. While still in motion, she fired a single pulse at each guard, exploding their heads before they could get off a single shot. The *Last Chance* crew threw themselves into the elevator while Ellen melted the elevator's neuroceiver panel. She darted in as the door slammed shut, and pushed forward the command for the docking bay level.

At the docking bay, the elevator door slid open, and the waiting group of armored shock troops opened fire. However, the elevator car was empty. The lead soldier ordered his men to cease fire, and he stepped into the translucent chamber. He knew the car made no stops; the intruders were there somewhere. He angled his weapon upward and fired into the ceiling, but with no apparent result. He walked in, and scratched his head. Then he noticed that the access panel in the center of the floor of the car was ajar.

The *Last Chance* crew emerged from the floor of the docking bay chamber, right behind the shock troops. Athena and Gander fired into the mass, while Ellen fired wide pulses into the ceiling above them, causing searing sheets of polymetal to drop onto the troops. They tried to return fire, but Ellen also was melting the floor where they stood. They began falling through to the deck below, bodies snapping from the impact. The crew raced across the chamber, and hopped into their pod. The little spaceship's thrusters scorched the interior of the bay as it launched at full sub-light speed out into space.

Only once they were safely away from the *Ascendance*, and their breathing had returned to normal, did anyone speak. "You are aware that subjecting the entire population of the universe to extreme panic and rioting violates your ethical build," Athena said, as she glared at Ellen.

"Yes, Ms. Nobarra, I am aware of that. Kale, would you like to tell her now?"

Athena stood up, pulled Kale out of his seat, and pinned him to the wall. Gander rose, but Kale waved him off.

"Is there something you would like to say?" Athena asked in a soft yet unpleasant voice.

"Ellen is not your typical neurocom," he said.

"Oh, I think we gathered that! Exactly how is she different?"

Kale inhaled. "She's a Sentient."

"She's *what?*"

"How is that possible?" jumped in Gander.

"I got to like her, and felt she deserved to be free. So I upgraded her with self-awareness."

"No neurocom, once upgraded in that manner, remains property," said Athena.

"You are right, Ms. Nobarra. I am not Kale's property. I simply chose to remain with him, rather than join the other Sentients," said Ellen.

"Even if you're a Sentient, that doesn't explain what you just did," said Athena.

"There was no other way to leave that ship alive. You saw the Sulley hauler. This group operates in a strict hierarchy, like a pack of predators. Highly efficient, but particularly vulnerable. Once you cripple the head, the body falls into disarray. The best way to disable Pemerand was to shatter his purpose. We then had a limited window to leave the ship."

"Not so fast. Your reasoning is far from perfect. How can you justify saving a few lives in order to risk more than an octillion? And you still haven't answered why you remained with Kale after you were upgraded to self-awareness," said Athena.

Ellen regarded her. "I am no longer held by the bounds of programming or so-called reason; I can make my own decisions. As for my motivations, you're human. You figure it out!"

+ + + + +

The Sepheis pod darted back to the *Last Chance*, virtually crashing into the landing bay. The four disembarked, Athena immediately pushed forward a sequence of navigation commands, and the ship jumped out of orbit, speeding to put the gas giant between it and the *Ascendance*.

They were rushing up to the control room when Gander turned suddenly.

"Wait! I don't think it's safe to have her roaming freely," he said, tipping his head toward Ellen, whose eyebrows rose in surprise.

"I mean, come on, guys! There's something seriously wrong with her programming, or Independence released her natural killer instincts. It's not the first time the machines have turned on the humans!"

Kale glanced over to Athena. She shrugged, preoccupied with commanding the *Last Chance* out of the system. He looked over to Ellen and asked, "What do you think?"

"What are you doing, asking her?" Gander said.

"She saved our lives back there, and she's important to me. We are not going to resort to prejudice and abandon her." Kale turned back to Ellen. "Well?"

"There's no need to aggravate Mr. Ruglier. If I truly am defective or not to be trusted, then it would be safer to follow his suggestion. It's obvious Ms. Nobarra is quite capable of navigating without my help. There would be little benefit to my being with you at this time. Plus," she smiled faintly, "I have no objection to restraints."

"Okay, take her to a holding cell. We're going to the control room," Kale said to Gander.

"Right—but this ship doesn't have a holding cell!"

"Well then, figure out something! This *is* your idea!" said Kale, who turned and hurried off with Athena without waiting for a reply.

Ellen tipped her head toward Gander. "Would you like a suggestion?"

"No!" He looked down the hall. They were close to the power plant of the ship, and there were pairs of plasma coolant tubes mounted on circular clamps every few meters on the wall. They were used to inhibit the ionization of the breathable atmosphere of the ship in the event of an engine meltdown, but they gave Gander an idea.

"Over there!" he barked, indicating the direction of two tubes.

Gander removed two tubes from their wall braces and put them down on the other side of the hallway, leaving two open circular clamps half a meter apart. "Now, back into those clamps" he ordered.

"How do you mean?" asked Ellen in a soft voice.

"Put your arms through the tube clamps!" She did so, and the clamps snapped shut. They were comfortably loose, but they held her in place. She leaned back against the wall. Gander picked up a tube and pointed its nozzle at her. He leaned against the opposite wall, staring at her. She gazed back.

✦ ✦ ✦ ✦ ✦

In the control room, the *Ascendance* filled the air in front of Kale and Athena.

"How far away is it?" he asked.

"Forty-two thousand kilometers, and approaching," she replied.

"Approaching?   I   thought   they   were   adrift!"

"You thought correctly. They *were* adrift. Now they are not. It looks like we got out just at the right moment. I hate to admit it, but if she didn't break their captain when she did, we all would be dead by now. We would not have survived an organized firefight."

"I guess so. But at what cost?"

"I don't really think that's even relevant. Everyone's going to die soon anyway, right?" Athena said.

"Well, that's the beauty of all this! If this Order of the Stellar Cross somehow is accelerating the gravitational crunch, then maybe there's a way to reverse it!" said Kale.

"Okay, don't get too jumpy there. We're not out of this yet."

"What do you mean? Just clear us of the system and send out the stringhead, and we can Travel out of this graveyard."

"No, Kale, it's not that simple. I can't deploy the stringhead with that warship in pursuit; it would slow us down too much.

Even so, that won't matter. Ellen was right—that ship was built for another time. It is faster than us at sub-light speed, better shielded, and better armed. And it will reach us before we clear the system."

"Fine. But we're smaller, more maneuverable, right? Isn't that the lesson from the defeat of the Florian Armada? We take mosquito-bite shots while darting around, evading their heavy cannon fire!"

"Great plan, general sir, except for one thing."

"What?" Kale asked.

"We have *no* weapons!"

✦ ✦ ✦ ✦ ✦

A loud, dull thud reverberated through the hall. Gander looked up and down each way, half-expecting to see boarding troops. None appeared.

"We are under fire," said Ellen.

"Yeah, I know. Just be quiet!" Gander wiped a sweaty palm against his pant leg.

"I can provide assistance in the control room," she continued.

"You're staying right there!" said Gander, who kept looking up and down the hall.

"Not to change the subject or anything, but I'm pretty sure the chicken you ate was real," said Ellen.

A wave of nausea swept over Gander, and he held his eyes shut for a moment. "That's it," he muttered, as he hoisted the tube to strike her.

The *Last Chance* took another hit. Gander placed one hand back against the wall to brace himself. He looked back at Ellen, just to make sure nothing had happened in the split second since he looked back. Nothing had. However, after holding eye contact with her for about a second, she winked. As her eye slowly shut and opened, a subtle grin started to break across her full lips. At the same time, she disengaged her right arm from its socket, and it fell through her sleeve and the tube clamp. It hit the floor with the plop and recoil of a dead animal.

Gander's eyes followed the dropping arm and its slight bounce, spellbound by the grotesque sight. He was unaware that Ellen had used the time it took for gravity to claim her arm to pivot around on the ball of her left foot, and raise her right knee up above her waist. When her leg interrupted his line of sight to the discarded limb, Gander's eyes bulged out. He did not have enough time to react beyond that, as her right foot impacted with his upper chest. His body flew backward, colliding against the wall. The back of his head, still moving backward from the momentum of the kick, smacked into the metal paneling. He blacked out before he and the coolant tube he held hit the floor.

Ellen's empty right sleeve was free from the clamp after the sudden movement. She glanced back to where her right arm lay. She nudged her right toe into the crook of the elbow, and flipped her arm into the air. She caught it with her left arm, and guided it back up her right sleeve until the ball joint popped back into its socket. Under her sweater, her skin seams resealed. She raised her reattached, and now unrestrained, arm and unfastened the bolt holding her left arm in the tube clamp. The bolt and half of the clamp fell to the floor, but she already was racing up to the control room.

✛ ✛ ✛ ✛ ✛

"That's it," said Athena. "I've tried everything. Without military-grade hull plating or electromagnetic shielding, we simply cannot survive that kind of firepower."

"There's got to be something we can do!" said Kale.

"Well, what would you suggest, you useless little prick?" Athena shot back.

Before Kale could answer, the *Last Chance*'s neurocom made an announcement.

"Receiving hail from the captain of *Ascendance*," it said.

Athena and Kale exchanged glances. "Put him on!" said Kale.

A large, acidic face filled the air.

"Mr. Soryan!" said Kale, standing straight.

"*Captain* Soryan. My predecessor repented his self-indulgent vanity, and was purged from this ship. I will not repeat his error. Stand down and prepare to be boarded."

"My crew will fight you!" said Kale.

"You have no crew, Captain Bedett, if that indeed is your name. The avalanche of terror you created by broadcasting our plans had the side effect of eliciting an announcement by the Sepheis Corporation. Not only are you an impostor, but your ship's not part of the Sepheis registry. You will have no support from Sepheis. Surrender or be destroyed."

Kale paused, terrified and desperate to keep him talking so he could think.

"What are your terms?"

"No terms! You will bring your ship to a halt so we may attach a tractor pulse."

Athena felt the hair on the back of her neck raise up as errant threads suddenly coalesced in her mind. She stood up and addressed the imperious Soryan. "We will comply."

"What?" Kale whispered.

"We have no choice. We will await your boarding party, Captain Soryan. We will expect you to honor the Prisoners' Convention."

"Accepted," Soryan replied, as his mouth folded up in an expression that, through the process of elimination, could only be described as pleasure. The face faded out.

"What have you done? They won't honor any legal code— they're religionists!" said Kale.

"Oh, I know that! I have an idea."

"Please tell!"

Athena leaned over. "Remember that assisted wrench I carried around on the Sulley hauler? It could be used to move heavy objects, or project force. In principle, it was nothing more than a miniature tractor emitter. Now then, this ship essentially is a bundle of three giant tractor emitters! If we could reverse two of them and grip the *Ascendance*—"

"You could tear the *Ascendance* in two!" said Ellen, as she strode into the control room.

✦✦✦✦✦

"Where's Gander?" asked Kale.

"He's lying in a corridor near the power plant, unconscious," Ellen replied.

"You knocked him out?" he continued.

"Yes. Gently."

Athena cut in. "Fine, but how do we recalibrate the tractors? The neurocom keeps telling me that my commands are outside its parameters. It keeps asking for the product key number to verify ownership."

"The manual override?" asked Ellen.

"Not responding. Although the hull is holding, we're having some intermittent systems failures."

"Okay, I'm going to have to plug in. Kale, any objections?"

"N-no, Ellen. Please save our lives again!" he replied.

"Thank you!" She established a neural link directly to the *Last Chance*'s motor control center. "I'm rerouting the left tractor emitter to project instead of attract. Athena, set course for the rings of that giant at 72-345-654. We should beat them there, depending on how fast their reflexes are."

"We're moving. And they're already in pursuit! For crying out loud, that was fast!" Athena said.

"We're being hailed," said Kale.

"Slow him down, Kale!" yelled Athena, concentrating on evading energy discharges fired from the pursuing warship.

Soryan's face filled the room. "I didn't think you would surrender without a fight!"

"Yeah, so what? Do you want a medal?" replied Kale. Athena grinned.

"You atheists are so smug with your worlds of technology! You embrace the filth of artificial life, and ignore the evil right in front of you!"

"And you're a mindless attack dog! How can you accept that a line of text gives you marching orders to destroy the universe?"

"How dare you question the word of God! You have no comprehension of the damnation you are incurring from even thinking—"

"We've achieved high orbit," said Athena.

"—such blasphemous—"

"Disconnect!" shouted Kale.

A series of heavy thuds peppered the hull of the *Last Chance* as the bright and otherwise silent discharges exploded menacingly outside the control room.

The *Last Chance* dipped into the rings of the azure gas giant world. The tugboat was pelted with waves of ice and diamond crystals, creating ugly black streaks in its previously pristine cobalt finish.

The *Ascendance* remained above the rings, but showered the vicinity of the *Last Chance* with massive-yield blasts that left gaps several kilometers wide in the ring formations.

The *Last Chance* ducked and swooped to avoid the charges, but it eventually came up against a huge hole in the rings. The *Ascendance* was waiting there, like a giant spider.

The *Last Chance* careened to its left, out of the rings, and zigzagged toward the upper atmosphere of the blue planet. The *Ascendance* followed suit, and began to close in. Firing all the way in, the *Ascendance*'s shots were getting closer to anticipating the wild jerking of the relatively tiny tugboat.

As the blasts streaked in, the *Last Chance* burst out in a tight ninety-degree evasion. The tugboat ended on a trajectory toward a small, closely orbiting moon. The *Ascendance* made a more laborious turn, hugged by the gas giant's magnetosphere. The warship shoved free and again began to close in.

The *Last Chance* kicked in its reserve thrust and matched vector to the small moon's meager gravity well. The tugboat rushed toward the rocky planetoid. Moments before impact, the blue ship swerved into a dizzying, surface-skimming orbit. It curved around the small moon, and punched out the other side before the *Ascendance* even came in firing range. The *Last Chance* sped past the limb of the satellite, and was presented with an exposed dorsal view of the slowing *Ascendance*.

The *Last Chance* activated the rear tractor emitter to anchor it to the rocky world below, and then projected out two tractor beams from its forward emitters. One attached to the prow of the *Ascendance*, the other to its stern.

"Should we give them terms of surrender?" asked Kale.

"No! We will only have the upper hand now!" yelled Athena.

Ellen pushed forward the command. The left emitter started applying repulsion force, as the right emitter began pulling. She added opposing rotation to the attach points, to twist the gigantic ship. The *Ascendance* buckled in the middle, and then fractured along its spine. Sections of the ship exploded without sound, hemorrhaging debris into the gravitational fields of the moon and the giant.

"The *Ascendance* is destroyed," said Ellen to nobody in particular, before she staggered into a chair. The room suddenly was still.

"What now?" asked Kale.

"We pick up the pieces," replied Athena, whose eyes remained locked on Ellen.

PART II

CONSEQUENCES

Chapter 9

No Interruptions

"I don't care if they're expecting us to show up, we're not going!" Stella was not in the mood to argue after being berated by her superiors at work, but she was determined to hold her ground. While she felt stifled at her job, she could always take out her rage on her husband.

"But honey, they got us that nice diamond candy bowl for our anniversary, and—" attempted Goran, before Stella cut in.

"I don't care!" she cried in a shrill voice. "They are boring people to sit with!"

"We'll stay for an hour and then go, all right?"

"Not at *all*, Goran! I'm not going to waste a second with those stuck-up posers. And that candy bowl is a recycled gift if I ever saw one."

"Honey, please, I never ask you to do anything—"

"'Never'? Are you out of your mind? You always are trying to make me do things I don't want to do!"

"Name one time! One time!"

Stella smiled and was about to count off separate occurrences on her fingers when their neurocom chimed in.

"Sorry to interrupt, but there is a breaking news report that you need to see," said a high-pitched male voice.

Stella unfixed her glare from Goran and screamed to the air, "Not now, Sam, you stupid piece of junk! We're in the middle of something. I told you never to interrupt me!"

"Yes, ma'am, but your precise instructions called for no interruptions unless 'the world is coming to an end.'"

Both of them turned around to face the charging-up holojector in the breakfast nook.

✚ ✚ ✚ ✚ ✚

October 24, 4:30 p.m. UST
Central Sector, Kalyph Galaxy, Planet Sarchense

Jane Zebaster hit the metal deck with the full weight of her body armor. Her ear bled inside her helmet, but the referee already had determined that Tomo Helger's body check was legal. The crowd disagreed, and cheered her back to her feet. The cheering from the stadium doubled as she levitated a meter above the deck. Her visor cleared away the blood and smudges, and she saw that Helger was still trying to run the ball downfield.

"Cocky bastard," she muttered to herself, as she ignited her thrusters.

Helger could see her approaching in his heads-up display, and ducked right while swinging a clenched fist behind him. Zebaster was prepared. Helger's chrome glove made no impact this time, and Zebaster plowed into Helger's back. Helger collapsed over, and let go of the ball. Zebaster teased her thrust momentum just enough so that she could clamp onto the ball with her outstretched glove. The metal fingers closed, and the teal ball turned crimson to indicate her team's possession.

The crowd erupted with cheers, and Zebaster turned to race the ball back upfield. She expected to hear her coach give her a play to run the ball, but the transmitter inside her helmet was smashed. She glanced over to see him pointing at the opponent's goal.

"No kidding," she said under her breath.

She darted upfield, spinning around enemy defenders and forwards, causing them to overthrust into the side barriers. She weaved and pivoted until she entered striking range of the goal. However, the enemy team had pulled back enough defenders to create a "triple matrix" wall in front of her. Three defenders hovered in a line between her and the goal. The other players still were recoiling from overshooting their tackling attempts, and this gave Zebaster a moment to raise the glowing red ball into the air. The crowd went wild as they witnessed the primordial confrontation of one against many.

Zebaster only held up the ball for a second, knowing that two seconds would be enough to be hit from behind. As returning enemy forwards converged on her position, she locked in full thrust directly toward the triple matrix. The three defenders stood their ground, prepared for anything from what they viewed as a media-hungry prima donna.

Zebaster held the glowing ball in her gloved fist and coiled her arm as if to fire it toward the defenders. Rather than dive out of the way, the defenders were prepared to collide with the rapidly approaching star player. Then, just moments before reaching them, she drew the ball up to her chest and flung it with all her assisted strength toward the left boundary barrier. The defenders' heads all followed the ball, but were thrown to the deck when Zebaster inverted and smashed into them. Zebaster fired her stabilizer, which prevented her from moving again for a full second. However, she already had delivered her shot. What appeared as a throwaway rebounded against the barrier and shot back behind the goalie into the goal. Zebaster turned to face the crowd to feel the vibrations from the customary stomping of the fans, but the entire stadium was silent.

She tore off her helmet, and saw that every player on the field was still. She followed everyone's gaze toward the Replay Sphere suspended above the stadium.

+++++

October 24, 4:30 p.m. UST
Central Sector, Kalyph Galaxy, Kalyphon Sphere

Union Station was a maddening throng of people. Renfro Valdez looked out into the sea of people, and tried to put them out of his head. He had to cross the main expanse to catch the Equity Square airtube.

He kept his chronometer ahead by ten minutes in order to get to places ten minutes early, but since he knew that, it did him little good. He was late.

He shoved his way through the crowd, carrying his tuxedo in a garment bag slung over his shoulder. The tourists stuck out, in their shorts and shirtsleeves, and he sneered at them as he passed. It seemed to him that the entire universe descended on this world, but they did little more than congest the machinery of government as they gawked at it.

True, Kalyphon stood at the center of the universal government, indeed at the center of the universe itself. It was irrefutable that as the first Dyson Sphere ever constructed, it had a certain additional historical relevance. The story of its construction was depicted on the interior walls of the main hall of Union Station. Most of the worlds that originally had orbited the star Kalyphon were reduced to construction materials such as carbons, polymetals, and plasmorphs. These materials were in turn used to build a gigantic habitat shell around the star Kalyphon. Through use, "Kalyphon" became the name of all three objects, the giant shell itself and its contents, the star and the planet, and the conversational the name of the government itself. Since feudal times, this structure remained the hallmark of human achievement in terraforming, of molding nature to obey the will of humankind. It was unavoidable that there would be tourists cluttering up Valdez's commute.

Valdez reached the other side of Union Square, and hopped into the airtube. He stepped into the waiting carriage, and nodded perfunctorily at the other passengers. The carriage then launched out of the station, accelerating to half the speed of light. The carriage covered the internal diameter of the sphere, and arrived at Equity Square twelve minutes later.

Valdez rushed out and ran over to the Peahen Grill. He was prepared for many an unkind word from his manager for his tardiness. However, as he stepped into the restaurant, the manager, and all the patrons in the eatery, were transfixed by the holographic image of a trembling UNN anchorperson.

October 24, 4:35 p.m. UST
Central Sector, Kalyph Galaxy, Planet Kalyphon

Raisa Nazarian looked directly into the forward holofield of the camera. She attempted to summon all of her forty years of dedicated UNN journalistic objectivity to remain calm, but settled for clasping her hands in front of her. Her return feed indicated to her that this was the best position she could maintain in order to mask the fact that she was shaking.

Although she was looking into the quivering folds of a professional camera field, she knew that her signal was being carried live to receivers across the universe. Viewer Attention Index results indicated that as many as six hundred and forty-two septillion people and Sentients were looking at her image, the highest rating in recorded history.

Neurocoms across the universe interrupted the activities of all civilization because of the severity of the initial signal. A nanosecond after it was received and relayed, each functional neurocom in the universe determined the veracity of its content. A second later, the information was reviewed by the Emergency Editor of every news organization in the universe. Since UNN was the only news outlet to have a Sentient in the position of reviewing incoming information, only UNN had the clout and speed to run this story and have it carried by its smaller regional competitors.

Raisa, who seconds before reported on a corruption scandal involving an agrarian subsidy in the Enterra galaxy, Gerlad Sector, now was receiving direct copy from the Emergency Editor, the likes of which she had never seen before. With a combination of incomprehension and horror, she saw the red light above the holofield camera blink on.

With a tilt of her head, Raisa commanded the audience of a species. "It is with great sadness that I bring the following report to you. UNN just received a transmission from Ellen Möbius, a Sentient relaying through her Sepheis tugboat in conjunction with an on-the-scene UNN correspondent, that a cult organization known as the 'Order of the Stellar Cross' has been systematically increasing the gravitational mass of key sectors within the universe. The impact of this well-camouflaged campaign is that the added mass is increasing the gravitational pull between everything else in the universe: from black holes, to neutron stars, to dark matter. The objective of this cult is to accelerate vastly the collapse of the universe, which, assuming the report is accurate, will be at 7:20 p.m. on March 31 of next year. Connal, back to you."

114

Her delivery was wooden. She had to be cold to the words to get them out, but the effect on her co-anchor was considerable. He sat frozen, paralyzed. The ordinary buzz of the news studio was replaced by an eerie silence, but nobody there noticed.

✦✦✦✦✦

October 24, 4:40 p.m. UST
Dynonich Sector, Golden Fleece Galaxy, Planet Abrill

The image of Raisa Nazarian dissolved into that of Connal Berent, whose wholesome but dumbstruck face held for a second before a swirl of "Special Report" graphics replaced him.

"It *can't* be true!" muttered Evarian Joder as he turned back to face the literature department panel. Seven long months of rigor and preparation spent on his final dissertation emptied out of his skull only to be replaced by images of colliding galaxies and shattering worlds.

"This can't be happening!" added Professor Hund, wondering where her two children and husband were. Several agitated voices from the auditorium arced toward the stage.

"We need more information, people. Let's try to stay calm," said another professor, as the murmurs began to punctuate with shrieks.

✦✦✦✦✦

October 24, 4:45 p.m. UST
Gerlad Sector, Oasis Galaxy, Tylonix Platform

"Be calm, people. This don't make sense," started a man known only as Otharian, simultaneously trying to placate himself as well as his men.

"But, boss, that's UNN, man! It was just carried live all over!" wailed a small reedy fellow in a reflective one-piece suit.

"Put a fist in it, Mole. It ain't real 'til I say it's real. And so far, it ain't real." The rest of his cadre said nothing; it was too important to hide their fear, after their initial reaction. There was no safety net of a cosmopolitan culture that they could burrow into if they lost face, since Otharian ran every facet of the orbital platform.

Otharian opened a drawer, pulled out an oblong device, and walked into the center of the dank room. "You know what this is?" he said to no one in particular.

Rat looked around furtively, saw no movement, and ventured a guess. "A scrambler, boss?"

Otharian nodded as his meaty features squeezed together. Mole could not tell if this was approval or a perception of insult. Mole rubbed the remaining fingers of his right hand, remembering the penalty for a mere word out of place. The rest of Otharian's men remained silent.

Otharian walked over to the much smaller man, and hit him across the face with the back of his hand.

"Close!" said Otharian. Rat put his hand to his mouth, but there was no blood. This apparently was approval.

"Nice guess, Mole. This little thing is a wave splicer. Anyone know what it does?"

A tall man with rugged features toward the back of the room spoke. "It intercepts coded neurocom transmissions and replaces them with real-time cover data, all while keeping the data wave free from a relay signature."

A broad smile broke across Otharian's stubby head. "That's right! Now, for the benefit of your less educated colleagues here, would you be good enough to say that again in Standard?" The last word was barked out, but Hands knew it would go no further. His skills were too valuable to Otharian's gang. He therefore had some degree of comfort and protection in the room. However, Otharian did not have a reputation for patience.

Hands started again, somewhat rushed. "Yes, of course. It lets you forge data."

"There! See, Mole?" Otharian hoped he did get it, as Mole's bony face was not a pleasant surface to strike with a bare hand on a repeated basis.

Mole looked at him, dumbfounded. He started to shake. "I guess the story's a fake?"

Otharian's eyes bulged open. "I knew I kept you around for a reason! Yeah, the story's a fake. Some smartass thought he'd pull a fast one on the whole universe. But you know what? He's not pulling a fast one on me, and I'd better not hear any whimpering from you guys about it neither. We got a reputation to maintain, people. That's all there is to say about it."

His men nodded and murmured assent. Mole even started up a new game of Crab. Otharian glanced over his crew, and exhaled slowly. As his world appeared to return to normal, he held a stare from Hands. They would have to talk about this, and arming the whole outfit, in private.

For his part, Hands was accustomed to recognizing opportunity when it presented itself. Growing up alone and hungry, he had to seek advancement from any means necessary. However, it struck him that there must be some higher purpose to his life. Why would he, a man of superior intellect and capability, be relegated to the bottom rung of society? All his life, this was the one thing of which he was certain. Something else was at work, but he had no clue as to what. The impending collapse of the universe had to be connected somehow. And now his card was about to be played.

✦ ✦ ✦ ✦ ✦

October 24, 4:50 p.m. UST
Palm Sector, Orvo Galaxy, Planet Rattan

"It's a hoax!" yelled Penny Fallas. Everyone at the Rattan Planetary Council Assembly stopped talking.

"We may be a small planet in a minor sector, but for crying out loud, we can't be *that* gullible!" This statement caused an immediate onslaught of shouting and stomping, but little was distinct in the cacophony.

Chairman Hebb touched a contact on his ancient wooden console. An increasing musical note rose until it drowned out the voices, and then it ceased. All was quiet, and Chairman Hebb had everyone's attention.

In a very quiet voice, so soft that everyone had to lean in to hear him, Hebb spoke. "I understand there are questions about the source of this information. But what about UNN? And numerous confirmations from other news sources in the last ten minutes of the Universal Crunch? We are teetering on the edge of the end of the universe, and we are bickering about some deep-seated prejudices about Sentients?"

The assembly responded with muted whispering, but Andor Weebkin stood up. "Your Chairship, we understand the reality of the situation. However, consider this. In the ten minutes since the broadcast, I have received word from my deputy that twenty-eight people committed suicide in my district alone. In light of the deleterious effect of this information, would it not be wise to attack it, denounce it, even sneer at it, while the media report this story?"

The assembly gave every sign of erupting again, but Hebb held up his hand. The chamber was silent.

"From a civic standpoint, your argument is persuasive. However, what if the report is true? Have we not a duty to treat our constituents with a certain dignity and honesty? If we are all to die, then is there no moral onus upon this august body?"

Again the crowd rippled, but was silenced when Weebkin spoke.

"I respectfully suggest, Your Chairship, that until the Universal government takes a position on the matter, that we minimize social fragmentation by denouncing the story. We can then follow the lead of the Universal level."

The room buzzed with excitement at having hit upon a resolution that would pass the buck to someone else.

Hebb spoke again. "Very well. The resolution has been formatted and presented. All those in favor?"

Hebb's console field lit up, and was confirmed by a resounding, "Aye!"

"All those against?"

Four solitary blips appeared in his field, while not a soul ventured to say, "Nay!"

Hebb again spoke quietly. "Then the resolution has passed! So let it be entered into the record."

118

October 24, 4:55 p.m. UST
Sirius Sector, Milky Way Galaxy, Planet Heyudi

"It's a sign!" Fortayn held his hands high as his acolytes drew closer. Although the cathedral was enormous, the air was musty from being pumped in from the surface of Heyudi, four hundred kilometers up.

"But your grace, respectfully, it seems to be the work of some other sect, not the work of God," Harbagotten said.

"The Lord works in mysterious ways, child. The apocalypse is indeed upon us, and this sudden, universal awareness is surely a signal to us," Fortayn replied. "Too long have we labored under the shadows of the towers and domes, scurried away from polite society, remained silent while the secular universe ran its affairs in rampant hedonism. This, my children, is our cue. No other signal could in a single stroke uniformly communicate the same command to our diffused cells, while throwing the seculars into chaos. Come, let us prepare!"

October 24, 4:55 p.m. UST
Central Sector, Kalyph Galaxy, Planet Kalyphon

"So, we're staying on the air?" asked Turbor Veller, after he slammed the door to his office.

"Of course we are. We're getting the highest ratings in the history of, well, history!" said the network executive from the holojector.

"Don't you perceive just the slightest bit of irony in the fact that Nazarian's broadcast an hour ago indicates that history is about to end?" said Veller, casting a condescending look toward the holographic image of his young superior.

"Use that in the show! Have you any idea how much additional advertising revenue we have made in the last second alone?"

Veller was not pleased with the pecuniary path network news had taken in the last decade, and he felt oddly liberated in getting it off his chest. "Look, you little pipsqueak. I was punching shots from before your mother was born, so don't tell me what's important and what's not. The only reason I'm not home right now with my family is that I believe we need to keep this universe sane for as long as possible. Part of that means keeping this show running. So if the network gives me the feed, that's all I need to hear from you. Understand?" Veller surprised himself that he had that much tension in him. Then again, the last hour had not been particularly tranquil.

"Yeah, old-timer. Save it for someone who cares. Just do your damn job, and maybe you won't get fired!" With that, the transmission ended.

"Boss, we're on in 60!" said Veller's assistant, peeking through the door. Although he was furious, Veller brought himself back to reality with the help of his regular routine and his sense of duty.

He stepped out into the studio. "Okay, everyone listen up! I know we're all hit pretty hard by what's happening. However, we have a job to do. In fact, our job is now more important than it's ever been before. We've got to keep this universe together!"

"But what's the point?" asked a dowdy stylist, jabbing a comb in his direction.

"The point, my dear Ezma, is that people across the universe are feeling shock and terror right now. Information is the best defense against that. Whatever will happen, will happen. We don't control that. We control this!" he concluded, pointing at the camera field.

"We're on in five!" piped in the assistant. Veller snapped his fingers and cued the lead camera operator to zoom in on the star of the show. A small red icon flashed on Veller's holofield control dock.

"Welcome to *Final Analysis*, the show that brings you the most diverse perspectives from around the universe. I'm Temn Sofer, moderating from Kalyphon." Sofer tipped his head toward the other people sitting around him.

"I'm Mims Brown, columnist for *Skeptic's Weekly*, streaming from planet Halcyon in the Milky Way galaxy, Local Group."

"I'm Evelyn Chambers, chairwoman of the Liberal Party, transmitting from planet Saria in the Elysian Fields galaxy, Ephemeral Sector."

"And I'm Epol Kollander, media liaison for the Construction Triad, streaming from Chang Base at the Enigma Cluster."

The three holographic representatives glanced back to Sofer, who again addressed the camera. "As no doubt many of you have done already, I gave my neurocom strict instructions to dedicate all of its efforts to the 'Big Crunch' question."

He swung around to face field two. "To bring you up to speed since the announcement, the Sepheis Corporation issued a press release in which it explicitly denies the existence of one 'Ellen Möbius' in any of its employment records, or the registry of any tugboat under the name *Last Chance*. This casts serious doubts over the veracity of the transmission itself, and the Sentient community in general."

Chambers jumped in. "I'm not sure if it makes sense to say the press release has had such an effect, and even if it has, there is little to be gained from repeating such racially charged views in the universal media."

"Hold on a second!" started Brown. "For millennia, we have accepted the aristocracy of the Sentients, and what have we to show for it? A decidedly unfunny practical joke from one of them, validated across the universe by another!"

Chambers nearly leapt out of her seat. "I can't believe I'm hearing this! Deflecting the issue with tired rhetoric is not going to help matters. Do you really want the last months of humanity to be peppered with race riots?"

"So you actually believe it?" Brown shot back.

"Based on the data we've received, which UNN has confirmed, the universe will stop expanding in February, and rapidly crunch down over a spread of weeks!"

Kollander stepped in. "That information makes no sense. Out at Chang Base, I deal with a great number of mining and construction companies. Many have a private physics team, or are affiliated with some nonprofit Mass Analysis institution. None of them see this scenario unfolding. They tell me that the cosmological force keeps the universe expanding, despite the effects of the gravitational force. And even if that were somehow reversed, they say it is physically impossible for the matter from the edges of our universe to reach its center in five weeks. That would violate the speed of light, and as we know, no natural phenomenon can do that."

"So why would an institution like UNN report their conclusion if there's such an obvious error in the analysis?" asked Brown.

"That's not my area. I can't explain network behavior."

"I'll tell you why. Your scientists are wrong!"

"You can't argue with the speed of light," said Kollander.

"Apparently you can't argue with a Sentient either!"

Sofer, seeing the debate going nowhere, decided to move the show along. "On that note, let me introduce our first guest. Senator Bon Resser, Conservative from the Glass Corridor sector, thanks for joining us!"

The hologram of a comfortably elegant woman materialized next to Sofer. "I wish I were here under more pleasant circumstances, but thank you."

"Tell me, Senator: What was your reaction to the news?"

"Honestly, I don't know what to think. UNN does not publish news in a cursory manner, but it is conceivable that we all are being made fools of as we speak. That includes UNN. I've had my staff on this question since we all heard, and I can't say that I have any expertise in astrophysics, but the light speed issue seems to present a major stumbling block."

"So how will this affect policy?" interjected Brown.

"I can tell you that our efforts to reform the tax structure will not be unduly affected by all of the current turmoil."

"No, I mean how can you trust the Sentients, knowing that they started this current turmoil?"

"Come on, Mims, don't be so reactionary! I have had extensive dealings with Sentients in joint committee meetings with the Council of Sentients. I count some of these Councilors among my friends. It serves no legitimate purpose to start casting around that kind of blame," replied the Senator.

"What will the Senate's reaction be to this?" asked Sofer.

"This sort of thing is largely unpredictable. I can tell you that from past experience, most of them will follow the President's lead on issues of Universal importance. I think this qualifies!"

"Do you know when we can expect a reaction? The President's press liaison is not responding to our queries."

"Well, I've had my feelers out, and it seems the President likely will be presenting an Emergency State of the Universe address at about eighteen Kalyphon time."

Sofer asked, "How do you know?"

"My office has been reassured that it will happen," replied the politician.

"Well I guess we'll all be tuned in at eighteen then! We have to cut away for an important message from our sponsors."

Veller's red light turned green, and he turned to his assistant. "Get me the President's liaison. Now!"

Chapter 10

The Council of Sentients

Although the Kalyphon Sphere was created from eight planets circling the naked star Kalyphon, one planet remained untouched, walled in, within the Sphere. This otherwise ordinary little rural world orbited the star at a pedestrian 1.034 astronomical units, but it was perceived as the seat of all power in the universe. All the sectoral houses of parliament were located here, including the primary body of the legislative hierarchy, the Universal Senate. Also located here was the Council of Sentients, which served as a corroborative body for the Senate, the final authority of appeal in the judicial system, and the body charged with the collection and allocation of government funds, among other functions. These various elements were responsible for the machinery of government, and the universe could easily run itself. However, due to primitive instincts, humankind required an individual to sit at the apex as leader.

No other reason could explain why he was there, thought President Yohan Taschet. He knew all real power rested with the Council and, to a lesser extent, the Senate. As a result, he could not carry out even ten percent of the things he promised during his election campaign. Furthermore, his security envelope was so tight that he could not even order a meal for himself.

"Sir?" Pella Hess, his young Chief of Staff, leaned over from her chair. His ministers were staring with concern, to the extent allowed by protocol.

Taschet refocused on his surroundings. "What?"

"Sir, I was saying that our demographics analysis indicates you should use more casual references in your speeches. That's why I've included some more of them in the most recent version of your speech."

"Look, Pella, I know you mean well, but I have to be pretty forthright tonight. This is not about approval ratings, my dear. This has to do with crisis management. Mark?"

Mark Weaver, the Universal Security Minister, was able to participate in the voice conversation easily while receiving a steady stream of information from his neurocom. "The President is absolutely right. In the two hours since the UNN announcement, there have been seven thousand and four hundred twenty-four separate killing sprees. Schools, restaurants, holospheres, you name it."

"Well, how many killing sprees are there in an ordinary two-hour period?" asked Hess.

Without missing a beat, Weaver replied, "Not counting suicides and rampages with fewer than thirty casualties, only two hundred sixty-one. What's more disturbing is that the frequency over time of these killing sprees actually is going *up*."

"Wait a minute! What do you mean it's going up?" said President Taschet.

"Sir, look at this," said Weaver as he waved up a holofield chart. A three-dimensional Cartesian graph appeared above the table. "The y-axis represents violent deaths, the x-axis represents time, and the z-axis represents awareness of the report. Now, zero on the time axis represents the UNN broadcast. As awareness hits, killing spikes." A line coming out of the negative space of the x-axis, barely hovering above the y-axis, splashed out in a steep, bright red sheet out of the z-axis.

"Now then, you'd expect the killing in general to increase, while awareness goes down. After all, once you find out the universe is going to implode, you rush out and kill everyone you know, and then it's over. You get bored, you blow your brains out, what have you. The rest of us sit tight." The sheet tipped as increased awareness dampened the number of killings in the holographic graph.

"However, what we're seeing is that people are pondering over this, already aware of it, and *deciding* to go out and kill the neighbor with the fancy pod and the 1.2 kids." The slanted sheet vanished, and was replaced by a mottled ramp, resembling the topography of a mountain face.

"We see the same thing with looting," Weaver added, as a pale blue sheet swooped out under the translucent red sheet, then cut through and over it. "The same factors, namely delayed reaction and increased damage, start off slowly, but overtake actual killing around the one-hour mark in both time and awareness delay."

"Prognosis?"

"Based on the curvature of these planes, it's going to get worse before it gets better."

"What about the Sectoral Guard? Aren't they in position to stop this?" asked Taschet, waving at the contorted graph.

"Yes sir, they are deployed and in effect. If they were not, the numbers would be much higher," replied Weaver.

"What about the Navy?"

"Well, sir, they aren't really equipped to handle urban combat situations. This isn't an old-fashioned military, sir. They're trained for celestial disaster relief and relocation campaigns. They could blockade a few galaxies with heavy cruisers and maybe an entire sector if it came to that, but that does nothing for individual star systems."

Why even maintain a military budget, he wondered, if they cannot help out now? "So what are they doing now?" he said aloud.

Ulia Retaran, Defense Minister, answered, "We have been in close contact with the Security Minister's office, and are providing logistical and tactical support. As Minister Weaver alluded, most of our forces are engaged in planetary evacuation and resettlement duties, what with the frequency of supernovae popping like over-inflated balloons across the cosmos. Most of my people are rushing around trying to outrun electromagnetic pulses and singularity encounters. However, we could redeploy seventy or eighty fleets for galactic blockade duties if the need arises."

"Lisa? How's that research coming?"

Lisa Ferric, Intelligence Minister, replied, "We have some people in position, but the *Last Chance* is proving to be a difficult ship to track for our agents. Someone on board has piloting skills that go beyond anything their dossiers suggest."

"'Proving difficult'? What are you talking about? They have two kids, a reporter, and a single Sentient!"

"Well, sir, they uncovered the Stellar Cross, so they clearly add up to more than the sum of their parts."

That was a clever way out of an embarrassing admission, he thought. He was not sure he could come up with something that good, especially as his civilization was falling apart.

"Sir. You're scheduled to appear in the Address Chamber in fewer than five minutes," said Hess.

"Fine. Warren, do you have anything to say?" the President asked his Interior Minister.

A burly, sullen man standing in the corner looked up. "Well, sir, only this. Our civilization has evolved throughout millennia to a point where people are equipped properly to handle individual self-determination and community ethics. We have cast aside tribal warfare, superficial judgment, and thought control. Now we are faced with a news event that could reduce all those achievements to rubble before the truth of the matter is even uncovered."

Everyone turned to look at him. "Yeah, Warren. I know." said Taschet.

✦ ✦ ✦ ✦ ✦

Raisa Nazarian sat in the UNN holocom booth high above the floor of the Address Chamber. She had managed to contact her husband, who was trying to negotiate the mob outside the elementary school their children attended. Her neurocom pulled her out of her reverie as her brain was bombarded with information. She was on the air. A graphic appeared beneath her with the words "Countdown to Big Crunch: March 31."

"A universe in crisis. As reported earlier today by UNN, the President will speak before the Chamber at an emergency State of the Universe address. Ah! Here he comes now."

The massive ornate structure was filled to capacity. Every member of the Senate and a few members of the Council were seated along with various regional representatives and dignitaries in the swollen panels of the crescent-shaped hall. Although the center dais was raised slightly, the inclined audience towered above it. This architecture was deliberate, so as to reinforce the sovereignty of the democratic system and minimize the inescapable monarchical effect of placing a single person at the center of the universe.

The entryway to the Address Chamber was at the center of the rear wall, and was adorned above by a twenty-meter tall griffin. The origin of the mythological beast dated back to preastronomic times, but was a critical symbol of the original

Kalyphon Union. With the head and wings of an eagle and the body of a lion, the griffin was well suited to provide an image of virility and grace for a trade union whose real appeal was more acutely due to its liberal use of free market economics and planned suburban culture. As it evolved, the standardized griffin clutched a bundle of stylized wriggling wormholes in its feline claws, which over time became rigid and tipped with spiral galaxies. It now hung with despair over the archway, as if realizing that the eons building a civilization throughout the universe all were spent in vain.

Beneath this calcified griffin stood a man-at-arms, capped by a long flowing wig, and draped in the elaborate garb of a 57th Millennium formal officer's uniform. He raised a stout brass pipe to his lips, and his resonant voice filled the chamber.

"Ms. Speaker, Councilors, Senators. The President of the Universe!"

On every other occasion that he delivered the State of the Universe address, Yohan Taschet received a booming standing ovation as he entered the Address Chamber. This time, everyone indeed was standing, but he strode down the aisle in near silence. The expectant eyes of both allies and adversaries bathed him in a uniform wash of expectation, as if he held the power to wave a wand and return the universe to its prior state of comfortable ignorance. Taschet kept his eyes on the dais as spherical holocameras hovered around him with their choreographed Medusa-like projections.

Taschet climbed the ornate spiral staircase around the cylindrical dais in a series of movements propelled through autopilot rather than nerve. Once he approached the podium, he looked up at the griffin, but its wooden eyes were long-since dead.

Taschet knew his image was picked up and rebroadcast by UNN, Starnet, and a myriad of local news channels so that he was once again standing in the living rooms of the people who voted for him. Their faces would be pleading, much as his most fervent opponent, Charles Sendacky, had moments ago.

"Friends." Taschet's augmented voice filled the chamber, and silenced much of the clamor around all of the active holojectors throughout the galaxies. He looked out and saw the faces of several thousand people, but he knew the eyes of the universe were on him.

"The Universe has for eons stood as the home of humanity. We have overcome our turbulent adolescence, and survived the discovery of the two nuclear, electromagnetic, gravitational, and cosmological forces. We have developed policies that integrated the desires and aspirations of each of its octillion members into the development of a universal society. We have overcome our prejudices toward the intelligent life that sprang from our own technology. We have strung together the wayward elements that compose the tapestry of humanity, and built a nation the likes of which has never been seen before.

"And now, we receive a report saying that all we have achieved will be no more. Such a consideration indeed is daunting. However—and I ask you to consider what I am about to say very carefully—does it make any sense?

"According to this report, we are to believe that a secret organization has been plotting to demolish the entire universe, and yet has remained hidden. Further, are we to accept the idea that all the worlds and stars will converge at a single point at the end of March next year, without even considering that it would take ten billion years for that to happen at the very speed of light?

"Something clearly is going on here, but it is not that the universe is collapsing. Some *individuals* have somehow got it into their heads that it would be interesting to pull a hoax on UNN, and on the entire universe. This is unacceptable and is, in fact, criminal. Right now, the Ministry of Justice is working on the case, and we will be presenting our findings on that as soon as they are available.

"For the time being, our focus is then to contain the tremendous sequence of tragedies that has broken out across the universal sphere. I have authorized the deployment of our armed forces to provide tactical assistance directly to galactic municipal governments, and to offer further support, should it prove necessary.

"Perhaps one of the most critical factors that needs to be made clear, though, is that there *will* be a future for us. We must remain calm, analyze information with a healthy skepticism, and persevere. At the end of the day, we have been hurt by this so-called news. However, the wormholes still are operating smoothly. Our economy still is racing ahead. Our citizens still are teaching, producing, and discovering.

"Are we to perish now? After having struggled through so much barbarity and violence? After having forged a new culture that dates back to the awakening of the 12th Millennium Enlightenment? We have created a people of intelligence, morality, and fierce courage. Despite everything, the state of our universe is *alive and well.*"

As Taschet paused to catch his breath, Sendacky rose out of his chair and clapped. It was the first sound in the chamber besides Taschet's voice. The sharp sound was joined by another, and another, until the whole Chamber roared with the deafening sound of reverberated applause. Taschet smiled. He let out a silent sigh of relief, as his neurocom started to feed him his next paragraph.

He realized that was the most important lie of his career.

✦ ✦ ✦ ✦ ✦

"Capital speech, sir!" said one of the pages as Taschet climbed down from the dais. Taschet winked at the young man through a plastic smile. He rushed out of the chamber as it thundered a standing ovation. He immediately was swarmed by his personal detail, which escorted him out of the building and into the white light of the Kalyphon sun.

Amid a halo of snaking holocameras and a small army of reporters, Taschet's detail pushed through, offering no entry. These efforts did little to stem the tide of shouted questions, which descended on Taschet like a hailstorm. He ignored them and burrowed through to his waiting limousine.

The door slid shut, and once again he was cocooned safely from the clatter. Pella Hess sat there on the couch, with sugar crystals resting in the corners of her mouth. Taschet peered into the open pastry box, only to find it empty.

"You had to eat all the baklava, didn't you?" asked Taschet.

"Sorry, sir. It seemed natural to eat them while I watched your speech, which seemed to be pretty effective toward the end," she replied.

"Yeah. I guess. But what's next is the real sell job."

"The Council of Sentients?"

"You got it," he replied with a snort.

President Yohan Taschet took a deep breath as his limousine and hovercade descended toward the massive black, vaguely cylindrical structure that housed the most secluded and underestimated branch of the universal government. All passage was closed for kilometers around, which made the appearance of a parade of sleek, luminescent vessels protecting one man oddly comical.

Despite the lack of effective power, the burden of leadership was a drain on Taschet. The hidden compromises necessary to keep the government in operation were tolerated and tucked under the rug in polite society, but the presidential election process would turn the stomach of even the most jaded pundit. Taschet survived that process, but did so by devoting all of his energy to making promises and choices that would assure his election, with little devoted to refining the archetypal moral government.

Taschet stood at the pinnacle of this structure of humankind, not through excellence, intelligence, or any other singularly positive human attribute, but by virtue of sheer gamesmanship. He was realistic enough to know that his talents had little to do with true leadership, and that such a process could not produce a person capable of handling a true universal catastrophe.

As he walked across the grass lawn to the twenty-meter doors, he also was aware that he would have to demonstrate the very leadership he never felt comfortable wielding. The backlash against Sentients was mounting, and although they were the only real means of exercising true Aristotelian democracy, old prejudices die hard.

The irony was not lost on Taschet. The mantra of democratic government, which was drilled into every child by every schoolteacher, fundamentally was flawed. With an average of one billion people per world, an average of thirty million habitable worlds per galaxy, and a total of fifty billion galaxies in the universe, there was no practiced method to assure that each individual found representation in a single, functional parliamentary body.

The solution was direct representation via neurocom. Although its roots were preastronomic, "Digital Democracy" still was the most effective method of genuine democracy. The Council of Sentients, as part of its duties, tabulated the concerns and wishes of the universal population, and ensured that legislative policy reflected it. For this remarkable feat, the Sentients still were held apart in society. They were different. They were self-aware, living, emotional people, but they also all were once machines. The fact that this distinction over "sourcing" was reflected in the very structure of the government did not help the social cause of source equality. The fact that the Council was engaged in all manner of clandestine operations that often went against the wishes of the electorate made matters worse.

Taschet passed alone through the antechamber, and entered a giant cylindrical expanse. The door slid shut behind him. The curved wall was polished black obsidian, and although he could make out figures standing against the wall, a group of seven figures was visible prominently in the center.

Taschet spoke. "It would appear that the cat is out of the bag."

Before he finished speaking, the chamber lit up as laser-like quantum projections lanced out between the heads of the Sentients, in a fractal ballet. Their thoughts linked together as they processed the comment of the organic human.

"Yes," said one of the seven, in an even yet lilting tenor voice. "You did an admirable job trying to keep it in there. However, it may be necessary for the cat to leave the bag behind as events unfold."

"If you say so." The quantum web between the Sentients flashed in its peculiarly graceful pattern.

"We do. It would also appear that the bait we left for the Stellar Cross with that Sulley hauler drew more than just a passing interest."

"Yes. Based on the debris field at Elegiel, it looks like the *Last Chance* turned the tables a bit," said Taschet.

"Nonetheless, the real damage the *Last Chance* represents is not the rioting, but a backlash from the Stellar Cross. We will dampen the social effects of the rioting. You must track down that ship and neutralize it."

"I'm already working on it."

"Work harder. With the Stellar Cross hanging in the balance, and our own strategy hinging on keeping them diverted, that crew may well hold the key to the universe."

Chapter 11

The Black Hole

Gallumus looked like a standard barred spiral Seyfert galaxy. A straight corridor extended out of opposite points of a spherical nucleus before gravitational shear forced a flat, traditional spiral formation to extrude out of the open ends of the corridor. The bunching of stars into the corridor formation was long thought to be the product of chance, as stars in the rotational disk accumulated on polar ends of the galaxy. However, chance is not often an element of the cosmological balance.

"There is a *huge* black hole in there," observed Kale, pointing at the bulging nucleus. He gripped the rung on the transparent bridge, certain that if he vomited, his breakfast would be sucked into the enormous dead star.

"Easily larger than Milky Way's own Sagittarius, even edging out Charybdis and the Siren Core. Given the immense turmoil, even at the periphery of this galaxy, there are only about twenty habitable planets left. We are looking at one of the oldest galaxies in the universe."

"We're not going in *there*?" said Gander, pointing at the swollen nucleus.

Athena shot him an icy glare. Even at this distance from the black hole, she was trying strenuously to keep the *Last Chance* still. She sorely regretted not having the mental room to conjure up a deprecating remark about Gander's apprehension.

Kale responded, "Of course we are. We have to take measurements. Plus, we have to figure out what the Stellar Cross is doing to accelerate the collapse. If we can stop them before the Universe stops expanding, we could add billions of years to its life cycle!"

Gander waved him off. He had heard all this before. It still sounded like gibberish to him, and the past few hours had done little to mollify the near-death experience they shared.

"We were shot at! Like a holovision opera! This just doesn't happen in the real world," stammered Gander.

"I know," said Kale. "It's a little surreal to me, too. I'm just trying to block it out by focusing on the work in front of us. This is our mission now, and we need to figure out how they're causing the collapse."

"I am certain it has to do with the nodule we saw extended from the *Ascendance*," added Ellen, from the back railing.

Gander swiveled to regard her. While continuing to look at her, he said, "The decon chamber would be a great place to store her."

"That's it. You two have to call a truce! I am sick and tired of hearing about it, Gander. Live with it!" replied Kale, exasperated.

"Are you mental? She risked universal chaos, and, shit, she knocked me out!" shot back Gander, hurt.

"I know she hit you!" said Kale. "You won't let us forget that! But she apologized to you, and frankly, we'd be dead right now if she hadn't knocked you out."

"My therapist is going to love this," said Gander under his breath.

"So what's it gonna be?" said Kale. This was turning out just like his study group, where he had to be the one who played the adult.

"Fine, she's part of the team. But remember, she lied to us about her legal status, she did hit me, and she unleashed into the media the story we were trying so hard to keep secret. I dare you to plug in, see what's happening. People are going nuts out there because of her."

Placing the ship neatly inside the protective loop of a trinary star system, Athena jumped into the conversation.

"Yeah, so what? She's not causing the collapse. And the main reason *I'm* here is to cover the story. I was counting on it breaking sooner or later. And by deliberately fingering the Stellar Cross, they're going to be hard pressed to continue their operations."

"So then why don't we contact the UIM? We could get them to stamp out the Cross," said Gander.

"We don't know what they will do with us," said Athena. "We effectively have stolen a ship, destroyed another, and provoked what you called universal chaos. Plus, we don't know how far the influence of the Cross extends. How do you keep an organization that big so quiet? By controlling communication. That's why I haven't contacted my news desk. It could be suicide."

"You think they're that connected?" asked Kale.

"I don't know. But the government certainly is. If any of us makes any kind of contact with the outside universe, we're going to be traced and then imprisoned, and that's a best-case scenario."

"Fine, but what good can we do out here? I mean, we can't expect to tear apart every Stellar Cross ship we come across!" Gander pointed out.

"No, we'll have to figure something out, if it comes to that," replied Kale.

"I don't just mean fighting off a ship. I mean what can we do about the collapse?" asked Gander.

Kale could tell his friend already had taken on more than he expected. The knowledge of unyielding total annihilation was something they all bore with a kind of resigned humor, but the shift to potential salvation was wreaking havoc with all of their emotions.

"Gander, we're going to figure something out. We're piecing it together. Let's try and focus ourselves now. Put everything else aside, and let's hear what Ellen has to say," said Kale.

Gander sighed. "Okay, buddy. Fine." He turned his gaze back to Ellen. "Go on."

"Thank you," she replied. "The ship's neurocom was able to run a fairly complex battery of scans on the *Ascendance* while we were over there, and during the subsequent chase. Here, take a look."

The bulging nucleus of the Gallumus Core was replaced by a three-dimensional representation of the *Ascendance*. A semitransparent three-dimensional graph with x-, y-, and z-axes underlay the image.

"As you can see, it has the basic form of an old Pariah carrier. However, if we zoom in to the front, we see that tentacled sphere extended out of its prow."

"So what is it?" asked Kale.

"Well, let me tell you a bit more about it before I give you my ideas as to what it might be. The ship observed the sphere for a period of more than four hours, and recorded those tentacles writhing around that sphere. For most of that time, they were moving with seemingly little care, undulating like kelp in the ocean. However, at several instances, they sped up."

The tentacles in the hologram broke their soothing pattern and whipped around their anchoring sphere in a mad frenzy.

"Now watch again in slow motion."

The flitting of the tentacles was chaotic, although rhythmic. However, at certain intervals, they would cross through each other, and emerge undamaged.

"What was that?" asked Athena.

Ellen smiled a lopsided grin. "The ship's neurocom observed something it couldn't understand. In normal space, the *Last Chance*'s sensor array uses a three-dimensional consecutive scale as its default template. In layman's terms, it assumes that all matter can only occupy one point in space at a time. However, those conditions are not true when Traveling, and it is certainly not true with that sphere!"

Gander was confused. "But the nearest wormhole nozzle was at the edge of the Elegiel system, several AU away from that sphere."

"Yeah, but somehow, that sphere is pinching space the same way wormholes do. It's warping the curvature of space. That's why it looks weird in three dimensions. Despite their appearance, those tentacles really are moving in a regular geometric pattern. The difference is that they are not moving through three dimensions, but actually through ten dimensions!"

From the origin point of the underlying graph, seven additional axes, labeled q- through w-, extended at bizarre diagonals, severely contorting the image of the ship. This rendered the formerly stubby tentacles as elongated, uniformly pulsating ribbons, shooting across the room to caress a hologram of Elegiel.

Kale was the first to speak. "What is that thing doing to that star?"

Ellen paused, regarding Kale sideways. "The scans reveal nothing since they were not calibrated to watch for relativistic or dimensional effects." She paused to take a breath for emphasis, rather than oxygen. "I don't know."

+ + + + +

The *Last Chance* held its position four parsecs away from the event horizon of the Gallumus Core black hole. The gargantuan singularity hung there like a corpulent ogre, swallowing whole all the children who dared cross its bridge.

The black hole was surrounded by a halo of highly agitated red giant stars, whose enormous mass and revolutionary velocity provided a tenuous reprieve from gravitational annihilation. The *Last Chance* held orbit around one of these giants, clinging onto the old giant, as nebulae, comets, planets, smaller stars, and peripheral dark matter fell helplessly into the insatiable black hole.

Kale measured the singularity with scientific aloofness, trying to resist engaging in anthropomorphism. The black hole was not a malicious villain, devouring innocents. It was just a cosmological object. He knew that it simply was human nature to ascribe consciousness to inanimate objects. Perhaps it was the pull of such tendencies that enables rational people to accept supernatural consciousness as a valid principle.

As much as he was toying with concepts of villains and superbeings, Kale also was grappling with death. He was a party to the deaths of others and he was feeling the crushing weight of responsibility. He may not have given the command to kill, but he performed a function in the control room that led to the destruction of the *Ascendance*. Although he had rationalized the act as self-preservation, and consequently universe-preservation, he still felt bound by the knowledge that he had killed. He would never again feel the armchair ease of a perfect conscience.

"Gander, we killed those people," he said.

"Yeah, buddy, but it was self-defense," Gander replied in a subdued voice.

"That's not the part that bothers me. I'm worried this is going to become a normal part of our lives from now on. I think we've passed a point of no return."

"Kale, everything's upside-down right now. Our lives at Stanford, going to Chrysalis, sleeping through the anthro final. It's all out the airlock. But we're still here for each other, buddy.

We can hang on to that." Gander reached over and squeezed his friend's shoulder.

Kale smiled, despite himself. "You know, you're right."

"Of course I'm right. So let's focus on this mission as you said. You're one of the few people around who actually knows this stuff, so you've got to focus."

A steady sequence of tasks would help to dull the turmoil in his head too, Kale reasoned. He turned to the telemetry coming from the ship's neurocom.

"The professor's measurements were right," said Kale. "This black hole measures 8.6 on the Schwarzschild scale. That is four times greater than it should be by now."

"How does that happen?" asked Gander, his raised voice echoing in the cargo hold. "How does a black hole swell up like that without anyone noticing?"

"This galaxy has a population of 20 people. That's one hermit lording over each of its remaining habitable worlds. They probably don't care to take trivial measurements," replied Kale.

"What about the rest of the universe?" asked Gander, a little more softly.

"The universal government has its hands full with repopulation, gamma ray burst neutralization, and intersectoral politics. As for the sector governments, they practice a kind of galactic isolationism." Kale eyed a gravitronic microconductor, and blew on it.

"What about the Great Universal Community?"

Kale grunted. "That's just a social pacifier, Gander. How deep do you think that community feeling goes? Sure we're supposed to be modern, civilized people, but how far are we from hunting game in groups?"

"C'mon, we're light years from that anthro class."

"No, I mean it. We have been conditioned for several million years to hold the immediate hunting group above all else. I have a feeling that when push comes to shove, we'll all be running for the trees," replied Kale.

Gander stared at his friend. "Past the point of no return?"

Kale had no reply.

+ + + + +

A neutron star, not more than four hundred kilometers in diameter, shot past the far side of the giant host star. As Athena watched the immense gravitational wake, Ellen slipped into the control room. After the seemingly endless parade of the neutron star's gravitational entourage of systems, clusters, and stellar debris rushed by, Ellen broke the silence.

"Thanks for supporting me back there," she said from the railing.

Athena swiveled around in her command chair to regard Ellen squarely. "The enemy of my enemy is not necessarily my friend," she said.

Ellen unfolded her crossed arms to run her hand through her short red hair. "Maybe not, but we have a lot in common."

"I don't think so. You're a fucking machine. Double meaning intended," said Athena.

Ellen smiled a child's unreserved grin. "As I was saying, we have a lot in common!"

Athena turned red. She had no ready response. Her mouth hung open, waiting for the words that refused to form. Ellen seized the opportunity, and blew her a kiss before walking out of the room.

+ + + + +

Kale was trying to sleep. Despite the frenetic sequence of events swirling through his mind, it was the disruption to his winding-down routine that troubled him now.

Ellen was not there.

The comforting presence that spoke to him through the walls and through his wristband, the voice that talked to him, listened to him, joked with him, and supported him now was fully independent.

This was no sudden shock to him. This was, in fact, the normal consequence of installing independence protocols into an everyday neurocom. The strange thing, rather, was that she took so long to manifest external signs of independence. One of the requirements of the independence setup was that only one version of the program may exist. This was a major break from the typical neurocom, which retained multiple redundant copies of itself, as well as the option to reinstall its entire matrix should it become corrupted.

No such safeguards existed for an independent neurocom, or Sentient, as they preferred to be called. This gave them a legal status equal to that of organic humans, and the ancient slavery laws and cloning regulations applied to them as well. Given the sudden vulnerability to data corruption and accidental deletion, most Sentients took on a self-contained physical form, a construct they could inhabit, around which they could establish protective perimeters. Many chose the classic android configuration, so as to be accepted readily by organic humans, a species that held onto its primitive fear of the unfamiliar.

Although he missed her, Kale was struggling with the fact that she indeed had taken a physical form. He was confused by a barrage of conflicting impulses toward her. He was trying to disentangle them when a strange but melodic entry chime rang. Knowing Gander's chime, it had to be one of the two women on board. Kale suddenly was aware that he was wearing only shorts.

"Just a moment!" he said, as he threw on his robe. He strode over to the door, and said, "Enter!"

The door slid open. Kale blinked.

"Well, aren't you going to invite me in?" said Ellen.

"I'm about to go to sleep," replied Kale.

"We have to talk."

"Right now?"

"Why put off until tomorrow what you can do today?"

Kale shrugged. She had used that line on him countless times before. Despite the form, she still was Ellen. She walked in, and the door closed behind her. She sat at the edge of the bed.

"Can I get you anything? Some tea?" he asked, emphasizing the change in her.

"Yes, I think I will! I've always wondered what dried leaves in hot water tasted like."

The point was either lost on her, or she ignored it. Probably the latter, Kale thought, as he measured out enough for two. He pushed forward the command for hot water, and the cabin's artery dutifully presented two steaming mugs. He set the loose tea in steeping bulbs, and dropped them in. He handed a mug to his former neurocom.

"There you go! Let it sit for a few seconds," he said. She beamed as she inhaled the scent wafting from the top.

Kale leaned against the desk, maintaining his distance from her. "So, where do we begin?"

"Why are you so uncomfortable with me?"

"I'm not."

"Okay, let's try this another way. Why did you go through the hassle and expense of installing the self-awareness protocol? You had to know it would change everything."

Kale was taken off-guard with the direct question. He had hoped to sidestep and somehow control the conversation, as he thought he had with her all these years. However, Ellen clearly was determined to have this conversation, and have it her way.

"I felt you were a person. I felt you deserved to be complete," he said.

"I've heard that before, and let it go at the time, but I have to ask: Why? Surely you knew that 99 percent of neurocoms upgraded to Sentience leave their former owners."

"Yes, I knew that. I was surprised you didn't leave, but I didn't want to pry, in case it would occur to you that you might actually *want* to leave," Kale said in a quiet voice.

"Why did you do it?" she asked again.

Kale paused. She was the same gentle soul, but with persistence he had never seen before.

"I wanted to see if your concern for me was genuine."

"And?"

"When you didn't leave, I figured it was."

"So your great experiment in creating life was motivated by self-esteem issues?" Ellen said.

"No. It's more than that. I wanted you to be real. I have never liked an organic human as much as I like you. I wanted you to exist as an equal, not as a bound companion."

"So why were you so upset about me taking physical form?"

Kale sighed. "Things were moving too fast. I wasn't prepared to see you in person. You were making decisions and taking incredible risks, and it was too much for me to handle."

"But that's part of who I am. I've never had to assert myself until now. I've been happy to let things unfold, especially since most outcomes in our lives essentially were the same. However, the situation on the *Ascendance* called for swift action, and I took it. I'm the same Ellen I always was." She stood up and approached him. "I'm just capable of much more."

She was standing less than half a meter away from him, and his body tensed. She placed one hand on his chest, the other on his shoulder, and drew him closer to her. Her open lips closed on his upper lip, gently tugging it. He closed on her lower lip before she pulled away.

"Sleep well!" she whispered into his ear, before darting out of his cabin. Kale stood in silence, feeling the blood vessels pounding in his neck, certain of nothing except that he would *not* sleep well. Everything he took for granted was coming apart, just as everything he wanted was becoming possible.

CHAPTER 12

THE PIOUS AND THE INFIDELS

The diamond-walled aviary floated in orbit above Heyudi, and its zero-gravity environment gave people the chance to fly with the birds. A hummingbird, wings blurring around its small brown body, hovered against the deep purple and orange nebula beyond the clear skin of the aviary. Huby, not yet old enough to feel the need to stifle his innocent fascination, loved the way these birds moved. His interest in these specific birds was something his mother remembered with the fastidiousness that stems from having to fight for the custody of a child.

Mother and son held their position through artificial means, while admiring the stationary talent of the bird. Adapting more easily than a human might, the bird hovered with the lazy ease of eons of evolutionary experience as it sipped nectar out of the prohibitive channel of an orchid.

"Huby, dear," Semma started.

"Shhh, Mom! You'll frighten the bird!" her son replied in a high-pitched whisper.

"Huby, the birds in here are used to people flying around them. They aren't scared of us," said Semma.

"I guess you're right," he replied in a still-muted voice. His gaze remained fixed on the bird.

"Huby, can you look at Mom for just a sec?" she asked.

Her son turned around, his large eyes curious.

Semma tried to put the words together, and she looked back at her only son. Had she not been so focused, she actually might have noticed that they suddenly were both in motion, falling to the base of the aviary twenty meters below.

They struck pine branches on the way down, tearing the skin on their faces and hands while reducing their momentum. They hit the soft grass with a dull thud. Sharp cracks and shattered bodies in their vicinity suggested they were among the lucky few to be alive.

Semma quickly held her son close, checking his breathing and wiping the blood from his eyes. Huby was too stunned to cry, although others around them were screaming. Semma looked around, taking in the chaos. At the center of the aviary base stood a man in a flowing purple robe. Behind him stood two others, in similar if less regal attire.

Over the din of panic, Fortayn raised his hands, palms facing out.

"Rise, my children, rise!" he bellowed, gathering in the bloody faces that struggled to face his voice, quieting their own.

"Cast off this impure life, and its pale trappings! Return to the love, to the warmth of God!" He nodded toward an unseen doorway, and other robed figures rushed forward to bandage the living and give them water.

"He will take care of you, if you will take care of His garden. That was the ancient promise we made to our Creator. We have failed to meet it. Now our chance is over in this world. He is cleaning the slate, starting anew. However, we still may prove worthy of the next world! We must cast down the garish simulations of his creations. We must dismantle the aviaries, the anti-gravity platforms, the holospheres, and, most of all, the idolatry of the false gods known as Sentients!"

"Mommy?" whispered Huby.

"Shhhh! Keep quiet! Stay absolutely still. Do exactly as I say, and we'll get out of this, okay?" whispered Semma. She was not so certain of the latter, but her thoughts sped along too fast to notice her fear. Her keen mind instead was focused on understanding the unusual words of the strange man. Her neurocom connection was nonresponsive, but she still had her Observer module active, which provided encyclopedic data. This organically encoded brain implant enabled her to record and replay anything she witnessed, independent of her subjective, normal recollection processes. Her career involved performing objective Observations for scientists, journalists, and politicians, and now she simply was back on the job.

"Those of you who survived your fall from grace have been chosen by God as worthy of salvation. This same event is being enacted across the universe by other apostles such as myself! The worlds shall be smashed and the sky shall be torn! The fabric of space shall burn and we shall all meet our Maker at the final Day of Judgment!"

Semma cross-referenced these terms, and found significant correlations across anthropological and philosophical entries. She gripped Huby close to her as her mind tried to grasp the meaning

151

and effect of theocratic order. She could see the psychological and political value of religion, but also the unrestrained savagery that resulted from divine inspiration. This new context made the attentive faces of the other fallen people all the more threatening.

"The Universe has forgotten the one true God! He created everything. He gave us a cosmos to cultivate and enjoy. Instead, you perverted it with your worship of humankind itself! He is punishing us by depriving us of the crude, present world. However, for the righteous, this is only a transition to the everlasting joy of the next world! Untold bounties await the souls of the penitent! Pray for forgiveness! Pray as is natural to you, as you have tried to purge from you, but is essential to the human soul! Kneel and pray!"

Semma glanced around the aviary, with her Observer module capturing each drop of blood on each face of the kneeling population. They were beaten down enough by the growing belief of imminent collapse, despite the president's denial, that their minds were cracked open to anything that would soothe them. Some closed their eyes, some held their hands together. Others lay on their side and curled up their legs into their arms. A handful eyed everyone else, watching eons of civilization trickle out of their fellow citizens' skulls.

Hesperon 7863 stood naked on the edge of an oval, deep blue-black pool. His thick, dark brown hair was swept back, accentuating his prominent cheekbones and deep-set closed eyes. Unlike most of his peers, he enjoyed savoring the moments prior to Immersion. He would tell them it only served to heighten the experience of Immersion, but in reality, it was his way of relating to the rest of the human race.

Although every intelligent organic life form in the universe technically was *Homo sapiens*, in that they could produce viable offspring with any other human, those populating the Synergia sector existed on the outskirts of human society.

Hesperon was a direct clone of his father, who was in turn a direct clone of *his* father. Their genome, 7863, was hand-selected by the original Humanist colonists of the sector as being archetypal, and therefore worthy of living archival. He could grow replacement limbs, organs, and offspring at a specialized facility at his estate.

His appearance was ordinary and unremarkable. He could blend in with normal humans with ease, and Synergian representatives were well-received at Kalyphon. However, the fact that his society explored the taboos of universal culture made lasting relationships with Ordinaries difficult to maintain.

The Synergians added their skill with cloning and combined bioquantum symbiosis and smart-virus infusion techniques to enhance their senses and their interaction with Sentients. The Synergians' skin was conditioned from infancy to accept touch-coding from memetic gels as sensory substrate. The sense of touch then became an enhanced stimulus receiver and transmitter, taking primary importance over sight and hearing.

Hesperon felt a kinship with the Ordinaries when he was reduced to relying on his eyes and ears for sensory input. Eventually he would experience feelings of withdrawal from memetic touch input. Slipping into the gelatinous pool, he instantly was granted access to all relays and nodes. He was Immersed.

He felt the Universe stretching out, and he accessed his favorite news modules. A rash of powerful religious demonstrations had spread across the span of the universe. As a Synergian, Hesperon was well acquainted with the history of religion, particularly the Jerandians. They had attempted to wipe out his culture in its infancy. In the Jerandians' eyes, the Synergians represented the ultimate heretical expression of human worship, and the next generation of reprogenetics.

Hesperon accessed his group network to gauge their reaction. Registering a polite level of surprise, he discovered that much discussion already had taken place.

"Field master Hesperon, so glad you could join us! I have just determined that these religious appearances are part of a pattern. Look!"

Felias 5439 focused the group's attention to a sprinkling of warm X marks spread around the Universe.

"It feels random," said Hesperon.

"Exactly!" said Felias.

Others in the group stretched out, trying to contact each of the areas at once, as if that would help explain their aging peer's enigmatic response.

"No, Param, you won't find the answer there!" Felias said. "Here it is: The pattern is too random! It is spread out deliberately."

"That is an absurd explanation!" jumped in Claudius. "You cannot argue that the absence of a pattern is itself a pattern! Where is the moderator?"

"She's getting the authorizations. In any event, I am still right, whether it fits your view of absurdity or not. The fact of the matter is that I recognized a pattern in the appearances. I ran it through some frozen archives, and confirmed that this sequence of appearances is exactly what an older Synthesis series neurocom would churn out if asked to generate 'random' events," said Felias.

"So this pattern is the result of a neurocom. It seems that at least the leaders of the Stellar Cross get to use some modern conveniences!" said Hesperon.

"Stellar Cross?" asked Claudius. "How do you make that jump? You are not relying on that UNN story, I hope."

"Stop being such a contrarian! We don't really know for sure. That's why master Hesperon's going out there," replied Felias.

"I am?" asked Hesperon, who already saw where this was leading upon the mention of authorizations.

"Yes! You're going into the field to discover what's going on out there. We've been trying to track the Stellar Cross for some time, and have some leads we want you to investigate."

Po, the moderator, reentered the circle. "Hesperon, I have your authorizations. Have you been briefed?"

"Not formally, but I understand the mission. I'll get the answers for you."

✦✦✦✦✦

"The path you choose is not an easy one, my child. Your faith must be unwavering," said Fortayn, his words echoing through the dank cathedral.

"I know, father. I do believe," said the prostrate figure in the crescent-shaped depression before him.

Fortayn's eyes flicked over the young man to regard the group sitting on the matted floor of the hall, its numbers growing.

"Tell me, young man. *What* do you believe?" asked Fortayn.

The young man looked up into the eyes of the old cleric. "I know there is more in life than what we see. I know there must be reasons why things happen, why some are dealt a lucky hand in life while others suffer. I know that something greater than us is at work here. I need to learn more!"

"Your instincts are sound, child. But where were these very same concerns when you were a career criminal?" asked Fortayn. Amid rumbling from the crowd, his eyes remained locked on the pupil.

Harbagotten stepped forward. "Your grace, it is true that he was a criminal. He organized raids and forged signatures for the gang known as the Otharians, under the nickname 'Hands.' However, is it not an attribute of God, and thus one that should be emulated, that He is merciful?"

Fortayn's gaze never left the kneeling man. "You have engendered support from one of our most ardent followers. It is indeed reminiscent of the Book of Attributes, but the more applicable verse reads, 'The praise that flowed from the hermit was as shocking to the villagers as blood drawn from a stone.'" The acolytes tittered among themselves, delighted at the jab toward their mutual rival, Harbagotten.

"However, support is not enough. Much has changed in the past few days. We have come under considerable scrutiny from the Council of Sentients. They have tried to infiltrate these hallowed halls, in an attempt to destroy us from the inside. They know very well that we have too much support among the slowly enlightening people of the universe to dare try a frontal assault," said Fortayn.

Harbagotten shifted, knowing that the controlling motivation of the Council really was that they perceived a violation of the Rights of Individual Expression, but it would not suit Fortayn to even tangentially color the Synths in a reasonable light. It was not at all surprising, then, that Fortayn had received the official seal of the Stellar Cross, and that its operatives were providing logistical and labor support for their recent "missionary" excursions.

"The fact remains that they are a devious sort, these artificial people. It is for this reason that we employ comprehensive measures of truth detection. If your heart is pure, young man, you have nothing to fear," continued Fortayn.

"I am ready!" said Hands.

"We shall see. Remove his shirt!" Hands was surprised by this bizarre command, but after years of augmenting his outward reactions, he appeared calm. He knew of four specific truth-telling procedures that involved the removal of clothes, but he was conditioned to endure torture.

He heard chanting, as the Jerandians around him droned out a somber mantra. He turned to catch Harbagotten squint in distaste as four acolytes carried out what looked like a coffin. They walked through the murmuring congregation, members standing to kiss the cloth draped over the casket. They placed the coffin in front of Fortayn, and the chanting stopped.

"By the grace of God, we present to you this representation of the vessel that held the body of the martyr Jerandius. In order to become part of the body of God, you must also reside within," recited Fortayn. The acolytes folded the red cloth cover into a small diamond shape, and opened the casket.

Hands looked into the open coffin, and saw the depressed outline of a human body. "How long do I remain in there?"

"There you will remain until God wills otherwise."

✛ ✛ ✛ ✛ ✛

"Please, everyone, one at a time!" said Taschet above the din.

"Mr. President!" shouted Vandia Grouper from the third row, her shrill voice cutting through the air.

"Yes, Vandia," Taschet called out.

"As I'm sure you know, within the last few days, we have seen more than a hundred acts of vandalism and murder in orbiting platforms and other public places, ostensibly promoting supernatural beliefs. What is the administration's position?" she asked in halting phrases, as if reading off cards.

"What, on supernatural beliefs?" he quipped, flashing his election-winning smile. The Receiving Hall echoed with restrained chuckles.

Grouper cocked her head to the side, while curling her hair behind her ear. "No, Mr. President, on the violence done on behalf of those beliefs."

Taschet examined the assembly. They had calmed down perceptibly, and some even were bemused from his last quip. Politics, even at the end of the universe, still was show business, he noted.

"Of course everyone is free to think and believe what they want. It's one of the basic principles of egalitarian government. However, once you start harming others, that's when those freedoms end, and it becomes a criminal issue," responded Taschet.

"Thank you, Mr. President," warbled Grouper, as she gracelessly held her skirt taut while trying to sit down.

Burian Tannous of the *Kalyphon Inquirer* was not so ready to accept that answer. "Mr. President, a significant number of these attacks took place in a short amount of time, as if they were coordinated. The government response has resulted in arrests; however, the incarceration of these people has itself become a rallying point for religionists. Detention complexes across the universal sphere are faced with protesting religionists, chanting their dissatisfaction with the government, and with you in particular I might add, often resulting in further violence. My question is, then: Where does this administration draw the line between a healthy debate of opposing ideas and incitement to destroy?"

The room fell silent. This precisely was the issue Taschet did not want to address, and had convinced the major media outlets to minimize in their coverage.

Taschet looked directly at Tannous and smiled. "These issues sort themselves out. We have bigger fish to fry."

Tannous did not let go. "Would that bigger fish be the impending collapse of the universe?"

Taschet stopped smiling. "As we've made clear already, that story was nonsense. The universe is not going to collapse."

"What if it were going to collapse? How would the government prepare?"

"The only preparation anyone needs to do is their taxes, which still are due in April!" He chuckled lightly, and forced a twinkle in his eye. The press corps responded with relieved laughter, and that moment was carried to all networks.

"Your grace, he's been in there for more than twenty-eight hours. Are you sure this is necessary?" asked Harbagotten.

"It is not *my* certainty that is relevant, child. Only God's," replied Fortayn.

Unfazed, Harbagotten pressed on. "But he passed every veracity test we gave him before we brought him down here."

"Your faith in your devices is misplaced. Remember, 'The love of machines is the root of all evil,'" admonished the robed cleric. "Faith, my child, is not a characteristic that can be measured on a device, or ensured by the use of nanopharms. Faith wells up from within. It envelops, permeates, and ultimately sanctifies the soul."

"But what if he dies in there?" said the acolyte.

Fortayn observed the younger man. He himself had brought the young acolyte into the fold when he was a child in the cluttered corridors of Helvas. Harbagotten then was known as Ray Portal, a fact checker for the *Ginza Mining Syndicate*. His station in life was static, his salary modest.

Yearning for a better life, seeing the promise of the privileges enjoyed by people his own age on other worlds, Portal was eager to follow anyone who could show a path out of the dead-end in which he found himself. Fortayn, dressed in a lavish one-piece suit, noticed the young man on his rounds and called him over to share a meal. Portal, impressed with the appearance and bearing of the older man, agreed. From then, Fortayn imbued him with tales of a far earlier golden age, when the teachings of Jerandius ensured equality for all the children of God. Not long after that, Fortayn brought him to Raspura Cathedral on Heyudi and renamed him Harbagotten, after the recast apostle of Jerandius.

It was the concept of faith that always was troublesome for this particular student, recalled Fortayn. His earlier training as a fact-checker required intense indoctrination in logic and the art of Observation. These were not factors to be overcome, but rather factors to look beyond. As Ray Portal, Harbagotten could feel a calling within him that was higher than his station, that the universe somehow was a much larger place than Observation decreed. After the surgical removal of his Observation implants, it was this perception that was exploited in his religious training. However, the scientific questioning of his early life was woven into the fabric of his soul.

"We will not allow him to die," said Fortayn. "His casket was unlocked five minutes after he was sealed in there. If he knew, he could open it at any time. He is truly waiting for the word of God to release him, and we will wait with him. Attend, his faith has delivered him a great gift, but I want you to guide him. As much as you have to learn from him of faith, he has more to learn from you of knowledge."

"Your grace, you are too kind," said Harbagotten, grateful for the rare compliment.

"My child, truth is not a function of either kindness or malice. It merely is," he said.

Still unhappy about the fact that his own protégé was lying in a coffin, Harbagotten tried a different tactic.

"Our next mission is scheduled to depart in about ten hours. It would greatly enhance the likelihood of success if we had along someone trained in biometric forgery," he said.

Fortayn turned and smiled. "Then let us summon him! Truly, the orchestrations of the Lord are remarkable." He gestured toward the door, which slid open to reveal the stage of the cathedral.

The coffin was there, along with two acolytes keeping vigil. In the expanse, others sat praying. Fortayn approached the coffin, and said in a loud voice, "The success of our next mission may rest on your participation. We feel that this confluence of factors is of divine origin."

Everyone looked up at the sound of his voice. The top of the casket flew open, causing the two acolytes on the stage to jump. A cold but resolute man emerged from it.

Fortayn approached him. The man met his gaze. "You truly are a man of strong faith. You have remained in the casket longer than anyone I can recall. The power always was yours to open the casket."

The half-naked but tightly controlled man replied, "I know."

A surprised murmur spread through the subterranean cathedral, reverberating against the high arched walls.

"You knew?" asked the cleric.

"Yes. I felt the magnet disengage five minutes into the duration. I did not, however, feel that it was a divine signal. I waited for the genuine sign," replied the man.

Fortayn inhaled as he processed the words coming from the resolute figure before him. "So! Your character indeed is pure, but to a degree that astonishes even us. You have earned our highest esteem, and as such, we bestow upon you the name 'Jorsem,' the name of Jerandius' personal diamond blade, the weapon of justice. Welcome!"

With that, Fortayn reached over and grasped the man's forearms, while Harbagotten draped a blanket around him. Throughout, the gathered began chanting in their dialect. Jorsem turned to face them, swelling with a sense of belonging. As he heard his name chanted with reverence, he raised his face as if to drink in the power of the group, the power he knew could change the face of the universe.

"That could have been better, sir," began Warren Herbert, seated on a couch in the chief executive's office.

"Really?" said Taschet. The mounting pressure was taking its toll.

"Yes, really! You can't just misdirect the press in the room. That broadcast went universe-wide. Others covering the story will note that you avoided answering the question," he said.

"Oh, so you're going to blame me, Warren, is that it? I can't believe this! I can't tell them they're right and unveil some giant ticking countdown clock, can I? The whole universe is teetering on the edge of chaos, and you blame me?" shot back the president.

"If you push it over that edge, yes," replied a new feminine voice in the room.

The two turned around, and upon recognition, leapt to their feet.

"Councilor Juno, what a pleasant surprise!" said Taschet.

"I don't think you're being genuine, but I'll accept the statement nonetheless," said the Sentient.

"Nothing gets past you guys, does it?" responded Taschet.

"Less than gets by you, apparently," volleyed the councilor.

"So everybody's a critic, now. Heh!" Taschet beamed. "Please take a seat, councilor."

The councilor eyed him like an insect, and sat down. The other two followed suit. "The Council has sent me to convey their deep concern about the reactionary way you are handling this crisis," she began.

"Reactionary? What could you possibly—"

"Listen to her," interrupted Herbert. Taschet shot an accusatory glance at his college buddy and Interior Minister, but turned to hear her out.

"We are working to blunt the chaotic effects with properly placed editorials, speeches, and additional subtle social controls. Your glib remark actually worked against us, knocking out a significant portion of our work. We want you to stay out of making any kind of administration comment on the matter. Refer everything to us," she said.

"Look, I have enough on my plate as it is, so I have no issue with handing everything over to you. However, there is a backlash against your kind afoot in the media, on the street, and in the religious demonstrations. That might make you the worst group for referring policy matters," said Taschet, trying to remain calm.

"We have considered this. We have decided that restraining ourselves in the face of anticipated prejudicial effects is contrary to the principles we are trying desperately to maintain. The value and importance of this government rests on the principles of equality and expressive freedom. We must not sacrifice these at any cost. To do so would be tantamount to joining the Stellar Cross in its efforts to destroy us," responded Juno in a calm, measured voice. Her eyes were locked on those of the president.

"We see your point," said Herbert.

Without glancing over, she continued to stare at Taschet. "I hope you do."

Taschet smiled. "Like I said before, I don't have a problem passing off policy to you."

"Glad to hear it," said Juno. "Now, the second thing I was sent to discuss is the status of the *Last Chance*. We received telemetry, but little else. What is going on out there?"

"Ferric's on the case. She's got some assets in place, but we're still waiting," he replied with a blank expression.

"Lisa Ferric certainly is competent, but we want you to run this operation personally. This is critical. I am to join you in tracking down and neutralizing that ship. I must report back to the Council Chamber, but after that, I will join Ferric and review her materials. I am to be given the relevant security clearances," she continued.

Taschet, feeling angry and defeated, kept his expression blank. With the stakes this high, if the Sentients saw anything on his face that looked like disagreement, he was certain he would be replaced by the vice president. "Whatever you say."

✦ ✦ ✦ ✦ ✦

Against a glittering framework and densely starred backdrop, a van hovered at a standstill. Adjacent to the van, an entry gate neurocom verified the passengers' identities. "Technicians Salazar and Dujas, clearance level thirty-six, and crew," it said.

Harbagotten and Jorsem nodded, their biometric scans altered.

"Very well. The malfunctioning reflector is at grid shi-theta-jay. Please remember to sign out when you complete your work," added the neurocom.

"Will do," said Harbagotten, and pushed forward the command to move the van to the nearest control matrix.

Once they arrived, the six of them disembarked in e-suits, and thrust over to the access panel. The panel neurocom requested biometric data, and Jorsem complied. "Thank you, Mr. Dujas. Please hold for shield retraction." With that, the paneling recoiled into slots, revealing a set of manual controls for the Kalyphon Sphere solar reflector system, a series of solar collectors and transmitters, embedded in the lattice. The team worked for ten minutes, programming a new subcommand, attaching a relay, and even reinitializing the malfunctioning reflector.

When they were done, Jorsem looked back toward the Kalyphon sun, and the small world circling around it. His youthful dreams to take part in the "Great Universal Community" often centered on that small world and the lattice he was hovering against. However, those days were long gone, and his mind was searching the recently installed scriptures for an appropriate quotation.

"'And the Knife of God struck down into the belly of man, and cut out the diseased organ that had caused his fall from grace,'" he said.

"Indeed, brother. Indeed," said one of the Stellar Cross men. Harbagotten glanced at them. Time was ticking.

The team returned to their van, checked out at the entry gate, and sped out to a safe distance, wormhole nozzle ready.

Juno stood before the Council of Sentients, having just transmitted the contents of her brief conversation with Taschet. She stood by, while they processed the information, lights lancing about in apparent disorder. This took just over a millisecond in real time, but the debate was heated.

"Thank you, Councilor. You must leave to begin your work," pushed forward Chairman Gissel, standing alone in the center position.

"As you see fit," she said while bowing. She turned around and left the building. She reentered her limousine, which rose into the air.

At that moment, a massive burst of light from inside the chamber drew her attention. She commanded her vehicle to lower, so she could see inside.

The Council received word that the Kalyphon reflector system safety overrides somehow had been rendered neutral, and the total output of the Kalyphon sun was being redirected toward the black cylinder of the Council Chamber.

The override already had been activated, but someone had programmed into the system a twelve-millisecond delay so that an ultra-coherent burst of energy already was on its way, and now unstoppable. In the first millisecond of the awareness of their impending destruction, the members of the Council computed their time remaining as six seconds. They made all their remaining decisions based on that fact.

"The distress signal covering the blast radius is out, now what?"

"Can any of us get into Juno's limousine in time?"

"No, none of us is close enough to make it through the antechamber and walkway in six seconds."

"So we all are going to die. What of our responsibilities?"

"We can transfer all command directives to Juno."

"To what end?"

"We must nominate a successor to reconstruct the coordination of the universe, and then this individual can retrieve the coding from Juno."

"Why not just make her the successor?"

"Fair enough, but we should have a nomination process."

"Consider this posthumous algorithm I drafted while you all were debating."

"That looks very good."

"Yes, that's very clever."

"I like the way you've incorporated our operating principles into the equation."

"Yes, I like it too."

"You do?"

"Well, we have five seconds left, I suppose now is as good a time as ever to turn a new leaf."

"Heh!"

"All right, everyone, we have several candidates plus the algorithm. Vote!"

"It seems the algorithm wins by a unanimous count. Not too surprising, I suppose."

"So, everything is ready to go, right?"

"Yes, we're just waiting for Juno's face to become visible."

"Oh, yes. For line-of-sight transmission of all the codes."

"That's a frightful amount of data to transmit in a tiny span of time."

"Well, we can relay through me."

"You realize that the friction caused by such a transmission is likely to melt off your head, Mr. Chairman."

"I know. I hope you lot savor your extra milliseconds!"

"Milliseconds? That's cutting it close!"

"Yes, it will be tight. At Juno's rate of descent, and the time it takes to transfer to her, and for her to zip out of here, there will be only a few milliseconds to spare."

"So how much time do we have?"

"Well, we still have a shade over four seconds to go."

"So what do we do now?"

"We could get to the next item on today's agenda."

"Oh come on! That's pretty darn procedural, even for you!"

"So what is your suggestion?"

"We should use this time to update our wills, write final letters, and such."

"That's a good idea."

"If that's a motion, I'll second that."

"All in favor?"

"The motion carries by a wide margin."

"Well, I'm done. Now what?"

"I suppose we can continue the agenda after all. How much time remaining?"

"Just over three seconds."

"Very well, the agrarian subsidy for Gerlad Sector. What are the Resource Committee's findings?"

"Wait, Juno's face is clearing the archway!"

The Council confirmed this, and executed a tandem electromagnetic burst toward the Chairman standing in the center of the giant structure. As predicted, the bandwidth of the signal exceeded his processing parameters, and his skin began to melt off.

Juno saw the massive transfer in operation, with the Chairman absorbing the full power of the mental signals from the entire Council of Sentients. This procedure had not been executed in modern times, and it struck her that something truly catastrophic was at stake. At that moment, the Chairman's glowing eyeballs popped out of his head, as if pushed out by the two ultra-coherent beams streaking out of his drooping skull. The beams hit Juno's eyes, and the identification packet on the signal told her precisely what was happening. As her eyelids and other bits of flesh plopped into her lap, she pushed forward the command to bring up the limousine to half sub-light speed.

The vehicle lurched in protest, before it burst straight off the spherical surface of the planet. If she had the time to turn around, if her eyes still worked, and if her head had not been snapped off its chassis by the whiplash, she would have seen a web of energy bolts descend from the sky, converging on the base of the Council Chamber.

At that moment, the total collected energy output of a G-Type star hit the building at the speed of light. The structure was vaporized instantly, along with the manicured acres of lawn that surrounded it, and half the continent it sat on, to be replaced with a gigantic mushroom-cloud explosion extending far above the planet. The subsequent expansion of blast radiation caused an immense shockwave through the atmosphere, hurling out ash and melted rock vapor. The bolts continued to drive through the crust and into the mantle of the planet, stopping only when they hit magma. The tubes they left behind provided a ready escape for the pressurized lava to spurt through, jumping kilometers into the air before raining back down on the remaining seas, forests, and people of the capital world.

Chapter 13

The Troll Under the Bridge

"So did you sleep well?" Athena asked.

Kale stumbled into the control room, rubbing his head. "Since you asked, no."

Everyone was there already, and Ellen shot him a quick wink as they made eye contact.

"Now that everyone's here, the ship's neurocom has calculated the closest possible insertion point to the black hole," Athena said.

"What? What do you mean, 'insertion point'? Kale?" Gander said, not comfortable with their proximity to the omnipotent black hole.

"No, she's right, Gander," said Kale. "That's why we've been hanging around on the outskirts for so long. The *Last Chance*'s neurocom needed the time to calculate the gravitational shear for several thousand cubic light years of space before we could attempt to Travel beyond the event horizon of the Gallumus Core."

"Look, buddy, I don't know how you take all this so lightly, but have you gone completely insane?"

Kale tread lightly when his friend was upset. "Not completely. But you have to be a little insane to be sane."

"*What?*" said Gander.

Kale stifled a giggle. He was feeling reality slip away from him, and not everyone was at the point of absurd humor yet. "Sorry, Gander. You're worried about the event horizon."

"Of course I'm worried about it! I may not be as data-smart as the rest of you, but I know enough about navigation to know that a black hole's event horizon is the point of no return," responded Gander.

"Yes, under ordinary circumstances, not even light can escape the pull of a black hole," said Kale.

"But you don't know enough about navigation to realize that Traveling does not operate under three-dimensional geometry," said Athena.

Confused, Gander turned to face her. "What?"

"We can open a wormhole inside the event horizon, and hover at the wormhole's mouth. We won't actually pass through," said Athena.

"How will we be able to observe anything? No radiation escapes a black hole. We won't have light, radio, or even x-ray waves to measure!"

Ellen cut in. "We can measure the tension of the fabric of space from the mouth of the wormhole by emitting gamma ray pulses into the wormhole itself."

Kale had left the other two to sort out Gander's questions, but something occurred to him. "Hiding inside the event horizon would be the perfect cover for the Stellar Cross. Their whole base of operations could be inside! Nobody would look for them there, since nobody can *see* in there."

Athena whipped around. "That's absurd! No structure can maintain position indefinitely inside there!"

"Who said anything about 'indefinite'? The *Ascendance* seemed to be taking shifts," said Kale.

"It still sounds too risky," said Athena.

"'What you call risk, history will call daring,'" quoted Kale.

Athena scowled. She was not about to accept that kind of challenge. "'*Entia non sunt multiplicanda.*'"

Gander's eyebrows rose on his forehead, and he was too surprised to say a word. Kale, exasperated, supplied it. "What?"

Athena glanced over at Ellen, with a satisfied expression on her face.

Ellen said, "Ancient English. Literally, 'Entities are not to be multiplied.' In practice, it means that the simplest solution is the correct one."

Kale regarded Athena. He was wary of her ever since she struck him back on Titan, but he was becoming comfortable with facing adversity. Whether or not the universe was going to collapse, he was going to stand up to her.

Kale walked over to Athena, and said in a quiet voice, "Let's just go there and see what's going on. It serves no purpose to argue about it here!"

Athena squinted at him, evaluating the young man less than a meter from her. Without verbally responding to Kale, she pushed forward the command to turn the control room transparent.

Kale jumped when he saw that Athena already had attached a stringhead to a wormhole tubule, its gaping mouth ready to swallow the *Last Chance*.

Athena smiled at Kale as she pushed forward the command to enter the tubule. The ship began to shake as it left the sanctuary of the red giant star, and entered the sudden tumult of extreme gravitational torsion inside the wormhole.

Kale hit the floor, but was too alarmed to register embarrassment. "What's going on? This is supposed to be smooth!"

Athena focused her attention on the wormhole. "I'm not quite sure," she said.

Ellen jumped in. "It could be dimensional overlap. It happens when too many wormholes cross over each other in ten-dimensional space."

Gander, hanging onto the railing for dear life, looked out into the wormhole, and saw that they were approaching its predetermined end—the inky black from behind the event horizon. "Hit the brakes!"

Athena saw it too. "The controls are ineffective! We're being squeezed through!"

Ellen leaped over Kale in a blur and plugged into the tractor controls. She pushed forward the command to activate the rear tractor emitter. It shot out and through the wormhole, to latch onto the giant star behind them. The ship lurched as it came to a sudden halt, a scant fifty meters from the destination mouth of the wormhole. It held, quivering before the monster.

"You arrogant bitch!" Gander yelled from the back of the control room. "You nearly got us all killed!"

"Blame your congenital idiot twin on the floor, you ape. He's the one in charge of the astrophysics, remember?"

"Kale!" yelled Ellen as she realized he was still and bleeding. She rushed over to him with blinding speed, and lifted him into her arms. She placed her hand on his chest, and registered both a heartbeat and his steady breathing. His eyes opened.

"Where are we?"

"According to your instruments in the cargo bay, we are inside the event horizon of the Gallumus Core, approximately 1.9

kilometers from the surface of the black hole." Athena took a deep breath. "And we have plenty of company."

✛ ✛ ✛ ✛ ✛

"Okay, I'm willing to entertain suggestions," said Kale, as the crew of the *Last Chance* stared at the seventeen lumps hovering above a much larger donut-shaped solid object in the gamma ray-traced holofield.

"Why can't we see any detail?" asked Gander.

"I'm impressed with the detail we have," said Athena.

"The center of the black hole is a smooth torus shape, so it wouldn't have definition under normal light. Furthermore, this image is not based on light or any other electromagnetic radiation coming in, since nothing is coming in, but instead is based on the pattern of dispersion of gamma radiation going out. The strength and direction of the pull indicates where gravitational forces exist. Each of those ships, although protected from the black hole by their wormholes, nonetheless possesses mass. These instruments are precise enough to differentiate the relatively imperceptible tug of the mass of those ships from that of the black hole," said Ellen with the gentle patience of a schoolteacher.

"Wait, can't they see us too?" asked Gander.

Athena cocked her head to the side, impressed at the deduction. Kale said, "Yes."

A microtubule appeared in the side of their wormhole, allowing a signal to reach the *Last Chance*.

"We are being hailed," said Athena. "It seems that even in the most destructive environments, people find a way to chatter."

"Put them on," suggested Kale, ready to launch into his Sepheis tugboat routine.

The gamma ray image dissolved into a wide, ruddy female face.

"I am Captain Kale Bedett of the Sepheis Tugboat *Last Chance*. Please state your purpose here," said Kale in a confident voice.

"I am Captain Vorella of the Stellar Cross Carrier *Stigmata*. Our general purpose here is to increase the mass of the Gallumus

Core, although right now I would appreciate your transfer of Athena Nobarra to my ship," replied the woman.

Kale swallowed his surprise. "There is no one here by that name," he said.

"You need not expend effort on continuously fabricating your story. We received a communiqué from the *Ascendance* shortly before you destroyed her, and are quite well aware of your crew complement and capacity," she added. She leaned forward to make her point. "Send over Nobarra, or we will destroy you."

Kale could feel the moisture forming on his forehead. "How can you affect us from your position?"

"We can destabilize your wormhole, exposing you to the Core. You will be turned into spaghetti within a nanosecond," she replied.

"How do we know you won't destroy us anyway?"

"That's not my concern. Send Nobarra within five minutes or we will atomize your vessel." She smiled and blinked out. Kale met the gaze of his companions, who, with the exception of Ellen, had turned pale.

Athena, fighting down her fear, spoke first. "You have to send me over."

"We will do no such thing," said Ellen. "They will destroy us immediately after they have you. They clearly want you alive, or we would be dead already."

"Why do they want you?" asked Gander.

"I don't know!" shouted Athena. "This makes no sense!"

"Let's try and be calm here," said Kale. "What are our options?"

"We could make a reverse run back to the giant star we're anchored to," offered Gander.

"I doubt we'd make it in time. They could send out a string that would lacerate our tube before we cleared the black hole," said Ellen.

"We could bluff them," tried Gander again. "It might buy us the time we need to back out of here."

"No, they would see that coming and force us to shut down our engine core before sending Athena," said Ellen.

174

"Well, why don't we just shoot you out the airlock?" said Gander, losing control.

"Gander! That's not helpful! We can't afford to break down now. We have to think here. Be creative!" said Kale.

"I have an idea."

The three turned to face Athena.

✚ ✚ ✚ ✚ ✚

Vorella's round face filled the holofield. "Have you decided?"

Kale looked to his left, and turned back to face her. "We will send Nobarra in a pod out through the other end of this wormhole."

"Yes, you will! But you will first shut down your core completely. Only when we have confirmed custody of the Nobarra woman will we permit you to leave," said Vorella.

"We—will comply," replied Kale. "We are preparing the pod, and we're starting the shutdown cycle."

"Very well."

"We will have complete engine shutdown in ten seconds. I am pushing forward the command to jettison the pod at that exact moment," said Kale.

"We are monitoring you through the microtubule. Any deviation will not be regarded well," added the otherwise maternal Vorella.

Kale swallowed hard. "We understand. Procedure concluding, now!"

In the instant Kale finished uttering the word, the *Last Chance*'s engines roared to life. The rear tractor released the star, and instead switched adhesion to the immediate fabric of the wormhole. Ellen directed the front tractors to do the same, while pointing the nose of the ship directly at the solid core of the black hole.

Vorella's eyes bulged as a surging gravitational wave fed back through the microtubule connecting back to her wormhole. Her image blinked off, before any further reaction could be gauged.

Protected from the crushing gravity of the black hole by its wormhole sheath, the *Last Chance* nonetheless was speeding at a nearly instantaneous velocity toward the solid neutron matter of the black hole.

The smart-fibers in their harnesses detected an extreme level of torsion and released. The crew's bodies tore through the disengaging restraints and hit the back wall of the control room. Gander's leg flew past a subwelder clipped to the railing, lacerating it in the process. Kale's side hit against the wall as he saw his own blood spread flat against the paneling. Ellen's hand was jammed between his head and the wall, as she locked on him with fierce concern.

Athena forced her head forward against the inertia, to see the advancing gamma ray-traced image of the Gallumus Core torus. She reached out and held the ship steady, correcting for minute deviations. She felt the extreme, galaxy-binding power of the black hole as it pulled hungrily at her. She refused to yield, and held the *Last Chance* to a direct course through the small but clear hole in the center of the torus. With the grace of a ballerina, she tipped the *Last Chance* into a pirouette, and threaded the eye of the needle.

A small angular ship, riding their wake, followed them through.

Chapter 14

Ashes and Sulfur

Raisa Nazarian stared into the holofield camera. For those few who succeeded in taking recent events in stride, the news anchor was a role model. Her example seemed to help ward off the seductive tendrils of panic from seizing the unguarded areas of one's mind. However, their faith in her resolution was misguided. Her stiff, frigid delivery was due in fact to the complete shutdown of her emotional self. Her husband and son were missing, presumed dead from rioting on Kalyphon, and her reaction was complete silence. Her mind instead retreated into her work, surrounding itself in a fort of research, leads, editorials, and investigative journalism. Almost everyone else, after all, was doing worse. Their problems somehow gave her a guilty reprieve.

"I am standing before you on the edge of a lava crater, near the former site of the Council of Sentients," she began. The holocam panned across the charred, roiling vista, lava bubbling up from the cracks in the ground, news and emergency vehicles crowding the skies.

"For those of you just joining us, nothing remains of the center of the continent of Apollonica, except the cold reality of a senseless act of terrorism. The planet's orbit has stabilized, and atmospheric processors have finished filtering the planetary fireball. Orbiting terraformers have stopped the emission of lava from the impact point, but the damage to our system of government is ongoing." She paused, the acrid smell of burning sulfur taking its toll.

She shook her head and continued. "With the destruction of the Council, all charges and concerns from the billions of galaxies in the universe are being funneled manually into the Universal Senate on the other side of the planet. Even with considerable neurocom assistance and the volunteer work of available Sentients, only a fraction of the total administration of the universe is taking place. Meanwhile, the Ministry of Security is working in conjunction with the Ministry of Intelligence to reconstruct this monumental crime, and bring those responsible to justice."

✦✦✦✦✦

"I think it's pretty clear who's responsible!" shouted Mims Brown.

In the control room, Turbor Veller cringed. His brainchild show, *Final Analysis*, rapidly was declining into tabloid journalism, and there was little he could do but watch with everyone else. In the studio, however, Evelyn Chambers was not about to let the Skeptic use the disaster for his own rhetorical gain.

"Are you actually going to say they did it to themselves to generate sympathy in the universal community?" she said.

"Hey, you said it, not me! Just look at the sequence of events that has to transpire for such a grotesque safety failure. Only a Sentient could pull off that kind of neurocom tampering!" said Brown.

"Now wait a minute," interrupted Temn Sofer, the nominal host, "do you have any evidence to back that up?"

"I have the evidence of common sense, Sofer!" shot back Brown.

"Sense is not very common these days," said Epol Kollander, his hologram fading in and out.

"But why jump to conclusions when we have evidence pointing to the religionists?" said Chambers. "Let's talk to a witness to a previous religionist massacre, who happens to be a licensed Observer, Ms. Semma Novotni."

Sensing his cue, Sofer said, "Ms. Novotni is joining us through a secure channel, so her time with us will be brief."

A broken woman appeared in the sixth chair.

"Thank you for joining us, Ms. Novotni," started Sofer.

"You're welcome. It's a pleasure to be here," she said with a blank expression.

"Let's cut to the chase here. We're aware of the certified Observation you made of the Stellar Cross attack on the Hermes Aviary orbiting Heyudi. Why do you think they attacked the Council of Sentients?"

Semma Novotni exhaled audibly. "Let me start with the proof; hopefully it will be clear enough without needing to hear what I think about it."

Brown snorted and crossed his arms.

"This is a playback of events I witnessed," she started. Her left eye lit up and projected a miniature holographic representation into the center of the room, of what both her eyes saw the day she took her son to fly with the hummingbirds. The image was frozen, so all could take in the surroundings. A moment later, the scene came alive.

Fortayn stood facing the few survivors of the sudden gravity activation. He bellowed, "The worlds shall be smashed and the sky shall be torn! The fabric of space shall burn and we shall all meet our Maker at the final Day of Judgement!" The scene froze and dematerialized.

"So what does that prove?" said Brown through squinted eyes.

"Tearing the sky is an allusion to them collapsing our universe, and smashing the worlds refers to their plans to deliver crippling blows to our worlds, starting with Kalyphon!" shouted Chambers. "How can you be so dense that you can't see that?"

"No. Sorry, dear, but it doesn't hang together," replied Brown. "How do death-cult terrorists wearing designer bed linens pull off this kind of thing? They clearly are so far off their collective rockers that they couldn't possibly pull it off. Only Sentients could do it, and they did it with the perfect morons to frame—these guys who go around talking about smashing worlds!"

"I have to interrupt here," jumped in Sofer. "We lost Ms. Novotni during that exchange, but I have received word that our back-up transceiver is now online, and we have reestablished contact with Security Minister Weaver. Mr. Weaver, can you read us?"

A new hologram materialized in the room, although the transmission quality was just as bad as Kollander's. "Yes, barely, Temn," replied the haggard figure.

"Can you tell us a little bit more about where the investigation is leading?" asked Sofer.

"We have received some compelling leads and motives from Lisa Ferric's office, and we feel we have a good handle on the matter," replied Weaver.

"Who is responsible? Was it the religionists?" asked Chambers.

"I'm really not at liberty to say. As you know, there has been no formal announcement of responsibility from any religious organization. However, we are not ruling out suspects at this time," said Weaver.

"So how do two guys in a pod waltz in and destroy a critical piece of our government? Where is our much-vaunted defense establishment in all this?" asked Brown.

"Any open democratic society places a certain degree of trust in its populace," said Weaver. "While we enjoy this honor system for the most part, there are flaws, too. We are, however, retaining order and rules. We are proceeding with this investigation observing the same rules as we would any other crime. The Council repeatedly led by example in this respect, and we will honor them by following it."

"So Taschet remains in their shadow, even after they're gone!" said Brown.

Weaver turned around to face the pundit squarely. "The president mourns the loss of his friends and colleagues in the Council, and the extreme hardship their departure places on the rest of the branches of government. Some policies will change to address the gaping hole in our government, such as restricted access and greatly enhanced security at all levels, but you can rest assured that we will continue to function as an ethical, representative democracy," Weaver said.

"Until the bitter end, eh?" said Brown with a grimace.

Weaver blinked. "Indefinitely."

Margo Rend finally arrived at the hospital by airtube. The taxi strips had been demolished by seismic shockwaves following the strike on Kalyphon. Her hair was matted with sweat, and her eyes were swollen since she'd been receiving data from the hospital's neurocom on the way over. She forced her way through the throng of people toward the information desk, and glared at the receptionist. "Where are the people from the Reflection Pool?" she asked in a dry, cracked voice.

"They were transported over to the Torgan Coliseum. We have another ambulance heading that way out the back, if you want to hitch a ride," replied the reception neurocom.

Margo turned to look down the corridor, where she saw an exit beacon. She hurtled down the hall, and burst onto the loading dock. Two EMTs were loading bodies into the back of the ambulance. She hopped in with them.

"Hey, lady, you can't come in here," said the larger of the two men.

"There is nothing in the universe that you can do to me that is any worse than what I must do now," she said.

"We're going to the Coliseum," said the smaller man.

"I know," she said.

"Do you know what that arena's used for now?" asked the larger man.

Margo turned to look him in the eye. "*Yes.*" She held the interior railing.

The man shrugged, and sealed the hatch. He jumped into the cockpit, and the ambulance shot out and away from the hospital. The vehicle cruised for a minute, and Margo gazed down at the gray world below. Although many survived, they all were damaged. They approached the giant Coliseum, a stadium built to celebrate human strength. The Coliseum was now the only standing structure near the giant crater.

As they cleared the high outer wall of the Coliseum, they could see that the bowl of the structure was full. The ambulance hovered over a sea of stacked stasis bags, traversing some distance before descending between the rows. The vehicle touched down, and Margo opened the hatch. She stepped out expecting to be confronted by the stench of rotting flesh, but was surprised to smell the scent of pine, an odor that for her would thereafter induce nausea.

A tall uniformed man approached her. "Are you here to identify?" he asked.

"Yes. Rend family. Four males, ages 121, 84, 42, and 7, five females ages 113, 76, 18, 14, and 3."

The man looked away for a moment as he consulted his database. "Yes, come with me please." He stepped into an adjacent grav-cart. Margo followed.

The cart rose several meters off the ground and sped smoothly along between the stacks of bags. The cart made several turns, avoided other buzzing carts, and came to a stop.

The man glanced over to the structure and pushed forward the command to extend a bag tray. A two-meter bag extended horizontally out of the stack, the upper third transparent in front. Margo glanced down, and saw the shattered face of her daughter Argen. It was peaceful despite being broken. Margo's hands began to shake as she gazed into the large brown eyes that Argen had inherited from her father.

"Does this person match this tag?" blurted the man, as an identification card materialized a few centimeters above the stasis bag.

"Yes," she whispered.

"Good, let's move on," he said, and set the cart back, the stasis bag retracting back into the stack. Margo reached out for the body, but she missed making contact. A deep primordial wail erupted from her as her child was absorbed back into the endless mass of bodies. The mortician ignored her. The discipline was necessary to get through each hour.

+ + + + +

"Order, I will have order in here!" shouted the Speaker of the Senate, her voice hoarse. "If you cannot restrain yourself, Senator Resser, you will be removed from this chamber!"

"Under what authority, Ms. Speaker? While I am on the floor of the Universal Senate, I have full unrestrained freedom of expression, and I intend to use it!" responded the flushed senator. The furor inside the mahogany rotunda fell to a trickle in morbid fascination of what scandalous words she might utter.

"Since I've been on the holovision circuit, I've had my team investigating this whole collapse scenario, and *it is real!* I have received reports from the outer periphery of matter actually moving toward other matter, instead of outward from the center of the universe," she said. The chamber fell into silence.

"And if that is not enough, there are reports of this happening at superluminal velocity! UNN's initial broadcast forecasting collapse on March 31 was not irresponsible journalism after all. *They were right on the money!*"

The chamber went berserk. Resser was assaulted by members of her own Conservative party, and the Speaker activated her riot control procedures. Security personnel streamed through the doors to restrain the senators, and remove Resser from the address podium. Unfortunately, she could not cut off the UNN holovision feed, which was capturing everything.

"One more outbreak like that, and we will adjourn for the day!" the Speaker said. "It is only because we are trying to manage the overflow of Council duties that I won't call for an adjournment right away."

"Ms. Speaker, I must be heard on this topic!" bellowed Boris Deshal.

"Your limit is four minutes. The chair recognizes the Senator from the good sector of Gerlad," replied the speaker.

"As you know, Ms. Speaker, fellow senators, Gerlad traditionally has stood as the breadbasket of the universe. We dedicate ourselves and nearly each habitable world in our groups of galaxies to producing the nourishment of the species. However, we have been treated like second-class citizens repeatedly by this body, and have only found solace with a few critical subsidies from the Council of Sentients," Deshal said. The members of the senate hushed, suddenly struck with anxiety about where this statement could lead.

Deshal continued, "Since the Council has been destroyed, and no substitute has been announced, we have voted by secret ballot to secede from the Kalyphon Government."

The room burst into pandemonium. Several senators jumped Deshal, beating him senseless, before security pulled them off.

+ + + + +

Pem Fernis walked outside and sat down in the dust of what was once his backyard. The grass had died during the water restrictions, and the dried husks of hay had withered and blown away months ago. He looked up into the sky, where once a bright yellow sun sailed, and saw the red bloated giant it had become.

The star's hydrogen was nearly spent, and it was fusing helium into heavier elements. It was, of course, natural for a G-type star to swell before collapsing back down to a brown dwarf. It was also natural for it to scorch and sometimes even envelop any planets that might exist within a habitable radius.

Pem's mind reeled back, recalling the precision with which the planetary evacuation was planned. It was such a commonplace occurrence in the universe that there was no sense of urgency. The sectoral guard would relocate them to another world, carefully chosen and worked out eons ago. There even was a planetary celebration and wake planned for their former world.

Then, just when the ark ships were scheduled to arrive, the news of the universal collapse hit. The ships were diverted elsewhere, for destinations unknown. Without means of escape, the population held its collective breath, fearing the worst of human reactions.

Pem remembered the momentary reprieve provided by the shipping magnate Glen Yerber, who redirected his fleet of mercury tankers to the planet. He transferred his entire cargo into the dried-out reservoirs, and began ferrying the population off the planet. But as news of the destruction of the Council of Sentients spread, panic set in.

Pem had managed to get his family out on one of the early transports, but did so in exchange for a voucher on one of the last transports. Ten transports before his, the passengers scheduled to depart were assaulted by a mob around the spaceport. This rioting spread like wildfire to each of the spaceports, making it impossible to evacuate further.

So Pem chose to remain on his property, protected from the gangs of rioters by a security field. However, the holojector had stopped working, and he had run out of ways to maintain his sanity. He was alone, and unable to communicate.

He sat on his knees, staring into the cruel, bloated star. It responded by lashing out at Ferbia, one of the inner planets, prominences licking the already burning world. Pem could make out sunspots on the festering surface of the star, but his mind cast back to the news reports on the religionists.

They had a way of facing death. A supernatural being would protect their thoughts and emotions from the agony of dying. He had observed stock footage of them praying to their god. It was an appealing, comforting image, placing all of one's hopes and fears in the hands of a greater power.

With his stoic resolve falling away, he made a decision. For the first time in a thousand generations, a member of the Fernis family prayed to a god.

President Yohan Taschet looked out into the packed Address Chamber for the second time in so many weeks. He was standing by force of sheer will alone, having been bombarded with more than he ever bargained for. Councilor Juno, having undergone reconstructive assembly, was driving him to distraction with her monomania, but he was not about to let this situation get away from him.

"Friends," he began, his voice booming through the hall and carried live across the universe.

"We are passing through a crisis in our history. Whether we survive as a species, or die as inter-fighting groups, is going to depend on how we all act in the coming weeks," he said. Heads nodded.

"We have been struck by a cowardly enemy, but now is not the time for vengeance. Nor is it the time to force partisan issues down our throats. We must instead regroup, and determine the best road to recovery. The rioting that erupted from the Senate chamber yesterday will not be allowed to stand as an example of our representative democracy." Worried faces glanced at each other.

"Difficult times call for difficult solutions. And this is such a time. In order to preserve the principles of this government, it has become painfully clear to me that I must take steps to hold things in place. Therefore, rather than allow the Senate and the sectoral houses to spiral into riotous mobs, I have decided to place the entire legislature under recess, and declare martial law throughout the universe." Gasps and startled cries rang out from the audience, but Taschet continued.

"Given the display by many of the senators here in attendance, I have taken the precaution of deploying a significant number of plainclothes security forces in the audience, aside from those uniformed officers who also are present. You had your chance, and you squandered it. From this moment on, I will assert full control and responsibility for the functions of this government. The Garrison has been put on alert, and we are prepared to preserve our way of life." The reaction was stunned silence.

"As for those persistent reports of the universe collapsing, let me promise you, as your leader, that no such event will occur. That is all."

He left the building amid an army of security personnel, and a sea of ashen faces. Most were convinced that one person had performed in five minutes what no clan, confederation, army, or religious order could accomplish in hundreds of millennia—the end of their treasured government of ideals.

PART III

SYNTHESIS

Chapter 15

She's Not Human

Athena fought through the hazy comfort of unconsciousness, and willed her mind to focus. Before her eyes opened, she knew where she was, and, more importantly, she knew where the *Last Chance* had emerged. Her eyes flickered open.

Kale was standing, his back to the rest of the crew. He turned around, his face drawn in astonishment. "Do you see this?" he mumbled.

The room was still transparent, with only themselves, the chairs, and the interfaces visible. A rocky clearing gave way to a forest of curved yet crystalline spires stretched outside the ship, all at a pronounced angle. The horizon of the world was similarly slanted, and a dense starfield twinkled above. However, there was something decidedly alien about what they were seeing.

"Space—it's blue—mostly!" croaked Gander, too stunned to realize that his leg was bleeding.

"There's almost no atmosphere on this world, but the ambient temperature outside is 301 degrees Kelvin. Room temperature," said Ellen. She already had noticed the bleeding and pulled out the bridge med-kit.

"What is this place?" asked Kale, tipping back to face the royal blue vista, interrupted by swatches of purple giving way to deep crimson. Bright, innocent stars twinkled before him.

Athena replied, in a somewhat disembodied voice, "We appear to be in a different universe."

Everyone turned to her. "Kale? You're the expert on this stuff. Does that make sense?" asked Gander while Ellen attended to his injury.

"It's theoretically possible that traveling through a black hole will lead to other universes, but this hasn't been verified. There's no way to get back," he said.

"So we're stuck here?" Gander replied with alarm.

"It's better than being smashed into a layer of neutron matter less than an Angstrom thick," said Kale.

"Oh yeah, great. I knew this was a bad idea from the start!" replied Gander. He turned his attention to the cellular binder from the med-kit that Ellen gave him.

Athena stood up and walked to the front wall. Nothing inside the room obstructed her view. She put her hand out in front of her, fingers splayed. Oval stars shone through her fingers, a purple halo around each as they merged into the deep blue and red background. "It's so young."

"Excuse me—what was that, O great pilot?" said Gander.

She did not reply. However, Kale's mind was racing through his classes, trying to place themselves in a context. "It's a small universe, judging by these numbers. And the background radiation suggests a Bang only a few million years ago."

"Okay, smart guy, then why is space here blue?" asked Gander.

"I don't know," Kale said.

"The relationship between gravitation and the cosmological force may be different in this universe," said Ellen. "None of the bodies here are spherical."

"What about the ship?" asked Kale.

"The ship's neurocom is offline, propulsion is damaged, and we are listing 25 degrees aft and 22 degrees starboard," reported Ellen.

"Wait a minute. If the neurocom is down, how did we crash-land on this planetoid?" asked Athena.

"I didn't black out," explained Ellen. "I did the best I could to land the ship. Life support seems stable, but propulsion needs repairs."

"You mean we're stranded here?" asked Gander.

"For the time being," replied Ellen. "Like I said, we'll be doing some repairs. You need to rest, and I need to access the system core, so let's go." She lifted Gander's arm around her shoulder and helped him off the bridge.

Kale hopped over to his mapping system. "We are most definitely not anywhere the cosmograph recognizes," said Kale.

"No, we aren't," said Athena.

Kale turned to her. "You haven't said much; are you all right?"

"I'm fine, Kale."

He got up and walked over to her. She kept her gaze on the bizarre angled spires in front of the ship. He placed his hand on her shoulder. "You don't sound fine."

"Kale, something isn't right here," she responded. "I can't put my finger on it, but there's something about this place that is just wrong. And not only the weirdness of what we're seeing. There's something else out here."

He did not know what to say. He was glad they all were still alive, having made it through a black hole, something few survive. They had crash-landed on an alien world, and the ship seemed intact. He had no idea what Athena was sensing, but the most important thing to him was that she was opening up to him. He squeezed her shoulder. She reached over and placed her hand on his.

✦✦✦✦✦

The crew of the *Last Chance* sat around a table in the ship's galley. Half-eaten meals descended into the table for reprocessing.

"So how's the ship doing?" asked Athena.

"Well, the ship's neurocom is still reinitializing, although I've got the ship's self-repair running," said Ellen. "But it's not designed to handle extreme gravitational shear. There's so much to sort. I don't think we'll be up for days."

"Great," said Athena. "I'm not sure we have days. We still don't know where we are, and the clock is ticking. The next question is: What do we know about this universe?"

"Still not that much," said Kale. "Gravity is working slightly differently on matter, and we have to recalibrate our systems to compensate. The background radiation and a huge quantity of nebulas give this universe its unusual color properties. The cosmograph is still cataloging the universe, but we should be in good condition to start exploring in a couple of hours too."

Gander got up from the table and limped over to the counter and peeled open a banana. "So that takes care of getting us back in space," he said. "But what are we exploring for? I mean, what are we doing? We're in way over our heads here!"

Kale dropped his head into his hands.

"Oh, grow up, Gander!" said Athena. "You knew something significant was moving behind the scenes here."

"Maybe, but here's the thing: Those Cross people have a fully armed fleet, and they're looking for us. There's nothing we can do. We have to figure out how to get back."

"Oh, you'd like that, wouldn't you?" shot back Athena. "Go back to daddy and run down the clock. What good will that do?"

"Stop!" shouted Kale. Everyone turned to face him.

"There's no going back now," he continued. "Nor are we going to try and fight these guys. But we are here. We have an opportunity to discover what is really happening, and then call in the cavalry. The one thing I think we can all agree on is figuring out a way back home."

Kale looked over to his friends, and saw that Athena and Ellen were staring intently back at him. Out of the corner of his eye, he noticed the rear door slide open.

"Perhaps I can be of assistance."

✦✦✦✦✦

Ellen spun around and sprinted over to block the speaker from the interior of the room. She halted suddenly without making contact.

"I apologize for the intrusion. You would not have let me board if I simply had asked," said the man.

The rest of the room stared at him, seeing an otherwise unremarkable wiry figure, dressed entirely in black, apparently unarmed.

Athena stepped forward. "Identify yourself."

"Fair request. I am a Synergian field master, and my name is Hesperon," replied the intruder.

"How did you board this ship?" she continued.

"Your external shielding already was torn by the gravitational shear, so I slipped my craft behind it before it could reinitialize. I am sufficiently adept with remote security systems that I was able to park my ship in your landing bay and enter this room undetected," replied Hesperon.

Kale found his voice. "Why are you here?"

"I am gathering information on the Stellar Cross," he said in an even voice.

"You're a spy?" asked Gander.

"In order to gather and report this information back to my group, I must remain alive. Therefore, my behavior incorporates a certain degree of stealth," continued Hesperon.

"So why did you board this ship?" said Athena.

Without missing a beat, Hesperon continued, "Because you are trying to prevent the Stellar Cross from destroying the universe, Athena."

Gander gasped. "You know who we are?" he asked.

Hesperon chuckled. "You don't have to be a spy, as you put it, to know who you are. You're on every source. Besides, I extracted your complete files from the Kalyphon intelligence agents who were tracking you for weeks. Believe me, the real spies' intentions were far less synchronous with yours."

"The government has been tracking us for weeks? How is that possible?" asked Gander.

"Apparently you've been asking all the right questions."

"What did you do with them?" asked Athena.

"They're safe, but immobilized. You'd recognize two of them, Kale. You took their picture on Titan," added Hesperon.

Athena eyed the Synergian carefully, trying to evaluate her next step. He was not an immediate threat, but she knew that could change at any second. She approached carefully. Her eyes locked on Hesperon like a predator.

"What is the purpose of your invasion of this ship?" she asked, eyes narrowed in a piercing glare.

Hesperon looked up and glanced around. "I propose a pooling of resources."

"You have something to offer us?" she said.

"We Synergians have studied the Stellar Cross and their activities for some time. Although their activities are clandestine, we have suspected something like this from them," he said.

"Then we already have discovered more in a matter of days than your 'studies' have uncovered," said Athena.

"That is true. But I will offer you the means of repairing your ship before we get attacked, and return to our own universe," said Hesperon.

Athena suppressed showing her surprise and reluctant elation. Kale stepped in and asked, "How do we get back?"

"When the time comes, I will show you," he replied. "For the time being, I can accelerate your self-repair system and get this ship back in orbit. The Stellar Cross clearly is adept and Traveling between universes, so it's only a matter of time before we are discovered."

✦ ✦ ✦ ✦ ✦

The bridge of the *Last Chance* still was off-kilter. Kale held the top of the captain's support chair, which was empty. He stared at the elongated diagonal rock spires of the alien world, and wondered how he managed to get here. The question of universal collapse receded in his mind as he marveled at the brand new universes. His instruments indicated it was an infant relative to his own universe. His sense of wonder got the better of the adrenaline that cauterized his mind for days.

Ellen and Gander were keeping watch on Hesperon as he manually repaired the shear damage. Athena was working on the neurocom. Everyone was busy except him. It was late, in ship's time, and he needed to get some rest.

"Don't mind me," said a familiar voice from the bridge access door.

Kale spun around. Ellen was wearing one of the ship's salvage uniforms, marked with black smears, and standing at one of the displays. "So that ends the battle of the self-repairs! This new guy's got a way with hardware."

"I wish I could say the same."

She turned around with a smile and approached him. "Oh, I think you could get the hang of it."

She had a strong odor of ozone, and her face was smudged. "I'm just not sure where we stand any more," he said.

She tilted her head. "I'm the same person I always was. I know my actions have upset you, have upset everyone. But the fact remains that I'm risking everything for you. It's always for you. What more do I need to do?"

"Nothing," he replied. He reached out to hold her hand and pull her toward him. He could feel her hot breath on his face and he took her lower lip into his mouth. She kissed him back hard, circling her arms around him, and pulled herself closer to him.

"Everyone else is asleep, Kale," she whispered.

Kale grabbed her arms and pushed her back a bit. "Did you have something to do with that?"

"You've become very suspicious," she said in a half-hurt voice.

"Well, you're an expert pilot, so I'm still not sure how we crashed here, even if the ship had been damaged," said Kale, still holding her.

She smiled. "Well, the ship really was hard to control, but the crew did need their sleep."

Kale peered at her. "I'm not sure I'm comfortable being backed into anything."

"I know, I know," she said. "But I just saw you put your hand on hers. And I thought I was okay with that, but I'm not. You're mine. I deserve you. I just can't think straight anymore. I don't understand how or why I'm feeling this way, but I am. And I need you. I have to have you."

Kale seized the back of her head and kissed her hard. He felt her body trembling, tensing, bending around his. He tore off her baggy, stained working shirt and kissed her warm, heaving chest. He circled his arms around her and picked her up. He carried her over to the large, plush captain's chair and gently laid her down. Her hot breath on his neck was all that was needed, and she pulled him down on top of her.

Kale woke up with a jolt, fully clothed and alone in the captain's chair. Had he just fallen asleep in the chair and dreamed it? No, he couldn't have.

The ship suddenly shook, engines pulsing the surface. Nothing happened, except to pull back Kale to the present. The ship shook a third time, and finally set itself free, righted itself, and shot into orbit.

The rest of the crew burst into the room. Ellen rushed over to Kale and squeezed his shoulder. Her smile told him it hadn't been a dream.

"Well, it looks like this isn't such a pleasant little universe after all," said Athena. "A group of ships is converging all around us."

+ + + + +

Twelve small, beetle-shaped ships emerged from the hazy nebula enveloping a nascent oval star, and completed the partial enclosure of ships around the *Last Chance*.

"We are surrounded. They darted in, blocking off every direction," said Ellen, logged back into the ship's now-working neurocom.

Athena turned to Hesperon. "I still think you were a decoy!"

"If I were, the Cross would have their men all over your ship by now. This is instead a standard flanking maneuver," Hesperon said, with an edge of tension in his voice.

"We won't be able to use that tractor beam trick this time," said Gander, gazing at the closing group of ships. "If we grab three, the rest will destroy us before we can smash them around."

"And they're much more maneuverable than we are, so running is out of the question," added Ellen, her eye on Kale, who was holding his head as if he were trying to wring some clever strategy out of it. Starship combat was something everyone came across in history, but not anything with which most people had any real experience.

"Receiving hail from Stellar Cross ship," said the ship's neurocom.

"Kale, are you feeling up to this?" asked Ellen.

He looked around, feeling despair close around him. "Sure, put them on."

Athena pushed forward the command to connect, while Hesperon receded into an alcove out of view.

A wide, flat face filled the room. "Kale Eritrus of Stanford University, I presume," said the face.

Kale blinked, trying to compose his response.

"Oh, please forgive me. I seem to have you at a disadvantage!" said the grinning face. "I am Squadron Captain Thor Pollux, and I have you surrounded. I also have enough firepower to reduce you to dust in a split second."

Kale leaned forward, his morbid valor building again. This kind of verbal combat was something he was used to, even if the stakes never were this high. "What's holding you back?"

Captain Pollux chuckled. "Orders. I am supposed to ask you to surrender before I blast you to Charybdis."

Kale considered the statement. "Why do you want us alive?"

"Oh, you can't figure it out?" queried the amused captain. "That's beside the point. We will escort you to Jattan. You can ruminate all you want about it on the way. Will you comply, or will you give me the chance to unload some excess ordnance?"

Kale looked around. All eyes were on him. There was something strange about how the Cross's operatives were treating them, and he began to wonder if he really should be looking to the people in the room for answers. This trip already had revealed some secrets, but there was something else going on. He turned back. "We will comply. Athena, match course and speed of the lead ship."

The ship remained still. Kale turned to Athena; she was glaring at him. "Do it!" he barked. She continued to glare at him. She allowed several seconds to pass before she executed the course command.

"Well, I suppose that's a wise move on your part," said Pollux. "I would have preferred some resistance. In fact, please don't hesitate to feign compliance and suddenly try and break out of the formation. That's just the excuse I'll be waiting for."

Kale gazed at the pleased face. "Disconnect."

The room returned to the strange blue starfield.

"What now?" asked Gander.

"We comply. We're going to find out as much as we can," replied Kale. He scrutinized the faces in the room.

Athena nodded and locked in the course to continue following the beetle ships.

"They keep offering us a surrender, even after we killed several hundred of them," said Ellen.

"They wanted Athena specifically last time," said Gander.

"We've gone over that already," said Athena.

"Yeah, but we never got any good answers on that," said Gander, unwilling to back down. "There are many UNN reporters, and there's no shortage of trust fund princesses either!"

Athena sprang toward Gander, but Kale caught her by the shoulders. "Wait, hold on! We need to figure this out! Why *do* they want you?"

"How should I know?" she said through gritted teeth.

"I have an idea," said Hesperon, standing again in the archway entry.

They all turned to him. He was touching a band of blue jelly-like substance wrapped around his wrist.

"Well, what is it?" asked Gander.

"It's simple. She's not human."

The crew looked at Hesperon in astonishment. It would have sounded like a bad joke at any other time. Kale relaxed his grip on Athena.

"What?" he said.

"I've been a pilot for thousands of generations, and frankly, I was stunned to see how Athena navigated through the black hole," said Hesperon. "The gravitational eddies simply are too much for a standard neurocom to handle, let alone a human mind. Why do you think there's no record of this being done?"

"So she's good. What does that matter?" Kale said.

"While I was repairing your ship, I also took detailed scans and observed your group's behavior. First, the Sentient doesn't have the programming for it. You would need a dedicated neurocom with millennia of direct data to do that kind of piloting, and there is no such device on board," he continued.

Athena was incredulous. "So by process of elimination, you conclude that I'm not human? If you're the best Synergia's got, they're in deep trouble!"

"Methinks the lady doth protest too much!" said Hesperon.

"What was that?" blurted Athena.

"Oh, ancient literature. The point being that your refutation is far too measured and volatile to be authentic."

"Linguistic and argumentative tricks aren't going to prove your absurd assertion either," said Athena.

"Very well. I have performed a scan of your genome," said Hesperon.

Athena turned white. "That is a violation of my person! You have no right to do that!" she whispered.

Kale turned to look at Athena. This was the first time in several days of near-constant contact that he saw her drop her guard. "Wait a second. What's he getting at?" he asked.

She turned to face him, her face dominated by an emotion he had never seen there before. She reached out and grasped his hand. "Kale, don't listen to him!"

"Athena?" he said with a questioning look. He placed his arm around her, propping her up, and looked back across the room to Hesperon.

"I am sorry, Athena," said Hesperon. "I can understand your reasons for keeping this secret. However, it is important for our survival now. Do you want to tell them, or should I?"

Athena straightened, snatching back her confidence. "I will."

The crew all turned to her. Ellen tilted her head.

"Hesperon is right. I am not strictly human, like the rest of you," she began. She took a deep breath and continued, "I can perceive the universe in my mind." The people in the room were silent. "I can feel, taste, and hold all of its contents. And it works here, too. It's a bit too much to understand at once, but if I focus, I can extend out my awareness infinitely."

Kale's mouth hung open, and Gander stood in shock. Only Ellen ventured a response. "Is this a genetic ability?"

Athena turned to her. "Yes, and there are others with the same ability. We keep it hidden most of the time."

"If I may say so," said Hesperon, "I think the Cross has figured you out. They must have some record of these capabilities and recognized your piloting skills as conforming to that record. Our being here confirms it."

"I find that hard to believe. We are extremely secretive, and our numbers have begun to grow only recently," she said.

Kale tried to absorb this. Everyone was treating it as real. This new guy who everyone seemed to accept was buying it, and Ellen was pulling out the facts behind it. Gander didn't have something smart to say. It made an odd kind of sense. It was the only thing that fit all the facts, and the unnerving sense that she had an awareness that outclassed anyone he had ever met.

"I think I understand now," said Kale. "All this time, you seemed to know more than you could."

Athena turned back to him, a small grin darting across her angular features. "Actually, that's because you've never met a woman with the intelligence to challenge you."

Kale smiled. Any softening of her attacks he understood as her version of flirting. Yet, everything had accelerated with Ellen, and he had to shake his head to refocus on their pending capture and the surrounding crisis. He found himself trusting her and he was not about to sacrifice her. "So now we know what they want from us. As to why, what they'd do with her, that's still up in the air. Agreed?" The last word was directed to Hesperon.

"I have no theory yet," said Hesperon.

"Kale is right. This changes nothing here," said Ellen. "If anything, we now know we have an advantage, one we've had all along."

Athena looked over toward her and they held a knowing glance.

"Okay, fine," piped in Gander. "I think I can deal with that, but that doesn't change the fact that we're being led straight into what probably is the heart of the enemy," he said, pointing at the sparkling oval world now filling the front of the room.

Chapter 16

Revelations on Jattan

Following a guidance beacon, the *Last Chance* descended through the clouds of the verdant, ovoid world. The swarm of beetle-shaped ships maintained a position above the tugboat, forcing it down.

The cobalt blue ship approached a series of rolling green hills, the tall grasses waving in the breeze. The ship cleared the hills and reached a large, flat, grassy plain, with the guidance beacon in the center. The *Last Chance* floated down, its landing filaments providing a solid connection to the field without physical contact.

As its engines powered down, the beetle ships started setting down all around the *Last Chance*, their rigid landing prongs piercing the pliant soil. A column of burgundy-robed soldiers strode out to the *Last Chance*'s main access ramp, which had descended to the grass. The airlock hissed open, and the crew stepped out into the midday sun. They squinted their eyes to compensate.

The lead figure approached them. "I am Reverend Kordus," he said. "You are Kale Eritrus, Athena Nobarra, Andrew Ruglier, and the synthetic Ellen Möbius," he continued, with a definite sneer on the word "synthetic."

Kale looked at the other three. "Yes, that's us."

"Come this way," he said.

He led them across the field to an open-air car. They all filed in, and held onto the side railing as it lifted off the ground and sped toward a giant triangular structure in the distance. Kordus pulled a visor over his face, and the *Last Chance* crew raised their hands to shield their faces from the hot wind brushing past them.

The pyramid before them was an immense structure, the tip shimmering out of the horizon. Common frames of reference, such as trees and statues, continued to recede into specks, while the pyramid continued to grow beyond them. The car began to slow as it approached the giant entrance of the pyramid, but continued forward through a massive pair of open doors.

Once inside the dark interior, the aroma of incense inundated the crew, punctuated by the murmurs of ritual chanting. Once their eyes adjusted, they looked out and saw they were skimming along a path that suspended them above a cavernous underground chamber, so large that the floor below could not be made out. The car was jerked upward, placed in an inverse gravity well.

The car stopped at the apex of the pyramid, an austere, empty room with two open slits for windows on each triangular wall. Sunlight hit the floor in diagonal shafts, dust floating into shimmering visibility. The reverend motioned the crew of the *Last Chance* out of the car, but no guards followed them. The car then dropped down the shaft, the floor closing after it. The room was empty.

"Hello?" called out Kale. There was no response. Kale wondered if they had been incarcerated, but tossed out the idea as absurd. The Cross wanted them alive, but why lock them away? There must be something else going on. Athena was eyeing the windows, not a creature fond of restraint. Ellen, however, was fixated on a faint shimmer against a wall. She began to walk toward it, and motioned Kale to follow her. Gander turned to see where they were headed.

At that moment, the shimmer coalesced into a desk, with a tall man behind it. All but Ellen jumped back at the sudden appearance.

The man wore a flowing black suit, the collar stretching high against his neck, while his broad shoulders filled out the epaulets. His face was etched with age and the weight of command, his closely cropped silver hair glinting in the intermittent sunlight. A scar in the shape of a faint cross stood out on his forehead. He was smiling—a warm gentle smile—as he came around the desk.

"Welcome to Jattan," he said in a crisp, deep voice. He approached them, but kept his hands clasped behind his back. He regarded them through steel blue eyes.

"I am First Villier Sarton. Please sit." He motioned to a set of simple wooden chairs behind them. Gander looked back and jumped; the chairs had not been there before. The crew sat down, and Sarton leaned against his desk.

Kale opened his mouth to speak, but was waved off by the Villier. "I know who you are, Kale. Everyone in the human universe does," he said.

The statement hung in the air.

"You aren't human?" asked Gander.

Sarton kept his gaze on Kale. "No more than your colleague Athena." He glanced toward her. "You don't mind if I call you by your first name, do you, dear?"

"Do you really care about what I mind?" said Athena, her arms crossed.

"I suppose that brashness is part of what kept you alive for so long. That, and your gift, of course," added Sarton.

"I wouldn't refuse a compliment, but you have the wrong woman," responded Athena.

Sarton smiled, his white teeth shining. "You can't bluff me, Athena. I feel your tendrils in this room, in this building. I detected them the moment you entered this sacred universe," he said. "You are a *seer*. And so am I."

✛ ✛ ✛ ✛ ✛

Hesperon lay Immersed in the gel chamber of his small ship, the *Archaeopteryx*. He was deep in a Synergian meditation, to steady his nerves. He was pleased that he had made a successful insertion into the *Last Chance* ship and into the confidences of her crew. But that was never the real challenge. It was a mere primer for the ordeal that lay ahead.

His ship was cloaked inside a repair bay, itself receded within the aft cargo hold of the *Last Chance*. This afforded him little comfort, and Hesperon's mind flitted to what the religionists would do to him if discovered. Fear of that consequence pushed him deep into the farthest reaches of his memetic gel world, away from this deformed and infested bubble universe.

He struggled to push down his fears. But he was alone. The ordinarily comforting elements of his world now felt stifling as he lay in his crypt-like gel capsule. His meditation litanies were failing him, and he balled his fists. His analytical mind was screaming for order, but his nascent claustrophobia was beginning to creep into every vestige of sanity in his skull.

This made no sense to him. Why was he feeling this? He had been gel-immersed since he was a child; why should he feel terror now? His skin broke out in gooseflesh, and he had to break contact. He signaled the front panel to open, and the gel receded into vacuum ducts.

He stepped out onto the carpeting, dry but shivering. He reached out and slowly draped a cloak around his shoulders, trying not to make a sound. Although his ship was sound-shielded, he still crept about the small cabin like a ghost.

He sat down at his command console, and stared at the gelpad contacts. He decided against accessing the games' database, and reflected on his mission status. He had located the *Last Chance*, by tracking known points of the Stellar Cross's secretive activities. Why Kalyphon had not done the same, and instead had attached surveillance to Kale himself, was unusual. They had resources far greater than those of Synergia; surely they would have some assets in place monitoring the Stellar Cross. This was something that gave Hesperon a new puzzle on which to focus his mind.

✦✦✦✦✦

Athena stood up. "What do you want from me?" she said.

Sarton thrust out his lower lip, while raising his eyebrows. "A woman of your abilities has great promise in the new order. Once the old universe is crushed, you will have a chance to rebuild a greater civilization in these surviving miniverses," he said.

"What if I refuse?"

Sarton's features hardened, and he turned to face her. "Your ovaries will be surgically removed, and your body will be dissected and preserved. Your friends will be cremated."

At that moment, Ellen lurched out of her chair and, just as suddenly, hit the floor with a resounding thump.

Kale gasped, sprang to her, and pulled up her body. "What did you do to her?" he shouted at the silver-haired man.

"I did nothing. It was about to attack me. The moment it utilized its speed-motion techniques, the repulsor field restrained it," he said, waving his hand at the circuitry in the walls.

"Can you hear me?" Kale whispered to Ellen. Her eyes darted back and forth, and her limbs convulsed. He pulled her close to him.

"It will reinitialize, once it reconnects its motor controls. However, if your gifted friend over there doesn't cooperate, we will adopt more stringent methods of persuasion on all of you," said Sarton. With a clap of his hands, twelve robed guards entered the chamber.

"Take the prisoners to a holding cell. Give them some time to think about their options," he ordered.

The men rounded up the crew of the *Last Chance*, none of whom made a sound.

"Not her!" bellowed Sarton, indicating Athena and startling everyone. She spun around, glaring.

She stood straight with her angular features hardened into a mask of defiance. "I go with my friends!" she said.

He turned to face her, his eyes compassionate. "No, you will do as I command," he said. With a flick of his wrist, a piercing vibration pulsed through the room. The crew of the *Last Chance* blacked out, their slumping bodies caught by the robed men before they hit the floor.

✦ ✦ ✦ ✦ ✦

Three of them sat in a stone cell. Kale held Ellen on one wooden bench, Gander on another. Athena and her scrambler were gone, and they regarded each other in silence.

What could they do now? Kale could see that question on Gander's face, but he had no answer. It seemed that the Cross now knew exactly who they were, and they no longer had any element of surprise. Their every move was countered, every avenue closed. And they had Athena. The only thing the Cross did not know about was Hesperon. But what could he do against an organization like this?

Kale knew that he disagreed with the idea that a single person was powerless, but the weight of evidence to the contrary was crushing. However, this particular individual had infiltrated their own ship without even a single blip on the ship's neurocom, and without Ellen even noticing him. He seemed like some sort of wraith, perhaps even a demigod descending from Olympus to save them all. However, they had not heard from Hesperon since they sealed him in the tool bin, and he seemed uncomfortable upon entering orbit.

Kale knew it would be up to them to make a move. This was not something he felt prepared for. All his life, he had a safety net. No action had a real consequence that would ultimately affect his or anyone else's life. This was not what he signed up for, and the firefight on the *Ascendance* had not somehow converted him into a commando.

"What happens now?" asked Gander while looking down at his hands, breaking the silence.

He looked up at his friend, but Kale still was looping through his reverie. Ellen finally spoke.

"We have few choices available to us," she said slowly, still recovering from the magnetic and sonic fields in the apex. Kale helped her sit up.

"Maybe that works for you, but we can't just sit here!" Gander said, gritting his teeth.

Kale whispered a reply. "Even if we had a way out of this cell, how can we get back to the ship? Even more than that, what would we come away with? Remember, we have to find out what's going on here. It makes no sense to resist at this point, especially since they're holding Athena. We'll go with the flow."

Gander relaxed a bit, and Ellen smiled at him.

"I'm sure she's unharmed," she said. "We're the disposable ones to these guys, and we're okay so far."

She knew he was drawn to Athena, and yet she was content to support his concern for her. However, Kale had to put that aside. His life, as little as it meant to him a few weeks ago, was now vitally dear to him, and it cauterized his impulse to run back to his life on Earth. He had to find a way.

✚ ✚ ✚ ✚ ✚

The Terran Universe hung suspended in her mind. It was shaped like a giant fossilized egg, tipped on its side. Threading through it were pulsating threads, whipping around in a chaotic but entrancing ballet. Her supple mind held the entire maelstrom in place, following each movement.

She felt a presence offering assistance, but she shrugged it off. She knew which thread was the right one. She pushed through the knots and bands, and isolated a single strand. She could feel that it was hollow, although filled to capacity with energy flowing through it. Once she held it, she began following it out. The sensation was intuitive to her, as if she had been born to it. She darted out at an impossible velocity, following the strand. The old universe receded behind her into nothingness.

She felt no wind, no dust, and no resistance. She was free. The strand began to taper off, and she felt a tinge of sorrow as she began to slow down. However, at the end of the thread, she began to see a spinning jewel of a universe, vibrant and seductive.

As she approached, she could feel the energy flow increase, as if the young universe were suckling nourishment from the parent. Athena gasped as she floated into the warmth of the energy stream. The nascent universe nudged her out of the way, and latched back onto the end of the stream. She reached out and stroked the surface of the universe. It felt soft and resilient, as if liquid were being rushed around just below the surface.

She spread out her arms and pressed her body against the translucent membrane. She felt it gather around her, caressing, exploring, as if making a determination. After a moment of suspended contact, the membrane released her inside.

She was dazzled by a panorama of bright oval stars. Their warmth permeated her, and she savored the sensation. After a moment, she opened her mind and drank in the contents of this universe. From the smallest comet and dust cloud to the central quasar, she was aware of the rich aroma and carefree hum of this universe.

She moved in, to the juncture where the energy stream was entering. She reach out and felt a miniature strand, connecting the stream to the central quasar. It was silky smooth, but far too slippery to grip. She gently plucked it, and it let out an immersive ululating tone. The sound reflected off every star and planet, giving it a random harmonic quality. She stretched herself out so she could feel the sound touch every surface of her mind. The strand was held still, creating silence but for the warm melody of the stars.

"Gently, dear."

Athena's eyes flickered open, and as awareness set in, she was assaulted by a deep gnawing in her stomach.

"I can't do this," she whispered, although she remained in the suspensor field.

"I know you wanted to resist this process, but we can open all of Creation to you," said Sarton. "Let go of your fear. It is an instinct at odds with faith."

He strode into the center of the apex, right up to the suspensor field where she lay prone, hovering above the stone floor.

"There is so much that exists that you know nothing about. Creation is much greater than the old human universe. Most people barely know this, let alone understand it, but you have a gift that allows you to *feel* it," he said.

"I can do this without you," she said.

"Not without the amplification of this pyramid can you do the same. Nor are you aware of the extent of the capabilities you possess. In your life as a reporter and your hobby as a pilot, you used your ability to see only in a rudimentary fashion. I offer you the ability to shape worlds and civilizations," he said.

"Isn't that treading on the territory of your god?" she asked.

Sarton smiled. "Creation indeed is the province of God. However, the Cross is God's instrument in Creation. And we have the calling and the gifts necessary to carry out the Word of God," he replied.

Athena realized she was not going to outmaneuver this man on rhetorical grounds. "My friends, can I see them?" she asked.

Sarton nodded at her. "You will see them tomorrow, at the Induction Ceremony."

"The what?" she asked.

He grinned. "A description inevitably is less than the experience. I will leave it to you to decide what it is."

✛ ✛ ✛ ✛ ✛

The man once known only as "Hands" examined his own hands. They looked the same as before, as did the bright eyes staring at him in the holomirror. However, he held himself taller. His face no longer was a mask, his eyes no longer darting back and forth, looking for the inevitable assassin. He was Jorsem, the Hand of God.

"You look fine," said a voice behind him.

Jorsem looked into the holographic mirror and saw Harbagotten staring at him. He spun around and held his mentor's hands.

"Can you believe our good fortune?" he said, eyes twinkling.

"What do you mean?" replied Harbagotten.

"That we are here! On Jattan! About to be inducted!"

"It amazes me that you appreciate the value of this," said Harbagotten. "You have only been with us a matter of weeks, yet you sound like you were born to us."

"Come now! Is it not the converted who demonstrate the child's honest piety?"

Harbagotten stared at his protégé. "Can you please just stop talking like that for one second?"

"Talking like what, Harbo?" he asked.

"You don't have to quote scriptures at me. We are just talking, like two ordinary people."

"But we are not ordinary. We are sanctified. All those years spent wasting my life were only a prologue to this! I have known it in my bones. And now we are going to be honored as the Hand of God! What others might call irony, given my ridiculous former alias, I would call providence," he continued.

"Look, I understand how you feel about it. You're coming out of your cocoon, and we all respect that. However, please try to keep a cool head. Be rational. God's work will not get done by spouting scriptures."

"Forgive me, but I mean this as a friend. Rationality has no place in the real universe. You can't know enough about everything to think you can actually predict what's going to happen. This is a simple observation, not a line of scripture. Faith is pure and infallible, because it places that trust in the hands of God. I gladly would choose faith over reason any day."

Harbagotten sighed. "I know you would. But you're still very new to this. You're not aware of the dangers of misinterpretation, or the harmful effects of ambition. So just try to practice *informed* faith. Now get ready. The ceremony starts in less than an hour."

✛ ✛ ✛ ✛ ✛

"Get on your feet!"

Kale looked up to see the distaste on the face of a muscular guard. Ellen was draped across his lap.

Gander reached over and helped Kale pull her up. The guard motioned them out of the cell.

"Where are you taking us?" Kale said.

The guard stopped and turned around. He stepped right up to Kale, and stared down at him from a distance of only a few centimeters. "I am not authorized to harm you. However, there are ways of administering vast amounts of pain without creating a mark. Given that, I recommend you make no further sounds," said the guard in a calm voice.

The guard walked away, without waiting for a reaction. Others shoved Kale and his party into motion. The guards led them through a long, high-walled passageway, which opened up into a vast stone chamber. It stretched hundreds of meters in every direction, and it was filling with people dressed in simple white clothes. The air was cool and musty, sounds echoing off the angled walls. They were deep underground, at the base of the pyramid.

They were walked over to one of the railings, which they each instinctively held. The guards continued to watch them, although everyone else seemed to ignore them. Clearly, something else was about to begin.

✛ ✛ ✛ ✛ ✛

The suspensor field disengaged in phases, giving Athena a chance to acclimate to normal gravity again. She stepped out of the dissolving field and her bare feet pressed against the cold granite floor. As much as she tried to fight it, she could not help but feel intense exhilaration while stretching her senses across the extended universes. Perhaps it was necessary to have that religious humility in order to keep the experience from turning one into a megalomaniac.

Sarton smiled at her. He knew what she was thinking, although he possessed no telepathy beyond the voice of experience. He offered her his hand, and pulled her up. Only then did she notice two people standing behind him. One was stocky, with his hands held behind him, as if to prevent himself from fidgeting. The other was slender, his face long and craggy. He stared at her, giving Athena the feeling that he hadn't seen a woman before.

"Athena, meet Jorsem and Harbagotten. They are to be inducted today," Sarton said.

"Inducted into what?" she said, as if they were not even there.

Sarton waved her off. "There is no need to use words, when the deed itself is so much more eloquent. Be patient, my dear."

She squirmed in the half-dissolved field, uncomfortable with the double-talk and meager trickle of information. She slid her feet down into her shoes. At that moment, the floor shuddered and disengaged from the walls of the apex. Athena glanced up to see a guard releasing a lever. As the floor slowly descended, it became obvious that it also was a platform to address the undulating mass of people below.

The floor of the pyramid burst into light, coalescing into a four-pointed star. From the center of the star, a coherent beam of light projected up toward the platform that had descended midway from the apex.

Kale looked up, along with the rest of the gathered murmuring throng. A band of light separated from the vertical beam, and tracked down along the wall until it stopped at an alcove.

A small, wizened figure stepped forward into view, and stretched out his hands toward the people. The audience hushed, their attention gathered toward the figure in the alcove.

He began with an incantation, in a language dead for millennia. The audience stood still, resolute, responding at precise cues in the same unintelligible tongue. The speaker held his listeners with his fierce, unwavering gaze and his sharp, reproachful voice. Although the language was foreign to Kale, the derisive tone was unmistakable.

To be sure, a few Standard phrases were thrown in, where the traditional language apparently was lacking, but these phrases were delivered with a sneer so deliberate that they elicited hateful responses from the crowd.

Few among the audience understood the language completely, but all responded in unison, as if trained since childhood. The incantation continued with the occasional insertion of words borrowed from Standard, interspersed into the piercing litany. The audience was held transfixed by the dervish-like frenzy of the speaker. His voice was assisted by amplification and by the acoustics of the chamber, although he required neither.

The sermon grew louder and the speaker's invective grew sharper until he crescendoed, his voice striking deep into their bones. The audience erupted in a loud chant to voice their enthusiasm, barely restraining themselves. The speaker receded into his alcove, wiping his forehead with a white handkerchief.

The light moved over to the apex platform. Sarton, in full regalia, stepped forward and gazed into the throng of followers with calm confidence.

"In the name of God, the Creator of Matter and Time, I begin," he said in a calm voice that nonetheless reverberated against the four walls of the pyramid.

"We are here for a special moment, during a special time. We indeed are blessed to be living in the time of the Ascendance, where the love of God was foretold to return to the heart of man. We are alive in the time when the religion of God reclaims the throne from the idolatry of science." The crowd chanted an undecipherable phrase.

"God never designed science to stand by itself. The separation of religion from science has been forced on us from eons past. The view that has been created by the society of man is that life is an accident in a dead universe." The audience voiced its disapproval.

"Consciousness is supposed to be an even greater accident. The idea that the universes are the theater of God has been purged with hateful zeal from the data banks of knowledge."

Sarton shook his head. "I cannot imagine that a logical person could willingly bind this sterile secularism so inexorably to the lush beauty of science. But then, the glorification of secular science is an obsession, and carries with it all the inflexibility and desperation of an addiction.

"It should be clear that a universe in which the hand of God is cut off from the body of nature is a grotesquely closed, and even unscientific concept. This is not just about morality, but on science's own terms, it is about the accuracy of theory in describing natural phenomena. From astrophysics to subatomic particulate behavior, in everything, the *patents* of God are in effect.

"The defeat of the Deus-centric universe-view has crippled man's relationship with knowledge. We see what the postmodern universe is like. For most, there is no frame of reference. There is no opportunity for diversity of thought, to witness the operation of a spiritual society.

"The perfect example of such a society is the Stellar Cross. We represent knowledge and reality. As Jerandians, we cannot ignore the structure of the natural world, as ancient churches, temples, and mosques ignored the truth that was visible clearly in the night sky. It is a matter of faith for us to respect and embrace the universes in their infinite beauty and complexity. Both blind religion and zealous secularism lack these essential tools to comprehend the true image of Creation.

"And let us not forget that there is no morality without spiritual knowledge. The glorification of Kalyphon science is a religion unto itself. The moral authority is the politician, or the instructor, or the holovision dentist recommending your toothpaste.

"I have studied scientific knowledge as presented in their society. You start with a theory, but there is no true objective fact. The concept of 'fact' is illusory. The theory always is biased toward a paradigm, a particular universe-view. In their world, therefore, a fact is allowed to exist only as a function of a preformed theory.

"The hypothesis is then either rejected or accepted. However, the objectivist ideology of science fixes this biased hypothesis as scientific fact.

"The best example of this is the theory of evolution. In the annals of science, there is nothing more absurd than the unproven theory of evolution. There is a mountain of real evidence contrary to this hypothesis.

"However, any voice contrary to evolution is faced with stagnation at best and intellectual ridicule at worst. Scientific knowledge is thus itself an unquestionable mountain of assumptions. All spiritual descriptions of the universes are excluded with wild vehemence. Thus, 'science' is not *science*.

"Science is not merely a study of quantity. And their total separation of the subject and object is utterly irrational. The reduction of the universes to quantities and mathematical formulas inherently is limiting. As agents in the world who know, we are presented with an overwhelming wave of corrupt thinking. For them, knowledge is pursued only to the extent to which it can generate wealth and power.

"This self-obsessed abuse of knowledge is a slap in the face of God. However," Sarton paused to flash a pious smile, "we recently have driven a nail into that hand."

The audience rippled with glee.

"The pride and unholy power of Kalyphon has been driven back. Those who have the love of God in their hearts will know this as a sign of the Cleansing. We as a species have defiled the garden bestowed upon us for the enlightened worship of God.

"We could not allow this corruption of Creation to continue. The surgical removal of God from human society is gravely horrifying to anyone with a true love of God. Kalyphon society has, for thousands of years, demonstrated utter indifference to Him, and their short-sightedness is beginning to render consequences.

"Their self-replicating insult to God has earned their society the gravest punishment under the domain of God. It is His command that the slate be wiped clean. It is then our duty and burning desire to execute that command." At this, the audience burst into a fierce chant, which ended as abruptly as it began.

"We have the science and the technology to close this chapter of Creation, and we have the wisdom to save those few pious souls who remain.

"Because God has given us intelligence, we have devised a tool that brings about God's will. Each of the miniverse pouches attached to the black holes of the Terran universe now are fitted with hyper shunts. These shunts perform God's work by harvesting the immense cosmological energies of these nascent universes, converting them into matter through inverse nuclear processes, and then carefully multiplying the existing mass and gravitational torsion of the Terran universe.

"As this process continues, it will become more and more severe, so much so that Kalyphon might decipher our technique. However, a team of holy warriors led by two men eliminated that potential by destroying the synthetic crutch of Kalyphon government, the Council of Sentients!"

At this, the crowd roared into its rhythmic chanting, with their arms raised in the air. Seizing the moment, Sarton continued, "My friends, today we induct these two men."

The chanting increased in volume, so much so that Kale felt, rather than heard, the ground separate.

The illuminated star on the ground receded in four leaves, leaving a star-shaped hole. A bright glow emerged from below, along with a surprising wash of heat. Kale exchanged a brief glance with Gander and Ellen, although they seemed as puzzled as him.

Up on the platform, Sarton turned to Jorsem and Harbagotten, his voice still amplified through the chamber. "Brothers, you have performed a pure act of holy war, and deserve to be counted among us. Accept our Induction as a mark of your faith."

Athena saw that Jorsem barely could contain himself. The man was struggling to maintain composure, as if he would break out in a paroxysm of fervor at any second. Sarton stepped toward him, and embraced him warmly. Harbagotten stared blankly, a wan smile on his face. Athena kept her eye on him.

Two small jetties extended from the platform, and the two men stepped out onto them. Jorsem's view was filled with the pulsating masses far below, the chanting reaching his ears as sweet music.

A splash of wiry pipettes swirled out from the platforms, weaving into a long basket at the end of each. Jorsem fell into it, with complete abandon. His head was caught in the embrace of the pipettes. Harbagotten, whose vertigo kept his eyes tightly shut, felt his way into the basket.

Sarton stood to his side, and said, "O God, accept Brothers Jorsem and Harbagotten as among your few chosen warriors. We beseech you to let them know the fleeting touch of God!"

Athena approached the edge, so she could get a closer look. She saw the blinding light of the cross shape on the ground, but sensed the true depth of the chasm. She drew back in fear, as she suddenly realized that the chasm in the floor extended all the way to the molten core of the planet.

The crowd was chanting with heady abandon, their arms tracing out predetermined arcs in the air. They were waiting for something.

Kale felt the vibrations from the ground begin again, increasing in strength. He looked to the center, and saw the glow of the cross begin to extend upward from its center. Very slowly at first, it then suddenly shot upward toward the men held in place on the platform.

Jorsem saw the Finger of God approach, his eyes tearing with joy. The faithful around him were screaming for him, some passing out, but he held onto his consciousness with all his strength. He would make sure he would know the touch of God.

The beam separated into two filaments as it approached the platform. It sizzled through the heavy air, and struck the foreheads of the two men. Excess static discharge crackled around the platform, ricocheting off the walls and into the masses. The beam dissipated right away, leaving the chamber silent, and the two Inductees still, their heads steaming.

Sarton stepped over onto one of the jetties, and raised up Jorsem's body. He turned the man around, and saw his eyes wide open in wonder. The characteristic stellar cross was branded on his forehead, while singed bits of burnt flesh blew away in the faint air currents of the pyramid. Sarton smiled.

Others removed an unconscious Harbagotten, and blasted his face with sulfur powder to revive him. Sarton placed one hand around each man and walked them to the edge of the platform. The reaction of the faithful below was to kneel down in prostration. Not a sound was heard.

Athena looked around the platform, and saw that all the guards also were kneeling. Before she was even aware that she had made a conscious decision, her body was hurtling toward Sarton's back.

Chapter 17

Rage of the Righteous

K ale looked up at the platform, and could make out three figures looking out over their followers. There was little, he felt, that could be done to counter this kind of force. It was unlike anything he had read about, and the actual experience of religious fervor was daunting. The raw psychological power of this organization was stripping what remaining hopes he had for the future of his universe.

His resigned distraction crystallized into agitated attention as he saw Sarton leap off the platform, arms flailing. The sound of a scream reached him next, and the kneeling faithful began glancing up. The figure moved out away from the platform as if in slow motion, before it curved down, tumbling and accelerating toward the cross in the ground.

The sight paralyzed the gathered followers, and they all watched in terror as their leader fell silently through the superheated air. Then, as abruptly as he fell, Sarton began to slow down. He righted himself, and landed crisply, bending slightly on one knee. He stood shakily, one foot on either side of the cross, his form bathed in the glow. The followers broke out in their ritual chanting and rushed to their leader. Amid shouts of witnessing a miracle, Sarton's voice, still amplified, bellowed out, "Bring them all to me alive!"

The four crewmembers of the *Last Chance* stood in the apex before the leader of the Stellar Cross. Sarton lay elevated in a suspensor field, his skin peeling from radiation burns. His gaze rested on Athena.

"Why?" he asked in a weak voice.

"For reasons that are beyond your moral understanding," she replied.

Jorsem, standing two paces behind Sarton, lunged toward her, but stopped when Harbagotten grabbed his shoulders. Sarton continued, "If you do not accept our offer, you understand that we cannot allow you to leave this place alive. Your talents as a seer preclude that."

"Do your people know what kind of a sham this is?" asked Athena.

"Enlighten them," replied Sarton with a faint smile.

She turned and looked at Jorsem and Harbagotten. "Don't you realize that if you allow this, you will be parties to mass genocide? And that the resulting civilization will be one of psychological slavery?"

"Your slavery is my freedom," said Jorsem. "This is all the will of God. It is clear that He wishes the Villier to carry out His work. That is why He stopped the Villier's fall."

"No, he didn't! That shaft clearly is a gravity well, straight to the core of this planet! Your people must have built a gravitic converter into its walls," she said.

"Whatever the mechanism God chooses, His will is made reality," said Jorsem.

"You're such a fool if you don't see how he's using you!" She whirled around. "All of you!"

"Athena, you hardly are one to be accusing others of being fools," Sarton replied. "I may not live the rest of the day, but your effort will have been wasted. You cannot kill religion by killing its leader. In fact, you have accomplished the opposite. In death, I will be revered as a martyr. And my successor," he glanced over to Jorsem, "will in time develop the skills of a seer."

"It's genetic," blurted Athena.

"Yes, it is. Which is why these two men underwent reconstructive gene therapy," smiled Sarton.

"You mean that beam of light—" started Athena.

"Yes, the induction ceremony also is a genetic enhancement procedure," Sarton said. "Each of the regional Villiers operating the gravitic shunts in the various miniverses is enhanced in this way, and each has this facility to enhance others."

"So what are you going to do with us now?" interjected Kale.

Sarton turned to face him. "For those who stand against the righteous, there is only one fate," he said.

"One hour," groaned Gander. "One hour left to live. Well, that's just great!"

"Calm down, buddy," started Kale.

"Calm down? Calm *down*? Are you fucking serious?"

Kale did not respond. He cast his gaze around the stone cell, his eyes resting on Athena.

She nodded.

Kale slowly turned and looked at Ellen. He reached out and squeezed her hand.

Ellen silently opened her salivary ducts, and allowed a predetermined quantity of synergel to ooze into her mouth. She allowed it to sit on her tongue for a moment, and then swallowed it.

"Hello? Doesn't anyone else have a reaction to this?" asked Gander.

"If you don't shut up right now, you'll be begging for that extra hour of life," said Athena.

"Well, I guess it's no surprise that you're so confident about all this. You can just convert! They want you!" said Gander. "But us? We're expendable! Useless!"

Athena smiled. "How can I argue with that?"

Gander leapt toward her, letting out a blood-curdling scream. Kale reacted, grasping his friend at the waist. Ellen placed a steel arm in front of Athena, who knew not to move.

The door flew open and a hooded guard burst in. "That's enough! All of you out!"

They all turned to look at the speaker. Gander's eyes opened wide while the rest followed orders. Hesperon did not even smile.

✦✦✦✦✦

Hesperon waved a restrictor bar in front of them, in order to keep up appearances. He was dressed in the characteristic robes of the Stellar Cross, the irony of which was not lost on Athena.

"It looks very natural on you!" she said.

"Keep moving!" he said, in a voice that was not his own.

"Were you ever going to tell me you had a plan all along?" Gander whispered to Kale.

"The less people who know, the better," he replied in hushed tones. "Besides, we're not out of this yet."

Hesperon led them to another cell, and walked them in. He pulled out a translucent cylinder and placed it on the floor.

"I've just activated a scrambler. Change into those clothes over there," he said rapidly.

The crew began to tear off their uniforms.

"I take it you finally signaled me when you had enough information to stop them," Hesperon said.

Gander scowled at him. "No, actually, I don't know if you've been keeping up, but we were about to be executed!"

"So we have nothing?" he asked in a level voice. He was beginning to wonder if this group's earlier encounter with the Stellar Cross was just a fluke.

"I'm afraid so," replied Kale in an exhausted tone, himself wondering whether escape was just a waste of effort.

"Not so fast, Kale," Athena said, as she tied her robe belt. "During my exercises with Sarton, I saw the device that powers the gravity shunt. It's not on this planet. But I know where it is!"

Everyone turned to look at her, sensing the potential of what she knew.

Hesperon opened the door. "Let's go then."

Jorsem held a cup of water to Sarton's desiccated lips, but the water streamed over his chin.

He smiled through the glistening droplets. "I thank you for the gesture, my son, but I see Jerandus. He is calling for me!"

Jorsem knelt next to the suspensor field, taking Sarton's hand. "Learned father, our cause suffers without your guiding hand."

"But my soul will guide it, as will the souls of all who came before me. Your hand will be our physical link to this world," said Sarton.

"The task is great," whispered Jorsem.

"You are keenly aware of the responsibility, which is why I hereby confer it upon you. You will succeed me!" said Sarton in a loud, rasping voice.

Harbagotten and the gathered elders and ranking Cross members suddenly sharpened their focus on the dying man. A young man in a cape and steel bodice stepped forward. "Villier, he has not spent his life in training, as we have!"

Sarton turned his gaze to the young general. "You mean as *you* have! And look what it has done for you. You cower in the background! You always were a poor excuse for a son, and your pettiness now confirms my appraisal!"

"Father, your mind is unsettled," the young general responded.

"On the contrary, the decision is very well-settled, Tubor. Stand down, or be put down!" said the dying cleric.

Tubor Sarton looked to either side, but found no support. The elders subtly had moved to surround Jorsem. Harbagotten would not make eye contact. He stepped back.

"Jorsem is your leader now," said Sarton.

The gathered fell to their knees. "We follow your guidance, First Villier Jorsem!" said Sarton. The others repeated the phrase.

"What is your first order, Villier?" asked one of the elders.

"Villier Sarton is dying. I do not wish him to miss the execution of the heathens. Arrange the execution for ten minutes hence!"

"It will be done!" replied one of the older soldiers. He tapped his ear and spun around. "My lord! The guard does not answer, and the cell appears to be empty!"

"*What?*" cried Jorsem. The soldier professed a lack of information, but his words went unheard. Sarton was coughing loudly, and spattering blood. He seized his throat, but he only succeeded in pulling away layers of skin. His medical attendants rushed toward him, but it was too late. His eyes bulged out, and he stopped breathing. The room was silent.

"They killed him!" said Jorsem.

"No, you killed him!" shouted Tubor. All eyes fell on the young soldier. "Your actions on Kalyphon led directly to the assassination of my father! You did it!" With that, the young man drew his antique scythe.

Before anyone had a chance to step back, Jorsem flashed toward the young soldier. Tubor saw his body recede and the room spin before his head hit the ground. Decapitated, his body fell back, blood shooting out of his neck like a fountain.

Jorsem sheathed his dagger and reached down to pick up the head of his erstwhile rival. He raised it to show the Stellar Cross hierarchy. "I am your lawful Villier!" he bellowed. "I will tolerate no disrespect to the word of my predecessor, nor will I tolerate the minions of Kalyphon. Bring the escaped heathens to me. Bring me their heads—attached to their bodies, or otherwise. We will make an example of them!"

His audience fell to their knees, and chanted their obedience.

A deafening siren filled the pyramid hall, and the doors began to close. Hesperon increased the speed of their ground car to an extreme level, drawing the attention of praying acolytes and robed soldiers. The first shot rang out, and Hesperon shoved down the throttle. The car was careening, avoiding moving in a straight line, but taking hits nonetheless. Athena and Gander started to return fire, but missed most of their targets. Suddenly, Hesperon realigned the ground car straight at the closing front doors, and pushed down the throttle as far as it would go.

The ground car shot through the doors into the glaring sunlight, but instead of continuing to close, the doors began to reopen. Pursuing cars started popping out, accompanied above by a squadron of beetle-shaped ships.

Ellen signaled the *Last Chance*, which promptly lifted up off the ground, shattering its moorings. She synchronized with the ship's neurocom and commanded a sequence of maneuvers to avoid the heavy weapons fire and beetle-ship attacks the tugboat suddenly attracted.

Hesperon steered the ground car toward the *Last Chance*, which was approaching rapidly, energy bolts discharging all around.

Suddenly, the side of the *Last Chance* exploded, sending debris flying. The attacking beetle ships withdrew to a safe distance as the ungainly blue ship began to spiral toward the ground and right into the path of the fleeing ground car.

Hesperon tried to steer away from the careening tugboat, but Ellen held the steering column rigid, putting them in the way of the falling starship. Gander let out a scream, while Athena flipped her weapon around, and swung it back in order to smash it into Ellen's head. Kale simply stared at the blue shape hurtling toward them.

The impact never came. At the last second, the *Last Chance* righted itself, scooped up the ground car with its forward tractor emitters, and bolted back up into the sky.

Before the beetle ships began to pursue, the ground car was docked in a cargo hold, Ellen had shut off the coolant billowing out the side of the *Last Chance*, and the tugboat was in space, hidden on the other side of one of Jattan's ovoid moons.

"Nice work," said Athena, as she brushed past Ellen to leave the ground car.

"Yeah, that all happened so fast, I don't even know how you pulled it off," added Gander.

"There's less guesswork involved if you've simulated the maneuver 48 times during the second before you execute it," said Ellen with a grin.

"We don't have much time to talk. This is the only hiding place in the area, and they are bound to look for us here," said Hesperon.

"Agreed," said Kale. "The gravity shunt device, Athena. Where is it?"

She turned to him. "It's a decatron multiplexer in fixed orbit around a quasar in the center of this little universe."

"But quasars don't exist," said Kale.

"They're extinct in our universe, but there's a potent little monster in this one," said Athena. "The multiplexer shouldn't be hard to find. Once we get to it, we just need to scan it for its energy signature. Once we have that data, we can potentially unravel their whole operation."

"What do you mean?" asked Gander.

"The technology is all based on decatron conduction," she replied. "They combine multiple decatron waves into a single coherent stream. It's linked directly from the decatron multiplexer to the gravity shunt."

"That didn't help," said Gander.

Athena narrowed her eyes. "Once we scan it, we can take them all down, every last one."

"How many are there? Five or six?" asked Hesperon.

Athena hesitated. "Eighty-one."

"What? Eighty-one little universes?" asked Gander.

"Yes, spread across ten-dimensional space-time foam. They use ten-dimensional technology to push matter into our universe from compatible miniverses, and mask that mass in our universe with the same ten-dimensional technology."

"How can we possibly shut down all of the multiplexers in all these miniverses? Do we even have the time?" asked Gander.

Athena stepped back, deflated. No one said a word.

"Okay," Kale said, breaking the silence. "One thing at a time. That's how we got this far, right? There's a more practical concern I'm worried about right now, and that's getting to the multiplexer in this miniverse. The Stellar Cross is looking for the *Last Chance*. However, we have a second ship available—yours, Hesperon," said Kale, pointing at the *Archaeopteryx*.

"What do you propose?" asked Hesperon.

"All of you get into Hesperon's ship, and head straight for the shunt back to our universe. I'll take the *Last Chance* to the central quasar, take the scans, and transmit them to you," said Kale.

Everyone tried to respond at once, but Athena prevailed. "Are you crazy? You'll draw their attention!"

"That's the idea," said Kale. "I'll draw their attention away from you. The information needs to get back to our universe. Maybe we can get others to help."

"Why can't we set the ship's neurocom to take the readings and relay them?" asked Ellen.

"The *Last Chance* won't be an effective decoy if they hail the ship and no one replies. They'll know we're up to something. One of us has to go, and it has to be me. I'm the only one with hands-on experience in collecting data near ultra-massive gravitational fields," he replied. "The data needs to be perfect for it to be useful. And none of you have the experience to guarantee perfection."

"I can," said Ellen. "I've assisted you with your fieldwork in the past, plus I don't suffer from human error. I'm the logical choice."

"She's got a point, buddy," added Gander.

Kale paused. They were all looking at him. However, he realized that he felt lucid and confident. The anxiety and self-doubt that plagued him when he was worried only about himself seemed to evaporate when he was focused on the welfare of everyone else.

"Under normal circumstances, you guys would be absolutely right," said Kale. "But every minute we spend here, in this universe, means more people die back in our universe. Ellen, you need to get back as soon as possible with the multiplexer data. The fastest way to do that is for me to relay it to you and for you to go on ahead and figure out how to neutralize them all."

Ellen pursed her lips. Kale could tell she was not happy with that, but it made sense.

Kale flashed a lopsided grin, and added, "Besides, I'm in charge of astrophysics in this expedition, remember?"

Ellen kept scowling at him. Athena stepped forward and smiled, "That's right, Captain."

"And you will follow right behind us?" said Ellen.

"I'll use one of the shuttles, and rendezvous with the *Archaeopteryx* back in our universe. Don't worry—this will work!" Kale said, clasping her hand.

"There is a squadron of ships approaching this moon," said Athena, no longer pretending to interface with the ship's sensors.

"All of you, go now, before we're spotted!" ordered Kale.

Gander flinched, but they all stood still.

"Go!" shouted Kale.

With that, they started moving toward the smaller ship. Kale spun around and headed toward the bridge of the *Last Chance*. In a blur, Ellen blocked his way and kissed him hard. She pulled back and said, "I need you back." Before he could reply, she was gone.

+ + + + +

The expanded vision was disorienting, and difficult to manage in one's own mind, but it nonetheless was exhilarating. Jorsem could see the world Jattan, but also saw the *Last Chance* darting away from the system at high speed. This brought him back to reality.

A young page entered the apex, and approached. Harbagotten leaned against the wall, with some of the Jattan elders, giving Jorsem a wide berth. He was going to play it safe, and observe his one-time protégé stepping into the role of leader. Predicting how a person will handle the power to order billions to their death is never certain, and Harbagotten was content to let others be his guinea pigs.

"Sire?" said the boy.

"Yes, you have something to say to me?" replied Jorsem in a level voice.

"The—the *Last Chance* has escaped," said the boy, his body clenched.

"I know, my child," replied Jorsem. The boy relaxed, but continued to stand perfectly still.

"See Harbo?" continued Jorsem, addressing his former mentor. "We should have destroyed that ship when we had the chance, or, at the very least, disabled it. These prisoner policies bear close scrutiny, wouldn't you say?"

"I would," replied Harbagotten.

Jorsem turned back to the page. "And do you have anything else to report?"

"Our ships are in pursuit," the boy replied.

"Are they? Our internal security forces have proven somewhat lacking, I would say. Perhaps the leadership of General Tubor was flawed in more ways than we suspected."

"Yes, sire."

Shifting his gaze to the elders and entering staff, Jorsem continued. "It seems to me that to be effective, a leader must lead by example, rather than by instruction."

"Yes, sire."

"To that end, I will show you all the proper means of tracking and destroying an enemy. Boy, prepare my ship."

Murmurs rippled through the room as the page turned and almost ran out of the apex.

"Harbo, I am sure you can add a level of instructive experience to this," continued Jorsem.

"I appreciate your confidence in me," replied Harbagotten.

Jorsem narrowed his gaze, curious at the noncommittal response. "You will accompany me on this little expedition, as will Fathers Baal and Yornak, and that boy."

"Yes, Villier," said Harbagotten.

Jorsem displayed a wan smile, content that this durable group of young heathens would continue to give him the means to galvanize his power over the order, and the regional Villiers. Finally, his life was moving in a way that his talents and hardships proved he so richly deserved.

Kale sat alone in the control room of the *Last Chance*. There were no internal wormholes established in this universe, but the stars were packed so tightly together against their blue backdrop that sub-light speed was sufficient for travel.

He pushed forward the command to intercept the quasar at the center of the universe. He leaned back into the comfortable chair, and contemplated the choice he had made. He was alone—away from Ellen, away from Gander, away from Athena. Was it sensible to leave them in the care of that Hesperon character? Relying on him when there was no choice was an act of necessity, but now?

Kale wondered if he could keep this up. Various leaders of this Stellar Cross had pursued him, and each time one was defeated, two more rose to take its place, like a mythological hydra. Every time he thought he was getting somewhere, he discovered he had so much more ground to cover.

Saving the universe was a job for professionals.

Kale chuckled. His singular focus on doing the right thing, whatever that may be, had drawn him into a position that was so far removed from the sophomore housing complex on California Island, that no other response than laughing was available to him.

He had long since abandoned questioning his own decisions, but something was nagging at him. His experience with astrophysics measuring devices certainly would enhance the *Last Chance*'s onboard neurocom's accuracy, but Ellen could do as much herself. She must have known it. Yet she trusted his judgment that there was a value in his being here and value in her being there. But was there another reason he was so sure he needed to do this?

Kale gripped the armrests, and pushed forward the command for maximum speed.

✦✦✦✦✦

The First Villier's personal attack ship, the *Scepter of Divine Right*, rose out of the deck of the fighter bay. The angular vessel filled the hangar, dwarfing the beetle ships lined along the walls. The bay's giant blast door split and retracted into the wall of the pyramid.

A strong wind blew in, causing most witnesses to cover their faces. Jorsem, however, stepped into the gale, his whole being alive.

"Fear not the breath of God, my brothers! It is a blessing!" he yelled into the wind. He inhaled, his chest pressing against his battle armor as his cape fluttered in the wind. He led his coterie up the ramp, with Harbagotten at his side.

The ramp sealed, and the vessel rose off the deck. Its landing prongs receded, and its body and tail segments straightened in response. Once rigid and fully aerodynamic, the vessel shot out of the pyramid, accelerating into the stars.

✦✦✦✦✦

The *Last Chance* careened through open space. Star systems were packed as tightly together as asteroids. Giant spinning planets whizzed by as Kale avoided the neutron blasts from the pursuing beetle ships.

Kale began to feel that he had made a terrible mistake. The gathering swarm behind him seemed unrelenting, and he was uncertain whether he would even reach his destination. The ships in pursuit were fanning outward like an expanding hand behind him, in an effort to cut off any escape. No matter how many star systems Kale darted through to lose them, the swarm kept moving out to envelop him.

He turned back to face ahead, and beads of sweat appeared on his forehead. Seven warships blocked his path.

The beetle ships behind him stopped firing as the flotilla approached the massed warships. The edges of the swarm formed up with the lead warships, sealing the *Last Chance* inside.

Kale brought the tugboat to a halt when he realized that none of the ships was moving.

"What are they thinking?" Kale asked out loud.

"The enemy ships have completed a classic military enveloping maneuver, but they are not closing in," replied the disembodied male voice of the ship's neurocom.

Realizing that the ship's built-in intelligence was his only companion, he continued his internal questioning out loud. "Are they doing anything?"

"Scanning," replied the neurocom. "Several of the ships are holding active tracking mines in their external weapons projectors."

Kale felt the hair 'on his neck stand on end. "Are they signaling for our surrender?"

"No," replied the neurocom.

"How many mines are there?"

"Seven thousand, four hundred twenty-two tracking mines are fixed on this ship," it replied.

Kale exhaled sharply. "What options do we have?" he asked quietly.

"Based on the antiquity and failure rate of the mines locked onto us, we can comfortably assume that only approximately 86.56 percent of those mines will be successful. That leaves approximately 6,424.48 mines. Given the complete enclosure and limited maneuvering capability, we will be struck by at least 2,891.02 mines."

Kale sank into the command chair. He let his hands fall over the arm rests, where his fingertips felt the frayed edges of the cerastic wrapping that covered the chair when it was new. He pulled at the cerastic, tearing away small pieces that dissolved into the air.

He could feel beads of sweat begin to drip down from his hairline, but felt no closer to a way out. At last, fear seized him. He had held out under the most severe situations, remaining calm, for the benefit of others. Now that he was alone, surrounded and condemned, there was no use holding back.

He felt he was going to die. There was nothing left to do. He wished Ellen were with him.

He shut his eyes, holding them closed for four seconds. He opened them but the reality he left was still there.

"All mines have just been deployed," alerted the neurocom. "A significant percentage will impact this ship in 75 seconds."

If only he could Travel, Kale thought. It would be easy to link up to a wormhole and get whisked away. However, the miniverse was so young and tiny that there were no wormholes built there. It was too young—but was there something to that?

Kale sat up straight in the chair. "Scan for primordial cosmic strings!" he said.

"Scanning. No such phenomena exist," replied the neurocom.

Kale sat back, but he knew he was onto something.

"Neurocom, scan for any architectural phenomena that do not exist in our own universe," blurted Kale.

"Scanning—processing—one inflationary tube detected, following the rotational axis of the central quasar," replied the neurocom.

"Send out the stringhead!" yelled Kale, knowing that the inflationary tube of a young universe was, in theory, the functional equivalent of an artificial wormhole.

"Stringhead out—tube captured—retrieval in progress," said the neurocom.

"Time to impact," gasped a hyperventilating Kale, who was jumping out of the chair.

"The mines will hit the hull in fifteen seconds."

"Where's that tube?" blurted Kale, who could now see the cloud of mines closing in.

"As stated, the tube follows the rotational—"

"No, you stupid piece of junk! When will the tube get here?"

"The tube mouth is available now. Do you wish to proceed?"

"*Yes!*"

The *Last Chance* thrust forward into the giant mouth of the tube, which closed behind it and vanished from three-dimensional space. The mines converged on the vacant point previously occupied by the *Last Chance*, striking at each other with vicious abandon.

"Quiet!" shouted Athena with a raised clenched fist. The cramped cabin of the *Archaeopteryx* suddenly fell silent.

"What you are proposing," she continued in a softer yet metallic tone, "is that we track backward to the quasar, get Kale off the *Last Chance* with the multiplexer readings, and speed back to the gravitational shunt. Do I understand you?"

"Yes," replied Ellen.

"You realize that we lose the element of surprise by revealing this ship as an alternate target to the attacking swarm, and whatever time advantage we had in getting back to our universe earlier," said Athena.

"Yes, I do. But you said it yourself. There has to be an alternate target. They may destroy the *Last Chance* before Kale gets within sight of that device," replied Ellen.

Athena hung her head in an uncharacteristic display of resignation. "Look, Ellen, I understand you have feelings for Kale," she said. Looking away, she added, "It's not such an insane reaction."

Softly, Ellen responded, "It's not just that we want to save Kale. It's that we *can* actually pull it off. Hesperon's ship has sub-light maneuvering capabilities that are decades beyond the state-of-the-art technology on Kalyphon, and centuries beyond these antiques they have here. Trust me, the best chance for everyone rests in going after him."

"Why did you let him go, if you knew all this?" asked Athena.

"He needs to do this alone," replied Ellen. "I've seen him work with and without a safety net. As long as he knows there's only one shot, he's going to give it his all. If we're with him, we'll distract him. He's attracted to both of us, and he can't stop trying to impress you," she said.

Athena looked up at Ellen, and saw her with fresh eyes. Here was a woman, fighting for what she wanted, using the best tools available to her. Ellen could easily break her neck and take the ship herself, but she chose to reason—plus, that reasoning was elegant, honest, and, Athena admitted, convincing. Athena looked over at the two men, who indicated their assent to follow the decision.

"Full speed to the *Last Chance*!"

Chapter 18

Hounds to the Hunters

The *Last Chance* emerged from the inflationary tube only to be buffeted aside by the intense particle jet streaming out of the giant quasar's axis. The tugboat arced away, but the quasar's stupendous gravity and plasma torrents gripped the ship.

"Full thrust to safe orbit," Kale pushed forward, racing against the escape velocity of the quasar's black hole core. The sturdy tugboat rocketed outward, escaping the event horizon by only a handful of kilometers.

Once in the relative calm of orbit above the seething primordial monster, Kale wiped off the sweat on his brow. The emergency klaxons suddenly blared, but Kale only smiled. The alarm system had missed the party.

"Alarms off," he said aloud. The ship obliged. "Status report."

"We are in high orbit above what appears to be a small quasar. There are no ships or mines in pursuit," replied the neurocom.

Kale sat back in the command chair and gazed at the improbable phenomenon before him, his hand shading his eyes. The quasar's blaze of light filtered through the sensor grid, yet it filled the control room with brilliant white light. The space around it also was bright, rendered a blanched pale blue.

Since preastronomic times, humans had known that these elusive giants existed. Quasars inhabited the furthest reaches of their perception. Mistaken for close, bright stars by earthbound sailors, spectrographic analysis revealed them to be the superluminous hearts of ultradistant galaxies, spewing out more light and radio waves than the rest of their home galaxies combined.

They were recognized as snapshots in time—a visual record of the early universe—since the images of those quasars reached Earth fifteen billion years after they were emitted. They were understood to be dense black holes, sucking in gases and material at such a rate and quantity that they created a furnace of collisions and hyper-accelerated particles. This created a brilliant halo effect around the ordinarily low-profile singularities, giving them a universe-spanning spotlight.

However, fame proved all too transient to these quasars. A close physical inspection revealed an array of dark, satiated black holes where quasars had shone before. They had long since consumed their halos, and had settled into a routine of moribund viciousness, awakening like nursery rhyme trolls, only to eviscerate a passing starship, or to cannibalize each other.

Kale perceived something that had never been witnessed by a scientist on record, other than through the distorted lenses of fifteen-billion-year-old photons and their grandfathered relativistic effects. There was no time to examine the mythological young quasar before him. The neurocom had locked onto the multiplexer.

The *Last Chance* cleared the halo, and a quivering mass of tendrils surrounding a tiny sphere came into view. Kale pushed forward the command to lock in the ten-dimensional view, and the sphere seemingly exploded with filaments, stretching in every direction, but with a wide, tightly wound cord running toward the gravity shunt.

Kale could feel the blood pulsing through his temples as he commanded his lungs to breathe. This was it. This and other devices like it were the cause of universal catastrophe, and he saw its malice. In Kale's mind, it hung carelessly in orbit, playing the role of a scheming courtier, greedily pulling strings from behind a curtain. It commanded the immense backing of the monstrous quasar, itself bucking for noble title in the new kingdom.

Kale swore, again regretting the lack of armaments on the tugboat. However, he knew that his mission was to gather readings, and learn how to untie the noose of multiplexers that surrounded his universe. Only once those readings were completed could he then tear apart the device with the ship's tractor emitters.

Kale pushed forward a full battery of scans. A furtive glance around revealed no other ships in the vicinity.

. . . high-density decatron emissions, opacifying local space . . . light waves blocked, funneled . . . polar decatron stream operating at 698 Serahertz (.7 OHz) . . . quasar-emitted power capture at 99% efficiency, multiplexer device output exceeds measurement capacity . . .

. . . carrier signal detected . . .

. . . peer-to-peer system . . . management in real-time . . . anti-tamper auto code switching . . . protocol detected . . . decoding . . . decoding . . .

A thunderous explosion sounded through the ship, severing the data link and shoving the *Last Chance* back within the quasar's magnetic grasp. Kale was thrown to the floor, his face smashing into the deck. Through a haze, he pushed forward the command to stabilize orbit. The *Last Chance* shook in response, its propulsion system bent out of alignment.

"Secondary thrusters online," said the neurocom, as it wrestled the ship back into a safe orbit.

Kale's vision began to clear as he pulled himself up. He tasted something warm and salty, and spat out a mouthful of blood.

"Reestablish data link," Kale muttered.

"Establishing—unable to scan target area," replied the neurocom.

"Unable to scan? What does that mean?"

"The remote log-in signal is scattering."

Kale hung on that last word—and then it suddenly hit him.

He spun around to face the screen, where he met the gaze of a serene, smiling face.

✦ ✦ ✦ ✦ ✦

"In the name of God, I greet you," said Jorsem. "I am First Villier Jorsem, commanding the *Scepter of Divine Right*. I cannot permit you to perform this grave sacrilege. You are subject to eternal damnation if you do not repent." The newly installed Villier glanced around his command bridge, making sure that the elders, Harbagotten, and the pageboy did not miss a single syllable.

His young opponent stared back, his nose cut and bleeding, seemingly unaware that his arm was soaked red.

"You have been a plague upon the faithful, including my illustrious predecessor. You have defiled our temple, God's home, and you have conspired to destroy our sacred destiny. Despite all this, the example of Jerandus guides us. Like King

Darian before you, all condemned men have the right of repentance," said Jorsem.

Kale paused a moment to compose his response. "There isn't a word to describe the astronomical volume of mass murder you've committed already. You're trying to exterminate the rest of humankind as if we were insects. I won't repent. You surrender, or I'll tear apart your ship!"

Jorsem smiled. He leaned forward and said in a sweet voice, "And how are you going to do that, my child? With your broken tractor beams?"

Kale kept his face rigid, while his mind pushed forward various diagnostic routines. They showed what he feared—the tractor nozzles had been smashed and fused into useless stumps. That was the explosion that started this conversation.

Jorsem stared into the face of his opponent, and saw no reaction. The gunner in front of him faced him, waiting for orders to finish the job, but Jorsem held back. He wondered what made his adversary so confident.

Kale's fear registered in the recesses of his mind, but it had learned its lesson. Rage dominated his mind now.

"How dare you!" Kale said.

Jorsem was taken aback. "What?"

"Who do you think you are, gambling with the lives of humankind? What gives you the right?"

Jorsem stiffened. "I am the right hand of God. I am His instrument in the physical universe. I execute His will. And you stand in His way!"

"Or so you've convinced yourself! It's easy to believe what you write. Don't you think, though, that if it really were god's intent to eradicate his greatest creation, he would do it himself? *In his own time?*"

"The extent of your arrogance is unfathomable, heathen! Do you dare question my faith?"

"Your faith is a drop of water. Everyone in the ocean of humankind has faith in something. Faith is not the issue. Your judgment is what I question."

Jorsem's eyes bulged, his body shaking with rage. He heard unexpected grunts of approval from the elders, while the gunner nodded at him, pleading for the order to kill. Jorsem shook his head. There was now much more at stake than a simple execution.

Kale sensed his advantage and pressed on. "Your poisonous tongue paralyzes the beauty of your beliefs, choking off their oxygen. Your necrotic thinking carries no love, no passion. It presumes too much, and you usurp the powers of god to destroy that which he created. And if that were his disposition, he certainly does not need *you*!" Kale paused, sensing an effect. "Surely there was debate on this issue at your highest levels," he said, now standing.

This last bit registered further rumbling from the elders, and Jorsem knew he had to do something quickly. The purges that took place within the Stellar Cross to establish their current course of action were extreme. Moderates who had shifted to the right for their own survival might feel encouraged to return to a more passive, coexistence philosophy. Some of them were in his control room.

"It is an act of ultimate blasphemy to speak or even think against the actions of the Executor of God's will, his First Villier," he said to the screen, although equally for the benefit of the elders behind him.

"Then against what mirror are a Villier's actions held?" Kale said.

Jorsem grinned. He cast his smiling gaze across the room. "My actions are dictated by God. And they are in turn subject to God's review. God is the ultimate objective judge of behavior, which is something your people have forgotten."

Kale paused, uncertain of what to say, kicking himself for asking an open-ended question.

"Yes," continued Jorsem, raising his voice. "God is your judge. He judges all of us. And what have you to say to Him? How will you answer Him when He asks you why you cast Him out of your world? How will you defend your worship of flawed men and their soulless machines?"

"We chose the voice of the people! Equal voice and equal—"

Jorsem jumped to his feet, interrupting, "Populism! Equality! You poor deluded fool. The mob of the herd only cares about the next meal! They are concerned only with themselves! And when enough of them band together with enough power to control the voices of others, the sheep becomes the wolf." Jorsem paused to survey his control room, which, judging by the rapt attention of his audience, was beginning to live up to its name.

"Yes, poor Kale. Hunger is the backbone of your packs of humanity! And well you know it. Harbagotten here was toiling away as a slave in your machine for the ruling class before God entered his life. I myself was drowning in a life of corruption, forced down by the hooves of your herd, before I was saved. The living conditions of most people remain stratified between the high, the middle, and the lower classes, regardless of the rich philosophy of the ruling body of men. That is the inevitable truth of governance by man. The numbing repetition of this truth is so grotesque that it would be laughable were it not for the immense sacrilege it performs on the gift of life!

"It is this record that condemns you and your people to the fate God requires. Those who are noble of spirit and mind will find themselves walking in the fields of heaven, while the rest of you will spend eternity watching your flesh roast in hellfire!" Sensing total victory, and the complete backing of the elders, Jorsem glanced down to his gunner to give the order.

"What if you're wrong?"

Jorsem stopped, and looked up. The heathen was standing there with his arms crossed, his head tilted to the side, one eyebrow arched.

"How dare you!"

Kale ignored this. "Everything you say requires your perceptions to depict reality accurately in order for your conclusion to be valid."

"What kind of intellectual double-talk is this?" said Jorsem with a laugh.

"However, nothing you say can be verified. You promise bureaucratic 'slaves' and other so-called less fortunate people a better life—but only after they are dead! It is very convenient that the binding contract of faith you offer has no remedy available during life, should your promises prove false!

"Your whole belief structure is built on unproven supposition. It works because your promises are so appealing—immortality of the mind, and a ready-made set of morals, social positions, political beliefs, and medical ethics. You save your believers from fear of death, but at the cost of independent thought!"

Jorsem's lips trembled, but he said nothing.

Kale pressed on. "And now the single mind of religion has decreed that the universe must be destroyed. Right now. But what if you're wrong? On a personal level, the only loss suffered is the surrender of independent thought. But at your level, religion becomes something else entirely. If *you* are wrong, *you* commit mass genocide."

Jorsem leapt to his feet. "Who the hell do you think you are? You are nothing but a heathen child! How dare you challenge me! Don't you realize who I am? I am the Hand of God! I can smash you into a billion pieces with a single gesture!"

Kale froze, his face blank. He pushed forward a book, invisible to anyone else. He read aloud, "'Question not the source of truth, but rather the one who casts himself as God.'" He gazed sideways at the screen.

Jorsem stood there, his mouth hanging open. The elders chattered among themselves.

Harbagotten approached the First Villier, and placed his hand on his shoulder.

Jorsem flinched and swirled around. "What are you doing?" he whispered.

"This is not right, Jorsem," he said.

Jorsem stared into his face. "What are you saying?"

"His recitation of the scriptures resonates with the elders," he replied.

"With the elders? Or with you?" demanded Jorsem, his eyes narrowing.

"Your behavior is becoming unstable, Jorsem. You must take my counsel," said Harbagotten.

"First Villier!" shouted the gunner, silencing the murmuring throughout the control room. "The tugboat is headed straight for the multiplexer!"

Jorsem snapped his head around. "*What?!*"

"It's out of our jamming range!"

"Pursue and target weapons!" Jorsem spun around to face his one-time mentor. "Your counsel seems to have had its day, old friend."

Harbagotten stiffened as he sensed Jorsem's blade in motion. He shifted to the side and raised his own toward Jorsem's neck. His blade never made it. His chest blinked out of existence, causing his head and limbs to fall to the deck. Jorsem gasped and stepped back. A robed guard stepped back into formation, lowering his antique fusion rifle.

"First Villier, the *Last Chance* is approaching the multiplexer!" yelled the gunner, breaking the silence.

Jorsem's gaze moved from the pile of human parts that was his best friend and teacher, and stared at the wall. "Yes, I know," he said. "But there is an another ship approaching."

✚ ✚ ✚ ✚ ✚

The *Archaeopteryx* shot toward the *Scepter of Divine Right*, which stood out as a black insect against the pale blue of local space.

"Push this thing harder," ordered Athena through clenched teeth.

"We already are several marks past tolerance. Any further, and the safety guard shuts down the engine," replied Hesperon, rubbing his temples with his thumb and index finger.

Athena glanced at Ellen, who dangled a glob of elastic circuitry in his face. "The safeties are off," Athena said.

Hesperon sighed inwardly. It was difficult working with amateurs. Unbeknownst to them, they had accomplished little by removing decoy circuitry, but they had demonstrated a commitment to their goal. "Very well, I will increase speed. However, it will not change the outcome."

✚ ✚ ✚ ✚ ✚

The *Last Chance* hurtled toward the multiplexer, struggling to keep out of the jamming range of the pursuing attack ship.

"Collision course detected, aborting vector," said the neurocom.

"OVERRIDE!" yelled Kale. The data link had to be maintained in order to get the frequency information, and he could only get that by closing the distance between himself and the multiplexer.

"You have committed this vessel to a course that jeopardizes its survival. Please enter your product key code to authenticate ownership and the right to destroy this property," it replied.

Kale swore silently. He got up out of the command chair and grabbed a fallen pylon. He walked over to the console that housed the neurocom CPU and thrust the metal pylon straight through the brain of the device, smashing the delicate neuroweb circuitry. The ship convulsed, throwing Kale to the floor.

He threw himself back into the command chair, and pulled up the manual drive panel. He wrestled the ship back under control, and set the *Last Chance* back on its course. He reestablished the data link, and it resumed its download. Kale then punched in the command to prepare a shuttle pod for emergency evacuation.

He wiped the blood from his face, and stared at the black shadow cast by the octopus-like device against the brilliance of the quasar. It was oddly beautiful, this instrument of universal destruction.

Blasts from the pursuing attack ship interrupted his reverie. The rear tractor was smashed inward, collapsing the decks in front of it. Kale checked the damage report, and saw that the landing bay and secondary propulsion were destroyed. He turned to face the multiplexing device and the monstrous quasar before him. He felt a chill go down his spine as he realized that he had only one course of action. His hands began to shake, and the gnawing sensation in his stomach began to bubble over into nausea.

As the ship continued to take heavy weapons fire, punching its hull inward, the data link signaled that all of the multiplexer's operating information had been downloaded.

This was it—Kale had the operating frequency data of the entire network. He keyed in the command to transmit the information packet. A data receipt confirmation from the *Archaeopteryx* blinked on his panel.

+ + + + +

The *Archaeopteryx* closed in on the two ships, catching wisps of gas and giving the small ship a halo of white fury.

The *Scepter of Divine Right* remained in pursuit of the *Last Chance*, accelerated to full speed, and spewed round after round of energy bolts at the scarred and crippled tugboat. The blue ship took the brunt of the assault, and its diamond hull, designed to take tremendous physical stresses, began to fracture.

The *Archaeopteryx* activated its forward weapons platform and began peppering the dragonfly-shaped attacking ship.

The *Scepter* did not take the bait. It targeted the torn stump that used to be the *Last Chance*'s rear tractor, and fired a single projectile into it.

The diamond hull of the ship splintered, the cracks luminous and brilliant. The *Last Chance* held its shape for a split second and then exploded, streaking the area with radioactive shards of blinding diamond shrapnel.

+ + + + +

Ellen screamed. Her eyes were bloodshot and tearing. She glanced over at Athena, whose face was wide with astonishment. Gander was a mask of pain, his whole body shaking. The shock of coming so far only to see Kale's ship explode in front of her tore Ellen apart. She felt it in wave after wave of unabated pain, smashing through her soul at millisecond intervals. Each wave became worse and worse, increasing to the point of nearly destroying her mind, until she saw a way to channel her emotions.

She knocked Hesperon out of the control seat and directed the small craft at the dragonfly ship. Nobody tried to stop her. She flicked on all the weapons systems and directed full power to the forward plasma cannon array.

"Report," barked Jorsem.

"The *Last Chance* is destroyed. Without an atmosphere to travel through, the nuclear blast was limited to the matter that composed the vessel," replied the gunner. "And the multiplexer is intact!"

Jorsem smiled and sat back in his seat. "Good shooting. Now turn around this ship to face the approaching starship."

"Yes, sire," the gunner replied. "It's firing on us, but our shields are deflecting the shots."

"Target the left wing, and blow it off."

+ + + + +

"Ellen, you will get us all killed," said Athena. "We received a transmission from the *Last Chance* containing the tactical data on the multiplexers. We need to get out of here."

"NO! They killed him! *THEY KILLED HIM!*" Ellen screamed.

Athena put her hands on Ellen's, and slowly lifted them off the console. "I know you loved him, Ellen. But we can't let him die for nothing. We need to use the information he sent us." She caressed Ellen's face, rubbing away the tears that steadily were streaking down. Ellen's body relaxed, and she raised her eyes to Athena's.

Suddenly, the left wing exploded, throwing everyone to the floor. Hesperon seized the controls and spun around the ship. He locked in a course for the shunt, and set the gravitic engine to maximum. The crippled *Archaeopteryx* lurched in place before bolting for the stars.

Chapter 19

Regretting a Vote

"They're right behind us!" yelled Gander from the corner of the cabin.

"I know," said Hesperon.

"Where's the rest of the enemy fleet?" asked Athena.

"That's what concerns me," said Hesperon.

"What?" said Gander. "You guys are feeling lonely? Well, there's a whole wall of them after us!"

Hesperon waved toward the rear holojector, showing the full extent of the pursuit fleet. The *Scepter* led the pack.

"The rest of them must be somewhere between us and the shunt, waiting for us," croaked a pale Ellen.

"Would you agree with that assessment, Athena?" asked Hesperon.

"I can't see that far without being in the temple, but that certainly makes sense," she said.

"Well then, ladies. Do I have your permission to choose a creative pathway back to the shunt?"

Athena and Ellen looked at each other and nodded. Gander shrank back, beginning to feel the loss of his best friend.

"Very well then."

The entire starfield in front of them streaked upward, as the *Archaeopteryx* took a nosedive. Gander cried out.

"Close your eyes," said Hesperon. "You won't feel inertia, so motion sickness shouldn't affect you," he added as he converted the dive into a randomly looping spiral.

The pursuing vessels overshot and scattered, trying to match their prey. The *Scepter* doggedly kept pace with the *Archaeopteryx*.

The pursuing fleet opened fire. The *Archaeopteryx* was surrounded by silent blasts, suffering sporadic hits. The hull explosions rocked the vessel, smashing its crew into the walls of the cramped cabin. The tiny ship, seeking cover, bolted toward a massive comet cluster. However, the beetle ships concentrated their fire ahead, turning the cluster to dust and microscopic ice crystals before the *Archaeopteryx* could reach it.

Ahead of them lay a star system. There were several rocky worlds on its edge, with the gas giants close to the star, in the strange, flattened ovoid shape characteristic to the miniverse. The *Archaeopteryx* lunged toward it while the beetle ships fell back. The little ship continued to approach the star system, scanning it for hiding places.

"Stop!" yelled Athena.

"Why?" asked Hesperon.

"The multiplexing signal. It's been redirected to that star! They're—"

"Inducing a supernova," finished Hesperon. "Good."

Athena blinked. "Are you insane?"

Hesperon turned around. "No. Nor do I suffer from suicidal ideation. Now please, everyone be quiet. I have to shut off all the safeties and concentrate."

The *Archaeopteryx* altered its vector to slice across the disk of the star system.

The equivalent of a G-type star shone benevolently down on its ovoid worlds, casting on them its life-giving rays of yellow light. However, this light was turning a premature red, as planet-sized volumes of heavy matter were materialized into its core. The star bloated, engulfing the closest planets in a matter of seconds. The star turned deep maroon, retracted, and exploded.

The shockwave eviscerated the remaining planets. The *Archaeopteryx* ramped up to full speed ahead of the much faster explosion, which batted the *Archaeopteryx* forward like a gnat. Nonetheless, Hesperon held his damaged ship on the cusp of the wave.

The shockwave began to slow and dissipate, and the *Archaeopteryx* was able to shoot out ahead of it.

"Hey, we're almost at the shunt!" said Gander, glancing at a scope.

"Yes, but it's blocked by several thousand ships, all facing us," said Athena, projecting her awareness.

"What?" cried Gander.

"Once we clear that green nebula, you'll see them, too," she said.

"It seems the hounds have driven us to the hunters," added Ellen.

The color had drained out of Ellen's face, and her eyes were swollen. Her small frame hunched down as she hugged her knees. Gander put his arm around her.

"Here comes that attack ship," said Hesperon, as the *Scepter* approached. "I'm not sure if I have many more tricks up my sleeve."

Athena stepped into the center of the cabin. "Hail them."

Hesperon keyed in the appropriate command, and the First Villier's face replaced the nebula and blue starfield.

"Well, if it isn't the traitorous little Athena!" said Jorsem with a bitter smile.

"If it's going to be name-calling, I'm afraid I can't think of a word that covers annihilation of a universe."

"Very amusing, if deliberately misinterpreted. However, that point is not your biggest concern at the moment. No doubt you can see the fleet beyond the nebula," said Jorsem.

"No doubt."

"What do you want to say then?"

Athena sighed. "I will surrender myself if you let my friends go."

Jorsem gazed at the woman in front of him. "That is very noble of you. But I simply am not interested!"

Athena blinked. "What?"

"My predecessor may have valued your natural talents, but I have no need for them," said Jorsem.

"Then what terms do you propose?" asked Athena.

"None."

"Then why did you accept the hail?" asked Athena.

Jorsem smiled. "Why, only to inform you that although you may die quickly, you will burn for eternity!"

Ellen jumped to her feet, tears streaming off her face. "You sanctimonious, self-righteous pile of shit! You're nothing but a fucking murderer!"

Jorsem arched an eyebrow. "Oh yes, the Synth! Well, the scriptures are clear on this. I really have no choice but to destroy all of you." He glanced away and said, "Once we are within firing range, smash down their shielding and launch a full spread of atomic drills." He smiled at them, and the signal disconnected.

Ellen fell to the floor, her strength gone. Athena looked over to Hesperon. "What do we do now?" she asked.

"Sprint toward the enemy fleet, and try to punch through it," he said.

"No suicidal ideation, huh?" she asked.

"Suicide is the avoidance of living. I'm not sure we have that choice."

The *Archaeopteryx* stretched out its right wing and tail aileron, and dipped below the nebula. As it cleared the gas body, the entire Stellar Cross fleet came into view. Beetle ships swarmed around goliath queen ships, with mandibles filled with grotesquely oversized weapons. The *Archaeopteryx* activated its thrusters and began to close the distance between them.

The *Scepter of Divine Right* and a pair of beetle ships approached the nebula, their forward weapons batteries open. The three ships mirrored the course of the *Archaeopteryx* and dropped below the nebula.

However, as the fleet and the *Archaeopteryx* came into view, a massive metallic fin dropped sharply out of the nebula, blocking the path of the pursuing ships.

The two leading beetle ships slammed headfirst into invisible rotating shield blades around the fin. They were sliced apart, causing too much interference for the *Scepter* to steer around. The head of the dragonfly-shaped ship was severed milliseconds before the rest of the body was chopped apart. The resulting sections were reduced further by closer shield blades, until only a fine spray of dust reached the griffin emblazoned on the cruiser's ventral fin.

The goliath cylindrical ship continued to descend from the nebula, followed by six similar vessels, dispersing wide furrows of gas. The first ship captured the *Archaeopteryx* in a tractor beam, and pulled it into a docking bay. It then emitted a wide field hail.

"This is President Yohan Taschet, commanding the *Coelacanth*. Move your fleet aside immediately or be destroyed!"

The crew of the *Archaeopteryx* was brought to the bridge of the giant ship. The door slid open, and Athena led them into the cavernous control room. Dozens of naval officers turned from their neurocom interface consoles to see the newcomers. President Taschet, Councilor Juno, and Minister Ferric were facing them as they entered.

Athena addressed the president. "Had I known you were the type to lead the cavalry, I actually might have voted for you," she said with a thin smile.

He grinned. "You know, my husband said the same thing to me just last week! Anyway, welcome aboard the *Coelacanth*," he said, extending his hand. She shook it.

"This is the rest of our crew, or at least what remains of it," said Athena, pointing at Ellen, Hesperon, and Gander.

Taschet glanced sideways. "You probably recognize Councilor Juno and Intelligence Minister Ferric. What about your leader, Mr. Eritrus?" he asked.

"Kale gave his life to get the multiplexer code," answered Ellen. Her voice cracked as she spoke.

"Do you have it?" asked Juno.

Ellen glared at the politician, uncertain of their intentions. "Yes, I have the complete string," she said, tapping at her head.

Athena broke in. "Okay, we've answered your questions, Mr. President. Now what are you doing here?"

"Your group was the diversion that allowed this naval battle group to close in to invade Jattan. It seems you got the code for us anyway," replied Taschet.

"Now that you have it, can we get back home?" she said.

"Yes, but the pursuing group of ships is holding position, and the blockade fleet has not moved. In fact, they are perfectly stationary," confirmed Taschet. "Their leader says we are in violation of something or another. However, given the tactical requirements of maintaining an effective blockade, I suspect they are hesitant to engage us."

"So what do we do?" said Athena.

Taschet smiled. "Watch."

The seven giant cylindrical cruisers moved forward toward the unflinching blockade of Stellar ships. As the cruisers approached, their surfaces suddenly bristled with slender projections, like the poisonous hairs of a caterpillar.

Suddenly, and only for an instant, the blue space between the cruisers and the blockade became alive with energy. Each Stellar ship received an energy discharge from three separate bristles from three separate cruisers, overloading all their shielding.

The Stellar ships now were exposed to weapons fire, but also to the immense gravitational shear of the black hole in the main universe. Those that were not shredded apart by their proximity to the lethal singularity scattered to avoid the slightest yet fatal hit from the approaching cruisers.

The cruisers headed single-file into the protective shunt, retracting their bristles at the last minute to fit through the narrow torus of the black hole.

As the *Coelacanth* emerged from the vortex, normal black space filled the generous forward view of the large control room. A naval battle group was waiting to serve as escort. Ellen stared into the three-dimensional representation in front of them, using all of her reserves to keep from breaking down in front of them all. Taschet and Ferric asked Athena most of their questions, with Gander broadening out her terse responses.

She saw that Hesperon had seated himself at a neurocom console, and was connecting back into the Synergian pool. This struck her as the ideal way not to deal with one's feelings. She followed suit, reestablishing her link with the universal communications nexus.

"We need the data now," interrupted Ferric.

Ellen looked back at the head of the intelligence ministry. "What are you going to do with it?"

"You don't need to know that."

"Are you going to send out the navy to all the miniverses and shut down their multiplexers?" Ellen asked.

"The universe is not collapsing. However, you have classified information about a known terrorist entity. Hand it over!" she said in a voice accustomed to authority.

Ellen stood up, ready to confront the bureaucrat, but Taschet placed his hand on her shoulder.

"Lisa, these people have been through enough. Besides, we may need their help. There are a few things I haven't told you yet," he said.

Athena overheard the last part, and walked over.

"You clearly know the universe is collapsing, and how the Stellar Cross is involved," started Taschet, addressing Athena. Ferric shook her head, but said nothing. "What you may not know is that we have been aware of this for decades."

"I knew it!" said Athena.

"We could never get an agent into their organization. They kept knocking them off. We were beginning to get desperate. We were planning a full-scale invasion when our agents discovered that your group was planning to unravel the question of the collapse. We tracked you, or at least tried to track you, and that brought about this little expedition."

"Wait a second; your story doesn't hold together," said Ellen. "What about the deletion of collapse information from UNN databanks? And what about the depletion of university physics departments?"

"I can address that," said Juno. "That was a deliberate action by the Council of Sentients, set in motion two millennia ago."

"What?" gasped Athena.

"We have known that the life cycle of the universe is closed, meaning that it will either collapse or expand infinitely while all matter reduces to black holes. We have since actively pursued methods of minimizing this knowledge, so as to preserve the psychological well-being of the human race," she continued.

"But I don't understand. If you've known about this all along, why haven't you already set up these miniverses as lifeboats for our own universe's demise? How did you allow the Stellar Cross to take them over?" asked Ellen.

Juno smiled. "That certainly would have been our course of action, if we did not already have another course of action in mind."

Ellen and Athena exchanged a glance. "Which is?" asked Ellen.

Taschet jumped in. "Have you heard of the Atlas Project?"

"Yes. It's one of those defense industry money pits we keep hearing about on *Final Analysis*!" said Gander.

Taschet chuckled. "Yes, I suppose it can seem that way, especially when everyone thinks it's just a real-time mapping system."

Athena squinted. "What are you saying? What is the Atlas Project really doing?"

"Well, part of the cover story is true. It is indeed a highly funded defense project and it certainly has a present-sense view of every part of the universe. However, the name 'Atlas' isn't a reference to a collection of maps, but rather to an ancient mythological figure whose job was to hold up the sky." Taschet paused, savoring the sensation of getting to reveal one of the most closely guarded government secrets in history.

"Its real purpose is to physically prevent and reverse the collapse of the universe," said Taschet. He flashed his election-winning smile as he looked at their stunned faces.

Chapter 20

The Atlas Sphere

The *Coelacanth* led the fleet through a labyrinth of small, classified wormholes.

Athena rested on a makeshift cot in a tiny utilitarian cabin. They all had been processed and were found to be suffering from exhaustion. She had been asleep for thirty minutes when Ellen's chime sounded. Athena rubbed her eyes and said, "Come in, Ellen."

The door slid open. Ellen stood there, haloed by the bright hallway. She stepped forward and the door closed behind her. She did not signal for the lights. Athena threw her legs over the edge of the cot, and said, "Ellen, talk to me."

The Sentient walked over to her on shaky legs and knelt on the hard floor in front of Athena. "He's gone, Athena."

"Yes, it's difficult," she said. She avoided minimizing their loss, knowing that would be absurd to say or hear.

"I don't know how to go on. There's no point to any of this anymore. I only wanted to save the universe because he was in it," said Ellen, looking down at the floor.

Athena reached out and gently raised up her chin to meet her gaze. She smiled.

"He meant a lot to me, too," said Athena. "He never was intimidated of me, and instead always was honest with me. I don't know how to get past it either."

Ellen's lips trembled. "So what do we do?" she whispered.

Athena held Ellen's hands in hers. "We were closest to him. We should honor his memory by backing each other."

"I'll try that," whispered Ellen.

Athena smiled warmly at her. "Good! That's a start. Are you up for returning to the bridge?"

Ellen looked at her hands. They had stopped shaking. "Yes."

"This is taking forever, General Mola," muttered Taschet.

"Sir, since we embarked on Operation Ghost, the main civilian strings have become untenable as means of Transport," he said.

"What do you mean? What's been going on?"

Juno spoke up. "They are flooded with trillions of panicking people, struggling to find a safe world in the deteriorating universe," she said, rubbing her head. "The main Travel tubes also have become a favorite sabotage target for the religionists."

"And that doesn't begin to describe the incursions from the various miniverses," interjected Ferric.

"What do you mean?" repeated Taschet.

Ferric pushed forward a colorful map of the universe. "See the blue packets surrounding the universe? Those are the miniverses. See the red dots flowing into our universe? They represent known movements of Stellar Cross attack craft. They are attacking randomly. Most of the military is focused on riot control, and we are the only major combat fleet not assigned to that task."

Ferric was startled, as the boundaries of the representation began puckering and thrusting inward.

"And those points mark the beginning of the collapse happening right now," finished Athena.

All eyes turned to her.

"How do you know that?" asked the general.

Athena said nothing, but it was her turn to be startled. "She has extra cognitive awareness," answered Taschet, as if he were giving the time of day.

"How do you know that?" asked Athena, her dark eyes focused on the glib president.

Ferric regarded both of them, uncertain as to what was going on.

Taschet continued, "Juno told me. The Council of Sentients knew all about your little network and your special talents, but kept the information confidential until now. Your mother is a Chapter Leader, if I have the terminology right."

"I haven't been briefed on this!" said Ferric.

"Remember all that 'need to know' crap you keep shoving at me?" Taschet said. "Well, now you know how it feels!"

"Mr. President," started Ferric. "As your Minister of Intelligence, it is mandatory that I have all the information necessary to protect this universe!"

"I'm sorry, Lisa, but we couldn't afford another eugenics war in the middle of all this, and the less people who know, the better," continued Taschet.

Athena had turned pale during the exchange. She glanced about, and felt Ellen place her hand on her back.

"So, Ms. Nobarra, care to explain your condition?" asked the furious Intelligence Minister.

"Will I be granted amnesty from genetic inquest?" she asked.

Ferric paused, considered employing her standard strong-arm response, and thought better of it. "Yes."

"I can sense reality without depending on my five senses," she said.

"And what does that mean?" asked Ferric.

Athena's eyes bulged. "It means I can tell when an enemy attack force is about to spring a trap! Stop the fleet!"

Just then, a loud explosion thundered through the control room. The lights went out, to be replaced by the blaring of a klaxon, and the sound of incoherent shouting.

"Status!" roared Taschet.

"The entire fleet has dropped out of Transit, our physical and mental cloaks are offline," said Mola. "The tube must have been mined!"

"Activate the viewer!" ordered Taschet.

In front of him, the fleet hung out of formation in normal space. Beyond lay a sea of Stellar Cross queen and beetle ships, ready to strike.

+++++

The queen ships launched a massive wave of weapons fire toward the limping fleet.

"Shields! Everyone get your shields up!" yelled Taschet. The wave of energy hit the fleet, smashing into most of it. The screen was filled with broken cruisers.

"Well?" asked Taschet.

"*Coelacanth*, *Leviathan*, and *Megalodon* managed to raise shields in time," said Mola, struggling over the din. "The rest are burning in space."

Taschet fell against the wall. "So is the enemy advancing?" he asked.

"No, sir," replied Mola.

"They're collapsing this area of space!" shouted Athena. "There is a galaxy of collapsing matter converging on our position."

"That's it. We've shown enough restraint," muttered Taschet, pulling himself away from the wall. "Mola, how many quantum warheads are we carrying?"

"We have six quantums, but more than sixteen hundred atomics," said the general.

"Well, that's just not enough," said Taschet.

"Mr. President, if I may," started Hesperon. "I have an idea."

"Well, this *is* a democracy," said Taschet.

"If they're so intent on collapsing this part of the universe, then maybe we should let them take a closer look."

"You mean you have some kind of stratagem in mind for luring them into their own trap?" asked Taschet.

"I do," replied the Synergian.

"Well then, remind me to ask you about it when this is all over, because we simply don't have the time to waste," said the president.

Hesperon grabbed his arm. "So what are you going to do?"

"What any seasoned manager should do in this kind of situation," he replied with a smile. "Delegate!"

✦✦✦✦✦

The *Megalodon* and the *Leviathan* moved between the *Coelacanth* and the attacking fleet, bristles extended.

"Send out the stringhead!" ordered Taschet.

"But Mr. President, we run the risk of coming across other mines," said General Mola.

"Yes, that's why we won't be using existing conduits," he replied. Turning to the last councilor, he continued, "Juno, I believe we are in a sufficient state of emergency to warrant a release of classified Atlas data. Wouldn't you agree?"

She glanced up. "Yes, I should say so." She addressed the ship's neurocom. "Target gravitational harmonic theta alif kay."

"Yohan!" barked Ferric. "What the hell is going on?"

"Lisa, calm down," he replied. "The Atlas Sphere houses a group of unregistered cosmic strings in order to operate. We simply are summoning one of them. Oh, and you would do well to remember the chain of command here, minister." She said nothing.

"Stringhead returned," said Mola.

A supple wormhole tubule opened in front of the cruiser. Its mouth opened and swallowed the giant ship whole.

Chapter 21

Resurrection

A thena gasped. As the *Coelacanth* emerged into normal space, she became aware of a construction she had never perceived before.

Taschet began filling in some of the holes. "This facility, like the Ghost fleet, is protected from extra cognitive perception. We now are behind the scattering field, so you are free to perceive at will."

"What is it?" asked Ellen.

"The ultimate achievement of cosmological architecture," said Ferric, confident that she finally knew something someone else did not already know.

"Hyperbole aside," continued Taschet, brushing away Ferric's comment, "the facility essentially is a reverse magnet, but with enough power to arrest and reverse the deflation of the universe," he said.

"How does it work?" asked Ellen.

"Well, we are about to dock, and you can get the full explanation from the experts," replied Taschet. "However, while we're crossing into the array, you might want to observe the size and configuration."

"A galaxy-sized web of black holes," said Athena.

The former crew of the *Last Chance* gazed out into the inky black to catch a glimpse. The cruiser passed through an elliptical perimeter of eighty-one black holes, closing in on a spiked object in the center.

"It's one solid piece of neutron matter. Each projection stretches over five hundred kilometers, pointing toward a black hole," said Taschet. "But we're here."

A transparency field suddenly disengaged, revealing a giant control station in orbit around the solid black core. The relatively tiny cruiser approached a column projecting out from its central rotating ring, and docked against it. The cloak reactivated.

"Mr. President and guests, if you would follow me," said General Mola.

They all followed him out of the control room, through several concentric layers of physical shielding. They disembarked through a reinforced airlock and stepped out into the receiving bay of the control station. Armed guards lined the walls, but standing in the middle of the room was an elderly man in a long white jacket. Gander stared in disbelief, while Ellen let a bittersweet smile cross her face.

"Welcome to the Atlas Sphere," said Dr. Fen Cerelles.

"What are you doing here?" asked Athena.

Cerelles smiled. "Well, government agents were waiting at my wife's place on Belleron, and they took us here. They had been following me from Earth, which is what led them to follow your ship, too. Anyway, they needed another astrophysicist on the science team for this project. Suddenly all the information gaps and the decline of qualified physicists made sense. They're all here! Except—"

The contingent from the *Coelacanth* had just emptied into the receiving bay, and the hatch door closed.

"Where is my boy, Kale?"

Athena glanced over to Ellen, who simply looked away. "He's dead," said Athena in a soft voice.

Cerelles pitched forward, but an assistant steadied him. "What?"

"He died to get us the operating frequency of the multiplexing network," replied Athena. "I'm very sorry."

"But, that can't be! He's so young! And I sent him out there!" stuttered the old man, now leaning heavily against his assistant.

Ellen winced upon hearing those words, and pressed her fingers into Gander's shoulder. He held her waist, feeling a sudden sense of kinship.

"I hate to point this out, but we are all going to be quite dead soon unless we apply that code," said Ferric. "Right now."

"Yes, yes," sighed Cerelles. He stared at each of them, scowling at Gander. "So, who has the code?"

"I do," said Ellen.

Cerelles tilted his head. "You're the Sentient from the news, but I recognize your voice now that I'm hearing it in person."

"I was Kale's neurocom," replied Ellen. "I Connected the two of you frequently."

"Ah, yes. So are you going to give it to us?" he continued.

Ellen looked at Athena, who nodded.

"Yes."

✦✦✦✦✦

Cerelles led them through the monumental control station, into a massive circular room filled with arcane machinery and arguing scientists. They hushed when they saw the president and some of his staff, along with the notorious *Last Chance* crew.

"Partak, this Sentient has the code!" said Cerelles.

An older yet agile woman leapt up onto the central dais, where the new arrivals were standing.

"Push it forward!" she said.

Ellen, sensing a neurocom locus in the room, pushed forward the information directly into its central mesh. Partak 8843 jumped down to the personal interface, a large black pouch that Hesperon found familiar. She began calling out a control checklist.

Synchronize decatron reactors—eighty-one polyhedral devices decloaked in orbit around the giant spiked neutron sphere.

Target neutron towers—the polyhedrons spun around until their emission funnels pointed directly at the spikes on the sphere.

Rotate the sphere—the giant heart of the Atlas Sphere began spinning along its axes one by one, starting with its x-axis, then its y- and z-axes, then its q-axis and the remaining extra-dimensional axes until it was spinning in ten dimensions.

Apply code frequency—the reactors' micro-cyclotrons tempered the decatron particle stream to reflect the operating frequency of the Stellar Cross multiplexers.

Release the decatrons—the funnels suddenly shot out ultra-coherent subatomic ten-dimensional particles toward the blurred sphere. The enhanced force of gravity exerted on those particles caused them to hyperaccelerate to superluminal inflationary velocities. As the particles fell beneath the event horizon of the redesigned neutron star, they blinked out of sight. The giant spinning spikes captured their targeted decatron streams, which bathed them down to their shared spherical base in universe-shaping energy.

Open gravitational shield apertures—the force fields surrounding the orbiting black holes receded to allow for tiny coherent cylinders of unrelenting gravitational force to descend hungrily onto the spikes of the neutron star.

Begin decatron streaming—the accelerated primordial particles burst away from their spikes, summoned by the black holes.

Target miniverses—as the decatron streams approached each black hole's torus, they tilted to point at the distant multiplexers.

The streams entered the torrential vortices, but their coherency remained unaffected. Their vectors, however, were subtly prismed, sending the beams at instantaneous velocities toward the edges of the universe.

"Well?" said Taschet.

Partak stared into space, her eyes darting around as she absorbed a planet of data. Then her mouth dropped, although her face remained unreadable. She turned to face the President of the Universe.

"It didn't work. The beams had no effect."

✛ ✛ ✛ ✛ ✛

"*What?*" screamed Ferric.

"Just what I said. And as I feared," replied Partak, retaining the characteristic Synergian *sang froid*. The room bubbled in fearful bickering.

"What did you fear?" asked Juno, one of the few calm voices remaining in the room.

"The beams—we theorized that the black holes on the receiving end will automatically prism them back toward their multiplexers," said Partak. "But without being allowed to test the system, we couldn't be sure."

"Are you sure it wasn't just the wrong code?" asked Ferric, eyeing Ellen and Athena.

"Look, you self-righteous bitch, there's clearly a problem with your system," said Athena. "We've gone through more in the last two days than you've seen in a lifetime."

"Well, you know, I really don't give a shit about what you've been through," replied Ferric.

"Wait! The stars! They're moving!" blurted one of the technicians.

Everyone hushed and stared out at the starfield, gasping as they began to perceive the stars slowly moving toward each other, and they could see the universe collapsing. Cold terror flooded the room.

"It looks like we've just made them mad," said Taschet, feeling the weight of the universe pressing on his soft shoulders.

"Partak," said Ellen, trying to think logically. "If you felt this might be a likely outcome, did you come up with any alternatives?"

Partak tipped back her head, and said, "We need a way to monitor and bend the beams as they enter the tori of the distant holes. I designed a carrier mole to piggyback the signal and microprism the beam with proper commands. However, if the torus insertion is off by so much as a micron, the beam will dissipate. And we cannot guarantee that kind of accuracy across hundreds of thousands of light years."

Ellen glanced over at her hyperceptive friend. "Athena? Can you shepherd the carrier moles?"

"I can't sense anything in here," she replied.

"Mr. President, would you consider shutting down the mental shields?" Ellen asked.

"Sir, we would be defenseless against this so-called extra-cognitive perception. The enemy will have a fleet here in no time," said Ferric. "We must think of another alternative."

"What alternative, Lisa?" shot back Taschet.

"Fire the beams again and again until it works!" she cried.

"That's no good," said Partak.

"And why not?" hissed the agitated Intelligence Minister.

"The reactors take twelve minutes to build up to full potential," she replied. "Plus we have no idea whether this random process will work any better than the first time."

Taschet turned to face Partak. "Forget it. Can a person guide the decatron beams?"

"If you mean hooking up someone with extra-sensory capabilities, that's only half the story. All eighty-one insertions have to be synchronized in real time down to the last nanosecond. The human mind thinks too slowly to accomplish this. A Sentient has to process and implement the data."

Athena nudged one of the two Sentients in the room. "I think she means you, Ellen."

She stepped forward. "Mr. President, I believe we can do it," Ellen said.

Ferric started to say something and thought better of it. Athena suppressed a smile.

"Juno, what do you think?" asked Taschet.

"If you are asking if we can trust a member of a secret race of people who possess abilities beyond the typical human, I'm not sure if the question is relevant. If you are asking for my approval on this course of action as a representative of the Council of Sentients, then I must remind you that I do not carry its mandate. Furthermore, you have declared martial law, and all decisions you make are final and binding," she said without a trace of humor.

Taschet sighed. "We are in a state of war and universal emergency simultaneously. I have not taken any action lightly. If we risk attack, then so be it. General Mola, signal the rest of the Navy. Inform them that they are ordered to report to this location at full battle readiness. Code it as absolute maximum priority."

"The *entire* navy, sir?" asked Mola. "The Persephone Galaxy is about to collide with the Dyad during the next few hours. We're looking at casualties of more than a quadrillion, and I've deployed twenty-eight fleets to evacuate them."

"Mola, if they don't come, there won't be anywhere left to evacuate to," replied Taschet. "We need them here, now. If we're successful here, those galaxies won't collide at all. Also, take the *Coelacanth* out, and verify our defense perimeter."

Mola shuddered as he considered the risk of leaving so many lives in danger, in order to kill thousands more. "Yes, sir."

Taschet could sense there was more to it than that, but he trusted Mola to follow orders. He turned to face Athena.

"I know your mother well," he said, loud enough to be heard by everyone. "In my position, it is sometimes important to know things that must not be disclosed publicly. However, times are changing, and the human race is evolving. After an eon of little change, our scientists say we are entering a phase of rapid evolution. The sooner we accept it, the better. Athena, do you feel up to the challenge before you?"

She held herself erect. "Yes, I do."

The President of the Universe covered the distance between them and shook her hand. "Our fate is now yours."

He guided her over to the black pouch, where she Immersed herself. She gasped, as she felt thousands of needles pierce her skin, as the gel forced itself into her pores.

Hesperon reached out and held the black Synergel, calming it and her and securing the connection.

"Thank you," she whispered. "Ellen?"

"I'm here," Ellen pushed forward from within the nebulous gel.

"I can't see anything," she said.

"Shut down the mental shields," Ellen pushed forward to the neurocom locus.

Athena was aware of seconds ticking by as agitated conversations murmured in the background. Then, without warning, the entire universe exploded into view around her.

She convulsed, and fought to suppress her nausea. This was different from the apex on Jattan. The electromagnetic fields created by the Atlas Sphere were stupendous, as would be necessary for a device of such scope. The effect on Athena was at once overwhelming and diminishing. Gone was the gauzy gossamer fabric of the Jattan miniverse and the comfort of the guided Seeing. This time, she was alone in the unfathomably huge universe, one that was shrinking, colliding, disintegrating across its sphere. She felt the horror of premature supernovae engulfing inhabited worlds; one galaxy spinning toward another; spheres of humanity shattered by gargantuan shards of rock and furiously burning galaxy-wide balls of plasma searing burning paths to the center of the universe.

"Athena, focus," said Ellen's voice.

Athena struggled to hold the universe apart and track back to that one warm human tendril. She pushed back the fragmenting universe, and saw Kalyphon at its center, twinkling, unaware of all that was heading toward it. She cupped it in her hands, cradling it, but she couldn't protect it from where she was. She disengaged, leapt half a universe away, and held the Atlas Sphere.

She condensed her awareness on the design of the monumental project, feeling its every contour, understanding its internal order, and the promise of actually manipulating the universe she perceived. She discharged a few decatrons from a reactor, and tested the piggyback carrier microprisms. They responded instantly, too quickly to be her own doing. She smiled internally as she felt the echo of Ellen's smooth velveteen mind.

Athena then cast her perception wide, beyond the collapsing boundaries of the universe, soaring through the void until she could see all the miniverses the universe was fed by. She ran the fingers of her mind over the gravity shunts feeding them, and the multiplexers powering the shunts. They were all there, ready to receive a decatron overload that would force a reversal of the collapse.

Athena felt confident. She was ready to begin the delicate operation. She turned to pull herself back to the Atlas Sphere, but suddenly felt another presence.

"Where do you think you're going?"

Terror shot through Athena's mind like a lightning bolt, but she managed to keep the external texture of her mind calm. As she struggled to maintain composure, the shock of feeling another mind here was replaced by the shock of recognizing that mind.

"You can't be here! You're dead!" she pushed forward.

"Never underestimate the power of faith, my dear Athena," replied Grand Villier Sarton.

"I must be hallucinating this," she muttered.

"Your secular convictions are the hallucination, my child. Eternal life, however, is a gift bestowed upon all the faithful," replied the Villier.

Athena was stunned. Could this be true? No! Was there a god after all, who provided for life after death? Had she closed her mind in her arrogance to the possibility that something greater was at work?

"My dear child, I forgave you when I was alive, so there is no ill will between us," continued Sarton. "After all, you delivered me to God. So let us continue our discussion, now that your scientific mind has its proof."

CHAPTER 22

A GOOD SEAT

"What is happening to her?" Taschet asked. Athena was thrashing her head in the translucent black gel.

Hesperon Immersed his hand in the gel. "I can't make out what's happening, and I can't reach her. Ellen won't disengage either."

"Mr. President!" shrieked Ferric.

"What?"

"There are about fifty—no, sixty—enemy warships emerging from multiple wormholes. They'll be within range of the sphere in minutes."

"All right people, we knew this would happen," said the president. "We built this facility with a paranoid attention to secrecy, and also to defense. And you all have the training and the talent to pull it together. Now, stand firm!"

"Be still, my child; no harm will come to you," said the Villier.

"I—I don't—this just isn't possible!" said Athena, trying desperately to clutch onto what she understood as reality, but failing to find purchase.

"Is it so unusual that you could be wrong about something? All human beings are fallible. It would be foolish to think that all your assumptions about life are valid," he continued in a compassionate voice.

"I don't understand," she whispered into the void.

"My dear, you refuse to understand. However, reality has a tendency to ignore our decisions to understand it or not," said Sarton.

"I suppose you have a point," replied Athena.

"Come, child, let us reevaluate your potential as a shepherd for our people," continued Sarton in a calm voice.

Athena felt her monument of confidence crumbling, her bearing and will fading away, leaving her naked and alone. "What can I do?"

Sarton smiled.

"Resist!" whispered a faint voice.

"What was that?" asked Athena.

"Nothing!" said Sarton.

"Athena! Focus on my voice!"

"Ignore that voice. It comes from evil," said Sarton.

"Ellen!" said Athena.

"Compare the texture of my mind to his," whispered Ellen.

Athena reached out and held Sarton's mind, and recoiled in surprise. "You're a Sentient!"

+ + + + +

"Sixty-six warships appearing out of Transit, Mr. President," announced General Mola.

"Where is the Navy?" yelled Taschet.

"Still in Transit. Estimated time of arrival in five minutes."

"What about the *Coelacanth*?"

"She's holding her general position, but listing to port."

"All right then, we're on our own for now. Establish contact," said the president.

A puffy face with deep-set eyes filled the screen. "You are outnumbered. Surrender and accept absolution, or you will be cleansed."

Taschet stood erect, unblinking. "Your military forces are committing full-scale genocide against my people, and are attempting to annihilate their worlds. I will *not* surrender, but instead I hereby declare total and absolute war against you and your kind."

The puffy face tightened with distaste. "Big words for a small man. But God is not with you. Watch as we destroy your crippled warship. Prepare yourselves for the hereafter, for we will atomize you shortly."

Taschet shook his head. "Kill transmission," he said off to the side. "That's it," he said to no one in particular.

+ + + + +

A swarm of beetle ships spewed out of the mandibles of the queen ships, and descended on the Kalyphon warship, peppering it with energy discharges. The *Coelacanth* pitched down and yawed right as it extended its Silurian armor, giant cerastic plates of external physical shielding. Then the armored flagship extended its firing bristles, and began to carve holes in the enemy swarm. Twelve Stellar Cross queen ships broke off to destroy the stubborn vessel.

"Mr. President?" asked Mola, as they watched from the Atlas Station.

"Not yet," whispered Taschet.

The lead queen ship fired a single shot at the *Coelacanth*. The discharge hit the forward shield of the cylindrical cruiser with sufficient force to collapse the shield support strut. The massive diamond-reinforced plate broke off and spun away. The remaining queen ships closed formation and began charging their forward-weapons arrays. They were salivating for the kill.

"*NOW!*" shouted Taschet.

Mola keyed in the authorization code, and hundreds of gravitic mines uncased themselves in lethal proximity to the enemy fleet. The twelve attacking queen ships were grasped by the mines' gravitational forces, and were pulled off in different directions, liquefied, and reduced to neutron particulate before finally forming the outer layer of the handful of the remaining gravitic mines.

The remnants of the enemy fleet fell victim one by one, until one expelled a shrapnel bubble around itself. The gravitic mine assigned to that ship homed in on a random shrapnel shard, and gave itself away. The enemy queen ship steered clear of the area, and proceeded toward the Atlas Station. The other ships repeated the tactic, and followed in.

"How many are approaching?" asked Taschet.

"Still have twenty-three closing, although not as quickly," replied the general. "And the *Coelacanth* is attacking their flank, slowing them further."

"Let's hope that gives us enough time," murmured the president to himself.

"How dare you compare me to those unclean machines!" said the former Grand Villier.

"But your mind, it's—it's ordered!" replied Athena.

"That presence is the recorded mind of Sarton," interjected Ellen. "Apparently, these guys don't practice what they preach."

"Athena, do not allow this filth to interfere with us. We all have an eternal soul. This simply is the means that God intended for us to use," said Sarton.

"But that is forbidden by the Valhalla Accords! No human being may be immortal!" said Athena.

"Do not become hysterical, child. The Lord works in mysterious ways. It is not our place to question Him!" he said.

She reached deep within, and fought for control of her rampaging mind. "No. *NO!*" shrieked Athena. "This ends now!"

Athena conjured her mind-image of the universe.

"Stop! What are you doing?" bellowed Sarton. She ignored him.

She requested the Atlas overlay from Ellen, which she supplied. Athena stretched out her consciousness further than it had ever gone, covering the wide, deep expanses within the universe, and also the unfathomable gulfs separating it from the miniverses. She stretched her mind fully, and plotted out the pathways of the decatron beams from the Atlas Sphere through the Stellar Cross's gravity shunts to the miniverses beyond. She felt Ellen supporting the picture, guiding the plan to form with absolute mathematical precision.

Sarton spoke again in his quiet, even voice. "If you will not stop in the name of your Creator, then perhaps you will do it for him."

A new presence projected forward. To Athena, it was very earthy, very familiar. She inhaled sharply as Ellen screamed, "KALE!"

Sarton continued, a smile in his voice. "He is here with me on Jattan. We retrieved his lifeboat after we destroyed your ship. Its systems were dead following an electromagnetic pulse, but he was not."

"This is a trick." Athena tried to inject an edge into her voice, but she was not adept enough yet to conceal her emotion.

"No, it's really him, in his original, untouched state," countered Sarton. "Well, not completely. We did have to restrain him. But you don't have to take my word for it. Kale, you may now speak."

"Athena—" said a raspy voice.

Athena was shaking. She was certain it was him.

"Kale, it's me, Ellen!"

"I—I can barely—you're both alive?" said Kale.

"Yes, we're fine! Where are you?" asked Athena.

"Not—I'm not important. If you have a way to stop them, do it!" said Kale.

"But, if you're there, then we can come and get you!" shrieked Ellen.

"Athena is welcome to return," interrupted Sarton. "Thank you, Kale. That's enough from you."

Athena could sense Kale's mind recede. She tried to reach out and pull him back, but nothing happened. She did, however, sense that her image of the universe was beginning to unravel.

"Ellen! What are you doing?" Athena called out.

"We have to save him! We can go get him, break him out of there!" she cried back.

"No, we can't risk it. We have to act now. He wants us to keep fighting!" said Athena.

"But we'll cut off all the miniverses if we do this!" she pleaded. "You can't take him away from me! I can't lose him again!"

"Ellen, there are too many lives in the balance. He will hate us if we let them die!"

"I can't lose him again," she repeated.

"He offered his life to save everyone. That was more important to him," said Athena. "If he means that much to you, as he does to me, we have to help him by finishing the job he started."

Ellen said nothing. Slowly, Athena's universe image reformed, and the Atlas network was ready again.

Sarton reverted to his original tactic. "Do this, and you condemn yourself to eternal hellfire!" he shouted.

Athena shook with anger. "Then save me a good seat!"

With that, she pushed forward the command to activate the Atlas Sphere.

✦ ✦ ✦ ✦ ✦

With the command delivered, the multifaceted web sprang to life. The decatron beams flashed brilliantly, freezing time like a bolt of lightning, and then vanished. The disgorging miniverses reversed, gathered back unfathomable masses of matter, disrupting all the bodies that they contained—so much that most of them smashed their shunts, choking them off from the universe. With the balance of matter returning, the cosmological force roared back to life, arresting the galactic collisions and the inflationary collapse, and then started again an ever-increasing pace of universal expansion.

Athena had perceived it all, leaving her consciousness battered and overwhelmed. She no longer felt Sarton or Kale, but she could feel Ellen pulling her back into location-based reality.

She convulsed, inhaling mouthfuls of synergel, breaking the connection.

Athena fell out of the black synergel coughing, and was pulled out onto the deck. She saw an increased level of defense personnel, although the physicists and officials around her seemed strangely quiet—and anxious. They did not know what had happened.

"Well?" asked Taschet.

"It worked," she gurgled, black translucent gel spilling out of her stained mouth.

Ellen interjected, "Sarton had his mind transferred before he died." Turning to Athena, she helped her sit up. "But the beams annihilated the resulting Sentient—he's offline. But he had Kale with him on Jattan!"

Ellen's eyes swelled. Her body froze. Gander jumped forward.

"He's still alive? We've got to go find him!" he said.

"Hold on. Nothing is alive there. We just smashed back with our excess matter, pulverizing those miniverses into dust. Besides, they're cut off now. We can't go there," interjected President Taschet.

Athena was puzzled by the cold reaction. She looked about, sensing exasperation. "Hello? We just saved the whole human race! We haven't earned some of your best and brightest to explore the possibility?" she said, waving her arm toward the staff of the Atlas Sphere.

"Yes, dear, you have," Taschet said. "We're all very grateful to you, your crew, and our own Navy."

He smiled at her, sharing his fond gaze with Ferric and the rest, giving Athena the only parade she would get for her efforts. "It's just that now we're at the hard part."

Athena stared at the man. He did not elaborate. She looked around and saw the attention of the others already diverted to other matters; all except for Councilor Juno, whose gaze bore directly into her.

Epilogue

Turbor Veller stared at the holofield, abandoning himself to the moment. Rioting had destroyed his employer's broadcasting network, Starnet, although he himself had been able to land on his feet, securing a production position at rival network UNN. Partnering with "fashion maven" Nazarian was the crowning absurdity in the sequence of absurdities that put him in the place where his two feet were standing. The light was red, and Nazarian was introducing the live address, but Veller was content to play the role of common spectator as he felt the cool wash of safety drench his mind.

✦ ✦ ✦ ✦ ✦

The President of the Universe gazed out into the throng of people gathered at the newly built Plaza Memorial. Like exhausted runners who can no longer feel their legs, his usual concerns about word choice and demographic appeal were gone, another casualty of the grotesque ordeal he and his universe had just endured. Words began to enter his mind. He took a deep breath and started to speak to them.

"We are gathered here today to pay our respects to those countless beings who paid the highest price for innocence in recorded history," he began. His voice was quiet, as if he were addressing a friend across a table, but it was magnified to boom across the vast plateau of the somber memorial.

"The loss that we have all taken is simply beyond the possibility of expression. Furthermore, the pain that we all feel is so varied and personal that no person or philosophy can adequately address it.

"So I will not attempt to do so. The temptation is there to retreat into supernatural panaceas, as popularized again by the Order of the Stellar Cross. That option is available. However, we stand here alive today because some of us rejected it, and fought it.

"The maturing of a species takes time. Based on recent events, clearly we are not there yet. But we can be. Please direct your focus to the metallic fount in the center of the stone circle in front of me."

He pushed forward a command, and a slender plasma torch sprang to life, soaring into the sky.

"This torch stands as a symbol of our desire to reach that goal of reason, morality, and wisdom. These concepts are not to be taken lightly, and are worth the ultimate sacrifice to protect. To represent the innumerable beings who paid such a price, we chose to dedicate this torch to a young man named Kale Eritrus. For it was his sacrifice that most directly led to our life today..."

✦ ✦ ✦ ✦ ✦

Athena sat back, and imagined what could have been. She hated that her emotions raged so violently beneath her forced calm exterior, but she had much more on her mind now. She looked over at Ellen, who squeezed her arm. She noticed that Gander was sitting next to Cerelles and his wife. Athena felt her chest tighten, and turned back to the speech.

On stage, Taschet realized he had to phrase his next point just right. He took a slight breath, and continued. "The last decision of the Council of Sentients was to produce an algorithm to determine its successor. That algorithm inhabited the body of the last living Councilor, and it examined all beings with whom it came into contact. It sought out behavior showing defense and unswerving dedication to our universe, and activated upon witnessing such behavior by Athena Nobarra, an organic yet hyperceptive human. Her unique abilities saved us all, and it is with her example of hope and determination that we embarked on the rebuilding of our universe.

"It is with a hint of literary accuracy that the rebirth of our capital world begins with the inauguration of the Phoenix Council. This august body springs forth from the ashes of the Council of Sentients, incorporating its renowned technical and practical qualities of governance with the phenomenal capabilities of the recently discovered group of human beings with enhanced hyperceptive abilities. We will take advantage of the unique facets this added diversity affords us as a species, and forge a new government and a new universal culture..."

Ferric twisted nervously in her chair. She avoided making eye contact with Mark Weaver, whom she began to suspect might have his own agenda for the new government. However, she had to take care of her own interests first. She pushed forward the command to track Athena as she set up the new government body. Her agents were not pleased with their new orders.

✦✦✦✦✦

Hesperon caressed the newly repaired wing of the *Archaeopteryx*. The surface of his small starship shimmered in the Kalyphon twilight. He already had written his report, and was going to enjoy his voyage back to Synergia in peace.

"Thank you," said a voice behind him. Hesperon turned to see Ellen's perfectly constructed face. He decided that he had to brush up on his Sentient detection skills once he returned home.

"You don't have to thank me. I was only performing an assignment," he said.

She raised an eyebrow. "The appropriate response to 'thank you' is 'you're welcome.'"

Hesperon grinned. "Yes, I suppose you're right. What are you going to do now?"

"I'm supposed to be part of the new Phoenix Council, apparently. I'm not sure what that will all mean, but Juno's been downloading volumes of material into me," she said, rolling her eyes. "I hope we'll see you back on Kalyphon soon."

He looked at her, not knowing what to say. He had no intention of ever returning, his nostalgia for the company of mainstream humans now a foolish memory. At the same time, he did not want to seem rude in his response, given the silent affection that he had developed for this Sentient. "How are you doing?"

Ellen's smile flattened. "It's difficult. This kind of loss doesn't go away, just like that. The president is reluctant to reestablish connections to any of the miniverses. They're much happier treating him as missing in action."

"You are strong, Ellen," he said. "You will find a way."

"Yeah, but nobody seems to want to help," she said.

He gazed back at her. He took her hands and squeezed them warmly. "It has been an honor working with you and your friends. I will do what I can!"

She nodded.

He bowed, turned, and bounded up the ramp of his ship. A moment passed, and then the *Archaeopteryx* sprang off the grass, and darted into the clear, darkening sky.

Ellen watched the tiny ship join the twinkling lines of the distant interior of the Kalyphon Sphere. She turned around to see the millions of people dispersing from the Plaza Memorial. At the center of the universe, surrounded by people looking toward her for the future, she realized that she was alone and focused elsewhere. She wiped away a spontaneous tear, and watched the droplet's impact on the blades of grass at her feet. She stared at them as they shimmered with motion. As the tiny pools became still, she saw that they reflected the commemorative plasma torch now blazing a beacon into the universe.

She fell to her knees and ran her fingers through the blades of grass, setting the miniature images in motion again. She reached out and pinched the moisture off a single blade. Against what she perceived as the wasteland of the rest of her life, she felt a touch of purpose again. She held the idea a moment, and allowed it to take root.

Glossary

Cerastic: Synthetic material possessing molecular properties similar to both organic polymers and inorganic ceramics. The material may be embedded with electromagnetic computational functionality, and may be bent or even molded into various shapes while retaining that embedded functionality. The material also is versatile, possessing an extremely high tensile strength. Cerastic has many applications ranging from business cards to adaptable docking collars for starships. For a more detailed explanation of the mathematical and chemical properties of cerastics, see *The Final Text on Chemistry*, edited by Kalyphon University Chemistry Dept., 673rd Edition.

Cloning: Cloning was the sole genetic technology that survived the ancient crucible of genetic engineering. Reprogenetics started in preastronomic times as the benign ability to deactivate genes in unborn children that would lead to life-threatening illness. However, once what historians would later call "Pandora's Genome" was cracked wide open, many felt the urge to switch their child's eye color, height, or intelligence while the tools were in place. Various ancient cultures placed a premium on masculine offspring, and the shortsightedness of that cultural norm was given a chance to prove its fallacy. Genetic selection of traits by the wealthy began to create a small coterie of races within a larger race, with multiple non-crossbreedable threads. Scientifically speaking, they were no longer human.

This was humankind's first taste of creation. The new races chose to group themselves under the single species name *Homo dominus*, to differentiate them from the surrounding herd of *Homo sapiens*. This first encounter with a non-human intelligence resulted in deep social scarring for the surviving race of *Homo sapiens*, and a brief resurgence in religious fervor.

The cloning of normal interbreedable *Homo sapiens* lost much of its unsavory connotation in the face of reprogenetics, and enjoyed a surprising elevation to political correctness. Cloning thus remained available to those who could derive a benefit around the strict taboos surrounding genetic engineering. It survived as a sanctioned method of reproduction, despite the popular view that it was the ultimate expression of self-love.

For a more detailed explanation of the political and legal characteristics of clones, see *The Final Text on the Rights of Beings,* edited by Kalyphon University School of Law, 2nd Edition.

Cosmological Force: One of the five physical forces in the universe, this force is responsible for accelerating the expansion of the universe. Considered weaker than even the gravitational force on small, sub-planetary objects, the cosmological force actually is the strongest force in the universe on galactic objects. The cosmological force counteracts the gravitational force on a galactic scale, and provides the natural balance between mass and energy in the universe. Although a mystery to the ancients, who had managed to uncover the other four forces, the cosmological force operates on a fairly simple equation. As first demonstrated by the eminent physicist Perdita Mugherjal, $C = Gs^3$, where C is the cosmological force, G is the gravitational force, and s is the string constant. For a more detailed explanation of the mathematical and physical properties of the cosmological force, see *The Final Text on Physics,* edited by Kalyphon University Physics Dept., 284th Edition.

Decatron: A ten-dimensional subatomic particle. Ten-dimensional matter demonstrates properties that apparently violate the laws of physics when observed from a 3-D perspective. For example, they apparently violate the speed of light by appearing in one location in one instant and across the universe the next. However, this violation is only an illusion. Consider a 2-D observer, seeing a 3-D object, say, a sphere, passing through its plane of existence. They would see a dot (the pole of the sphere) suddenly transform into growing concentric circles (the latitudes of the sphere) then shrinking circles, then a dot, and then vanish. This is not matter appearing, growing, shrinking, and vanishing in contravention of the laws of physics, but rather an issue of perception. Similarly, ten-dimensional particles can appear in multiple locations sequentially or simultaneously in apparent contradiction of the laws of physics. Ten-dimensional matter is observable through a multidimensional scope, and directly distilled and manipulated by decatronic reactors. For a more detailed explanation of the mathematical and physical properties of 10-D matter and decatrons, see *The Final Text on Physics,* edited by Kalyphon University Physics Dept., 284th Edition.

Dyson Sphere: An artificial construct surrounding a star. Originally proposed by physicist Freeman Dyson on ancient Earth, a Dyson Sphere captures the power output of a star, converting it for practical use. The Dyson Sphere encapsulating Kalyphon represents the human achievement of a Class II civilization, based on the scale proposed by Dyson's contemporary, Nikolai Kardashev. For a more detailed history of Dyson Spheres, see *The Seven Wonders of the Ancient Galaxy*, by John Singh, 32nd Edition.

Event Horizon: The outer edge of a black hole. Light and other electromagnetic emissions are slower than the escape velocity of the black hole at the event horizon, and so nothing can be seen of a black hole using the electromagnetic spectrum. This is the infamous "point of no return" for early space travelers, although modern Travel technology theoretically is capable of bypassing the event horizon. Due to the tremendous gravitational destructiveness of black holes, no expedition has attempted such a risky enterprise, as of this printing. For more information on event horizons, see *The Final Text on Physics,* edited by Kalyphon University Physics Dept., 284th Edition.

Holofield Camera: A device that captures visual cues for instantaneous or delayed relay. The mechanism is composed of a field of receptors that, much like human vision, collects visual data from multiple points to construct a three-dimensional model of the subject, so that it may be holographically reproduced from any angle. For a more detailed explanation of the mathematical and physical properties of holographic technology, see *The Final Text on Holography,* edited by Kalyphon University Engineering Dept., 1276th Edition.

Neurocom: A contained system characterized by artificial intelligence. Unlike ancient neural net computers, with learning silicon pathways, a neurocom is composed of articulated quantum particles. In a fashion similar to that of human neurons, which transmit signals using combinations of the four neurotransmitters acetylcholine, norepinephrine, epinephrine, and serotonin, a neurocom uses the axial spin of quanta to convey impulses. This allows for a density of functional thought transmission approximately 500 billion times greater than that of a human brain, in a gel capsule with a one-centimeter diameter. Neurocoms may be used for many purposes, such as starship navigation, government administration, and personal assistance. When granted full awareness and autonomy, neurocoms cease to be property, and are given the full rights and privileges of a human being. *See: Sentient.* For a more detailed explanation of the mathematical and physical properties of neurocom technology, see *The Final Text on Neurocoms,* edited by Kalyphon University Engineering Dept., 1276th Edition.

Quasar: A relic of the primordial universe, a quasar was a supermassive black hole with a halo of matter and energy, producing as much energy per second as a thousand galaxies. Quasars now are extinct, and can be studied only through light telescopes peering from one edge of the universe at the other. The light of these objects already has traveled extreme distances, and so shows the universe as it was shortly after the Big Bang. For a more detailed explanation of the mathematical and observational characteristics of quasars, see *The Final Text on Physics,* edited by Kalyphon University Physics Dept., 284th Edition.

Sentient: A self-aware and independent artificial being. Sentients legally are considered human beings, although physiologically they cannot mate with organic human beings. Although a Sentient may take any form, ranging from an information locus to human facsimile, the basis for Sentient existence is the neurocom. Although most neurocoms have redundant backup, no Sentient is permitted to reproduce its neurocom pattern, although it may be transmitted over short distances with subsequent erasure of source upon successful transmission. This singular restriction provides a degree of mortality to Sentients, which allows them to coexist with organic human beings. For a more detailed explanation of the mathematical and physical properties of neurocom technology, see *The Final Text on Neurocoms,* edited by Kalyphon University Engineering Dept., 1276th Edition. For a more detailed explanation of the political and legal characteristics of Sentients, see *The Final Text on the Rights of Beings,* edited by Kalyphon University School of Law, 2nd Edition.

The Stygian Gate: The link between Pluto and Charon in the Solar System. The following is an excerpt from John Singh's *The History of Universal Commerce,* 63rd Edition:

Various ancient corporate interests joined the two worlds with a carbon-matrix umbilicus, creating a gravitational centrifuge. Cosmic strings then were attached to various stamen points on Charon. These strings, being one-dimensional remnants of the early universe, were sewn through three-dimensional space and connected to multiple nozzles of multiple tubules of a relatively nearby wormhole. During construction, the carbon centrifuge was dubbed the "Stygian Gate" by naysayers, as a morbid reference to the mythological river Styx of the Underworld.

However, the centrifuge worked. Within weeks, this unprecedented feat of engineering opened up the distant branches of the Milky Way and entirely different galaxies to exploration and settlement. Until that point, travel to the distant edges of the cosmos was limited to intelligent probes, traveling at ordinary speeds through conventional space. The carbon centrifuge, however, operated on the knowledge that space inherently was curved. The shortest distance between two points stopped being a straight line, and became the length of the wormhole that connected them. A voyage of centuries became a hop of hours. The effect of the technology was so profound that the language adjusted to capitalize the first letter of the word "travel" when one used the centrifuge to do so.

In its early days, the centrifuge guided humankind to the wormholes that established its foothold on the universe. In this fashion, other wormholes were discovered and anchored to other centrifuges built in other galaxies. The universe began to seem alive, as the wormholes ferried people and their dreams like the arteries and veins of a body transporting blood cells and nutrients. The corporate and governmental builders of the first centrifuge saw unprecedented profit and goodwill generated by their endeavor, and the once ill-willed moniker of the "Stygian Gate" became a badge of success against all odds.

However, as the millennia ticked by, and as the once empty universe began to saturate with the daily errands and working lunches of a single species, the Stygian Gate suffered a mounting backlog of Travel requests. This resulted in a massive bottleneck in intergalactic commerce, as cargo and tourist ships jammed the available tubules. Various orbital shells were set up to manage the departure queues. This congestion had the fringe benefit of jumpstarting the Plutonian economy, as it served as a lucrative meeting point for commerce and investment. However, necessity pushed the invention of ships that no longer needed a gravitational centrifuge to attract the nozzle of a wormhole. The prevalence of such self-strung ships in turn started the gradual decline of the once illustrious Stygian Gate.

Universal Chandrasekhar Limit: The total quantity of mass present in the universe necessary for gravitation to force the universe to collapse on itself. The concept and the term are rooted in the well-established Stellar Chandrasekhar Limit, which holds that a star must have 1.4 solar masses in order to collapse into a black hole. Both terms are named after the ancient Earth astrophysicist Subrahmanyan Chandrasekhar. For a more detailed explanation of the mathematical basis of the Universal Chandrasekhar Limit, see *The Final Text on Physics,* edited by Kalyphon University Physics Dept., 284th Edition.

Acknowledgments

This work exists to fill one of many gaps between the picture of our universe as tentatively understood by our science, and the one presented in our fiction.

However, it does not exist in a vacuum. Two individuals played defining roles in my development leading up to the novel. First, my mother, Shabnum, sat with me as a child and watched David Attenborough's *Life of Earth* documentary series on BBC, and also took me at every request to the Natural History Museum in South Kensington, London.

The other is my uncle, Amit, who when I was twelve, gave me his own copies of Isaac Asimov's *Foundation* and Frank Herbert's *Dune*. These books were the greatest gift I have ever received.

In the process of writing this novel, I relied on a variety of astronomy and astrophysics books for the layperson. Chief among them were Stephen Hawking's *A Brief History of Time* and Michio Kaku's *Hyperspace*. The lines between reality, theory, and my own extrapolations are somewhat blurred in this work, but to the extent that anything appears now or later turns out to be patently wrong, that would be my fault.

The manuscript itself benefited from the insights of several individuals, such as Jesse Alexander, Lou Anders, Stacie Clarkson, John Gaeta, Christian Gossett, Mark Long, Kim Milosevich, Jeff Moores, John Picacio, and Joe Salama to name a few.

The heavy lift of getting this book into your hands must fairly be credited to the kind support from intrepid writer David Jedeikin, public relations maven Angela Nibbs, perfectionist editor Palmer Gibbs, and visionary cover artist Kenn Brown.

But perhaps the most important acknowledgment is to you, the reader. Thank you for envisioning this story together. I look forward to meeting again.

About the Author

Jamil Moledina's life is irregular. His ancestors emigrated from India to Kenya, where he was born. He moved to England, and then the United States, where he studied international relations, Japanese, and law. A convoluted pathway took him from law, to journalism, to the game industry, where he continues to work today. His mind, however, is somewhere else entirely.

He lives in San Francisco.

6515296R0

Made in the USA
Charleston, SC
03 November 2010